CARNIVAL CREEKE

BOOK 1

ANGELA FOY DAVIS

This is a work of fiction. The events and characters described herein are imaginary and are not intended to refer to specific places or living persons.

CARNIVAL CREEKE: VOLUME 1
All Rights Reserved
Copyright © 2019, Angela Foy Davis

Cover and illustrations by Angela Foy Davis

ISBN: 978-0-578-59306-7

Printed in the United States of America

*To my husband, who told me to "believe in this fairy,
clap my hands a little."*

*To Jeremy... Without your relentless encouragement, this
adventure would have died a long time ago.*

With thanks to God, because we're all stories in progress.

WANT TO KNOW A SECRET...?

When you see this little critter (or one of his friends),
it means there's more to the story.
Visit www.CarnivalCreeke.com and check out the
"Easter Egg Hunt" to unlock goodies, bonus artwork,
or listen to what's playing on the jukebox.

HAPPY HUNTING!

DAY ZERO

Lemon-scented ammonia. Or coffee cake.

Or both.

My eyelids spring open. I'm lying toes-up on a narrow bed inclined slightly at the head. A blue paisley privacy curtain encloses me on all sides, sterile fluorescent lights overhead. Likely a med center or a hospital...

My nostrils are assaulted again by the burn of lemon-scented ammonia, rubber, and iodine.

Definitely a hospital.

I stare up at the buzzing light fixture for a moment, utterly disoriented. Then I somersault off the bed, nearly sliding out of the baggy pink hospital gown I'm wearing. A plastic, kidney-shaped bedpan clatters to the floor. Apparently, someone thought I was going to ralph. Or maybe I told them. It's all pretty foggy.

I pat myself down, taking inventory of my limbs. Nothing is hacked off or missing, no broken bones or –

Hold on. There's something in my hand.

Curiously, I uncurl my fingers. A little keychain with a tiny plastic 8-ball sits nestled in the palm of my hand. Is this mine?

Never seen the doggone thing before in my life. Don't even remember picking it up.

Well, that makes no sense...

But then again, neither does the hand I'm looking at. My skin is pale like strawberry milk. It doesn't compute, because I have no earthly idea what color my skin is *supposed* to be. With a slight jolt of horror, I realize I have no memory of this hand. Or my feet, or my hair – which appears to be wavy, copper-colored and a royal mess, judging from the sweaty strands I keep having to flick off my face.

My face...

Can't remember my face.

Or my name.

Just a series of blank files. Cabinets with empty drawers, a vacant room with windows thrown open to repeated frustration in the shape of brick walls.

My vision lurches unsteadily, and I have to grab for the metal rail on the side of the bed. Dizzy and rootless, I stand there for a moment, clutching the rail like a kid in a carnival funhouse. Oh, heckfire...they must have juiced me with sedatives. I whip my arms palm-up and peer at them closely. The pale skin on the undersides of my elbows is still smooth, revealing no needle punctures. My elbows are dusted with dirt, but no tales to be told there. Weird... With no glaring reason to feel woozy, I force the rising panic back into one of my empty brain drawers and temporarily label myself as "fine."

My eyes dart quickly around the enclosed bed area. I must have had clothes at some point. No one gets admitted to the hospital buck-naked.

Please say I wasn't buck-naked.

Thankfully there's a plastic belongings bag sitting on the floor behind the bed; I grab it without looking inside. I have enough mysteries, and that bag's contents honestly aren't at the top of my list right now. In the same movement, I unhook my chart from the metal bar at the foot of the bed. I flip open the chart and scan for my name.

Female, age 19. Kyle, C.

Alrighty, we have a last name.

Every journey begins with a first step.

For good measure, I also grab the 8-ball keychain. Reckon I must have had some brilliant reason for having it in my possession – and right now, that ghost "I" is the most reliable person I have in my empty inventory of options to trust. This completes my optical sweep of the area. Time to peer out from the blue privacy curtain like a kid with stage fright.

A nurse in jack-o-lantern scrubs breezes by with an armful of sterile IV bags. My bed is the first in the ER row, next to a bathroom door with a poster displaying the warning signs of a stroke. A small reception cove is ten well-scrubbed floor tiles away. The secretary's back is to me, engrossed in her computer screen, her finger auto-piloting to a loose strand of hair.

Without warning, a countdown erupts inside me. It's as though someone clicked a stopwatch in my gut, triggering a sudden awareness that if I keep standing here, my seconds are ticking away, dropping like instantly ripe fruit, mounting to some awful unwritten climax.

Can't explain it...

Tucking the chart firmly in my armpit, I emerge from behind the curtain and move like a ghost along the wall of medic supplies. Now that I'm moving, I'm aware that my tailbone is throbbing. And my chest is hurting like a son-of-a-gun. I press my palm between my breasts. Hope I'm not having a heart attack...

Have I ever had a heart attack?

If I do blow a gasket, at least I'm in a hospital.

A plate of sliced cake sits on the reception counter right behind the secretary, a silver pastry knife beside it. Aha! So I *had* smelled coffee cake. Under different circumstances, I probably would have asked them for a slice. My stomach growls, unable to decide if it wants to eat or puke.

The pastry knife leaps into my hand before me or the doctor coming around the corner can breathe.

"What the devil–?" The doctor sputters, gaping at the knife in my hand.

Behind his glasses, his expression looks like a mole shocked by sunlight. I inhale, and his mole face puckers and turns pink; I twitch the tip of the knife, his hands jerk to the ceiling. It's like puppeteering with invisible strings from the blade. Oddly satisfying.

I glance down at the name tag pinned to his lab coat.

"Doctor Fairchild?" I know I probably look like a spit-crazed horse right now. At least I remember what a horse looks like.

"Now, honey," the mole-faced doctor speaks slowly. "Perhaps we could discuss things more freely without the knife?"

"Uh-uh, don't think so." Strange venom is coursing through me now, firing me up, inflating me with false confidence. "I'm saying your name, Doctor Fairchild. How come you're not calling me by mine?"

He blinks. "I-I don't know your name, honey. You've, ah, got your chart there."

I don't glance at the chart tucked under my armpit.

"Dang doctors," I mutter to myself, or maybe out loud. "Can't remember how to hiccup without a chart..."

My chest is throbbing again.

"What did you do to me?" I bark, trying to get a side-long glance at my chart without taking my eyes off the pink-faced doctor. "Weird tests? Brain scans? Government Roswell alien-baby stuff?"

"Nothing." He shrugs. "Not a thing." His glasses are fogged up.

"Sure, okay. Then what am I doing here, Doctor Fairchild?"

"I don't know."

I gawk at him, stunned. I want to lash back at this calm sadist, but all my spitfire apparently ran off and left me. Thank

5

goodness my invisible knife-puppet strings still seem attached. Pretty sure they're the only thing holding me up right now.

"Then what's wrong with me?" I demand, my voice drained of its punch from five seconds ago.

"I'm *telling* you, I have no idea. Because you haven't *told* us yet." He emphasizes each syllable, slowly and clearly, as though he's speaking to a two-year-old. Which I'm pretty sure I'm not.

"Why," Doctor Fairchild tosses me a light smile, fluttering his creased eyelids. "We haven't even had a chance to take your temperature yet."

I stare dumbly, trying to process what he's telling me. Bile rises in my throat. My stomach is threatening to empty right here on their white tile floor.

"You checked yourself in just fifteen minutes ago, insisting you would speak *only* to the doctor. Hmm?" He purses his lips, cocking his head in a gesture urging me to remember – or at least pretend like I remember and put the knife down.

My brain is spinning. I guess I don't say anything, because he starts clucking those slow words again.

"Now then, perhaps we could arrange–"

I don't recall what happened next. Only that the stopwatch inside me exploded and now I'm flailing around corner after corner down a carpeted corridor, a heavy metal door banging shut somewhere.

*

My exodus spits me out by a green dumpster in a side exit loading dock by the hospital.

Well, no pomp and circumstance here.

I quickly fling the pastry knife; it hits the bottom of the empty dumpster with an almighty and unnecessarily loud clang. There's a large truck with its rear backed up to the loading dock. I half consider whether I might be lucky enough to find the keys still stashed inside. Or does that only happen in movies?

Against my better judgment, I grab the truck's side-view mirror and swing up monkey-style, feeding myself through its open window. The cabin reeks of Copenhagen and vanilla cupcake air freshener. I yank the sunshade down, praying for keys. An un-opened fortune cookie falls out into my lap.

Zero helpful.

Hopping from the truck, I dart around the perimeter of the concrete alcove and slip out into the crisp autumn sun. The field that stretches out behind the hospital is split down the middle by a row of trees. A gaggle of boys in jackets are playing baseball in the grass, two players short of a team. They aren't looking at me, which is good. Pretty sure I look like something out of a Living Dead flick.

Mystery plastic bag tightly in hand, I trot barefoot across the leaf-covered pavement into a quaint downtown street.

It's a charming little speck of a town, the kind you'd need a magnifying glass to see on a map, the kind of town that probably still sings Christmas carols and holds barbecue-eating contests every summer. Rows of shops are spaced neatly along the tree-lined strip. Antique joints and book nooks, mostly, but I spy a hardware shop, a post office, and a handful of shoebox-sized mom-and-pop eateries. The afternoon sun bathes their striped awnings and patterned brick façade like butter wash on a pie. A perfect autumn postcard.

A maroon and orange banner stretched across the street announces Carnival Creek High School's homecoming football game this weekend; it bulges and flaps in a sudden up-gust. A herd of boys gallop around the steps outside the colonial-columned Post office. Crispy red leaves sweep down the herringbone brick sidewalk behind them, accumulating in a pile under the doorstep of Hank's Used Auto Parts. They're promptly broomed away by a man with a porkpie cap and a Jamaican complexion. I assume that's Hank.

My gaze drifts lazily to the horizon. In the distance, a water tower is visible. Its hulking shape is obscured by the firs beyond the tree line, only the piping of the tank's domed army-green head stands silhouetted against the blue sky.

The water tower. For absolutely no rhyme or reason, the sight of it fills me with creeping dread.

Shuddering, I shove the feeling aside.

Now that the adrenaline of my hospital escape has begun to burn off, my whole body aches. Every muscle is screaming how dog-tired I am. The earth spins slowly beneath me like a tilt-a-whirl, seemingly competing with my trembling jelly legs to see which can knock me down first.

I stay my pace at an unhurried walk, forcing the swing of my arms to appear relaxed even though I'm far from it. That silver-haired couple in matching velour jogging suits, eyeing me curiously from a secluded bench on the library lawn... A woman passes by, twisting to stare at me, her Golden Retriever tugging at its leash... To any of these people, I would appear completely normal.

Well, normal if I weren't still sporting a pink hospital gown.

I toss the plastic bag over the iron cemetery gate behind the library. With a quick glance over my shoulder, I join the bag and plop down behind a tombstone. Not that vaulting into a graveyard looks at all suspicious.

"J. Robertson," I mumble at the stone slab I'm squatting on. "Nothing personal, buddy. I'm a 'one-letter-for-a-first-name' kinda girl, too."

I rip into the plastic bag without bothering to untie the knot and root around inside. Clothes, sure enough – cargo pants (with a nice wad of cash in the pocket), a no-nonsense, off-white tee, and a creased red leather bomber jacket, buttery soft and well-worn, with some kind of funky smoke burn on the hem. At the bottom of the bag is a military grade wristwatch, which I strap to my arm. There's also a pair of oxblood leather boots that lace up to mid-calf.

I wriggle into the pants, sliding off the tombstone in the process and grinding a few pinecones under my butt. Just as I'm shrugging on the red bomber jacket, pain shoots through my chest. My stomach lurches; I clamp my hands over my belly.

Nausea, dizziness, sore boobs...

Holy cats, is *that* why I was at the hospital?

Am I pregnant?

My earlier accusation of Doctor Fairchild and his alien-baby experiments pops into my head with fresh cruel irony. No, this pain doesn't make sense. It's deeper...more in my chest than my stomach. A dull burning sensation, a hollow twinge pitted behind my sternum, burrowed uncomfortably between my lungs.

Something raw, something *inside* me...

Still, better safe than clueless.

Shoving my hands deep in the jacket pockets, I trot across the street. The General Store sits on the corner where the road splits off into a Y-fork on either side, like two streams around a rock. One direction leads toward the tree-lined Main Street, the other road narrowing and sloping uphill under a false dusk of chestnut trees. Pumpkins line the wide slatted porch of the General Store. A life-sized, carved wooden Native American chief in full feathered headdress glowers pompously at me, disapproving of my existence. Or maybe he's just ticked off because somebody left a pumpkin sitting on his head.

Cowbells clatter against the General Store's door as I enter. Okay, if I were a pregnancy test, where would I be? The aisle shelves are arranged neatly, but in no particular order. Tin stacks of beeswax lip balm sit snuggled amongst neat rows of canned beef-a-roni. I'm just passing the soda fridge when my reflection flashes at me. I freeze.

Tucked behind the safety of the chip rack, I lean in toward the fridge and study my facial features in the frosty glass.

So that's me.

C. Kyle. Nineteen years old. Though my forced smile might lie and say I'm cucumber cool, my rattled expression screams "little lost rabbit." Milky skin has a faint dusting of freckles that would probably disappear if I were wearing makeup. Under my bedraggled jungle of copper hair, my eyes are soft fawn brown, glazed and sleep deprived. They are a stranger's eyes, and that unsettles me to the core. That girl in the reflection is unfamiliar, but I simply have nothing to replace her with. No expectations. Nothing but a stranger's existence to pair with the name "C. Kyle."

The rack of newspapers catches my eye.

Thursday, October 19.

I grab a generic pregnancy test and a pack of turkey jerky and toss them onto the wooden checkout counter. The tall, lanky middle-aged clerk looks like he wandered off the set of some old Western saloon. The crisp white apron tied over his burgundy flannel shirt smells freshly washed. He picks up my turkey jerky with his long fingers, tapping his foot and whistling cheerfully through his woolly mammoth mustache, as if ringing up my stuff is the most exciting thing he's done all day. Maybe it is.

Small towns like this, everybody knows you. If C. Kyle lived here, chances are, everyone from the mailman to those kids running around outside would know me to the seventh generation.

I watch the tall clerk closely for hints that he might recognize me. But he's hard to read behind his mustache of award-winning proportions.

"So," he begins as I hang a little too eagerly. "Just passin' through Carnival Creeke?"

Well, that answers that. I'm not from this town.

"Yeah," I reply. "Guess I am."

"Didja see my Indian out front?"

"Yeah, I saw it."

"I'm thinking of puttin' him on wheels, just like in that book. Scarin' the kids for Halloween, you know? Boo!"

I smile as though I know what he's talking about. His face turns sly, waggling his bushy eyebrows at me.

"You like kids?"

He's holding up the pregnancy test box.

"Huh?" I stutter. "Oh...sure, if I get hungry enough."

His expression is horrified. I hot-foot it out the door without waiting for my receipt.

Why did I have to go and freak out Kindly Mustache Man like that? I decide my sense of humor is best left stuffed in my pocket with the 8-ball keychain. Now I just need to find a restroom to take this pregnancy test. Find out if C. Kyle's life is about to change.

Ha.

Can't believe I'm thinking of myself in the third person. No one should ever have to do that.

I lean on the porch rail, watching a spider climb the wood. Why can't I remember anything? My head isn't cut open and sewn up. Not even bruised. I'm telling myself I'm not worried, and that's the story I'm sticking to. Reports have shown that extreme emotional trauma can induce temporary memory loss. My brain will come back. It just needs a good jogging.

"What's up, Doc?"

The soft voice startles me; I spin around. For a second, I wonder if the scowling wooden Native American just spoke. But it wasn't the statue that just addressed me. It was the weird boy perched atop the statue's head.

With one hand, he flicks back the hood of his jacket.

I blink.

If he's trying to blend into this Norman Rockwell town, he's doing an astoundingly bad job in combat boots and black leather. He's my age, maybe a year older; twitchy as a barn cat, slender and sleek, and fish-belly pale. Despite the death pallor, he's a strikingly good-looking corpse. Under thick arched eyebrows, his eyes are delicately lashed and black as charcoal briquettes, his hair a wild tumble of coal-black curls. Small nose and high cheekbones, mouth like a Michelangelo painting, perfectly symmetrical, draped with a smirk that probably tastes like poison.

Atop the statue's head, he's holding the pumpkin whose seat he stole, rotating it in his hand with an unhurried, nonchalant twirl of his wrist.

Now, I'm positive this black-eyed pinup is no local high school boy. Something about him... The way his restless gaze keeps darting around, then landing back on me with vicious delight, assessing me, sizing me up, like a cat-calling construction worker who simultaneously wants to remove my liver with his teeth. He feels...misplaced.

Just like the water tower.

Just like me.

Under fingerless leather gloves, his long white fingers are dancing around, twitching and tapping against the pumpkin's shell, as if keeping to some silent rhythm inside his head.

He cocks his head, his black eyes boring into me.

"So. Are you having a good day?"

His voice is so soft it makes mine seem hoarse and squawky. I detect his accent this time – a careless Irish brogue that he speaks with a thick, lazy tongue, making the words "are you" sound more like "err ya."

And he's...tossing pleasantries about my day?

"Yeah, peachy," I mumble, hopefully leaving him no room to wonder whether I wanted to continue a conversation.

"WHAT'S UP, DOC?"

"So, Doc," he drawls like spun silk. "How ye liking Carnival Creeke so far?"

"It's nice, I guess."

"*Nice.* Ooh, she says the town is nice." He hops nimbly off the wooden statue, causing the studded chain belt around his hips to jingle. "And what ye think of the library?"

"The library?" I hesitate. "It's...full of books, I guess. You know, library-like. Listen, I'm gonna go now."

I start to walk. He follows me.

I make a stupid split-second decision to turn into the narrow alley between two buildings, as if I could vanish fast enough and Casper the Unfriendly Ghostboy would somehow magically lose interest and leave me alone. But he's right there behind me. I can hear his boots. Keeping up with me effortlessly.

So this is it. He's going to kill me. I'm going to get murdered in some alley between a bargain bookstore and the Pinkie Poochie Dog Day Spa.

Has C. Kyle ever thought about how she would die?

Well, I resolve wryly, *if he ditches my lifeless body here in the alley, maybe the town could serve me at their next barbecue-eating contest.*

"They don't do barbecue-eating contests in Carnival Creeke," the pretty weirdo purrs behind me. "Pie-eating contests, yes... But only in the summertime."

Wait, did I say that out loud?

"Dunno myself," he continues, gnawing twitchily at his thumbnail. "Ye take another gander at that library, ye start to notice things."

I stop walking. "Such as?"

"Why doncha try using yer eyes, Doc?"

Suddenly he's grabbed my head like a basketball, my skull knocking into his chin. Right in front of my face, he extends one gloved finger, pointing toward the mouth of the alley we came down. My skin is burning, my brain clanging around in the empty room where my defensive reflexes should have been.

Should have.

I have no choice but to follow his gaze.

The library is across the street. A red brick academy building with a bell tower and steeple; Colonial-era, probably a lot of history cemented in those bricks. Beyond the portico columns, wide stone steps yawn out into a well-manicured courtyard lawn shaded by peeling silver sycamores. The sun-dappled green grass is scattered with picnickers. A huge, ornate clock is mounted onto the belfry's spire, newer looking than the rest of the structure, probably added during the town's modern renovations.

The Irish jerk is having fun squeezing his cheek against mine. "Notice them ugly stone monstrosities decoratin' the roof?" He nods. "How many ye count?"

I look.

Just below the belfry, above the far-left drain spout, crouches a lone, ugly, smush-faced gargoyle. Hunkered on its perch, its enormous dry monkey mouth gapes open, its granite wings folded in perpetual rest. A stone guardian watching folk pass below with their library books.

Just *one* gargoyle. Not centered evenly on the roof, but way off to the left. This suggests there should have been a matching statue on the right.

Okay, I'll admit that's strange.

"All yer tax dollars at work," the feathery brogue hisses in my ear. "Seems a might odd that Carnival Creeke's founding fathers would go t'all that trouble to erect such a fine community monument, only to make it so bloody lopsided."

I shrug. "It doesn't really bother me."

I bet he's one of those super nitpicky people. Probably the kind of person, if his car radio volume is set on nine, he'll notch it up to ten just so it'll be even.

He sniffs my hair. "I don't have a car."

Okay, *I know* I didn't say *that* out loud. Either this guy is telepathic, or I'm seriously bad at the whole inner monologue thing. I decide not to ask him.

"Well," I squint at the lone gargoyle. "Maybe they had a reason for using just the one statue. Like those war memorials where the horse's hoof is lifted up if they were wounded in battle."

"General Simon Bolivar's statue has its hoof raised, an' he died at home from tuberculosis."

Fantastic. I was darn proud of pulling that little trivia nugget out of my amnesiac brain, and here it's thrown back in my face by some Irish psycho who watches too much Discovery channel.

"I don't have a TV," he purrs.

Yep. This freak is definitely reading my mind.

He pulls an old silver pocket watch from inside his leather jacket with his free hand, his other arm still pythoning my head.

"I'm gonna let ye go in a minute. Just keep yer mouth shut fer a sec and don't scream or nothin', yeah? What I'm about to tell ye... It's gonna change the way ye look at the world forever. I'm lettin' go now. No screamin'."

He does, and I don't.

A grin pulls at one corner of his poster-boy mouth, as if amused by my obedience. He raises the pocket watch and starts to swing it between both our faces. The chain sways between us. He studies me like he's doing laser surgery with his soulless black eyes. Strange eyes...eyes that neither glisten nor reflect any light. Makes my insides crawl. Like I need to shower off that look...

I wish he would just kill me or leave me alone. Get on with it. Whatever nastiness he dishes out, I'm fairly sure I could pop him a good punch in the throat before he could make me dead. But as long as he's feeling chatty, it means I don't have to put my theory to the test.

"Okay," I say slowly, ignoring the swinging watch and locking my gaze on him. "Tell me. Change my world."

He doesn't laugh.

"Well, I'll tell ye this," he purrs softly. A chilly edge creeps into his voice. "This morning there were *two* gargoyles on that roof."

He's playing with me now, I'm sure of it. Because I don't know a thing about gargoyles. For all I know, *I* could have carved the doggone thing. Or stolen it.

"And it wasn't stolen," he retorts, right on cue. "Or moved, or blown over by the wind. It's gone because it hiked up and *left*."

"You're not serious."

A slow, open-mouthed grin breaks his angelic face. "Serious as a heart attack."

He shoots me the most unreadable look, or maybe I just don't want to think about what's going on inside that head.

Then he turns and skitters up the alley wall like a spider.

I wish I could say this was the freakiest thing I would see today.

*

I'm hunched low on my elbows in a fifties-style diner booth. I'm starving, but I can't seem to stop chewing and actually swallow, so half of my hamburger sits shunned beside the empty box for the pregnancy test. The test was negative, by the way.

So, no babies, alien or otherwise.

But that means I still don't know what's wrong with me. Or why I checked myself into a hospital earlier this morning.

I take a deep drag of my milkshake. It's not helping; my stomach is churning like an acid-filled cement mixer. Against the wall behind me, a candy-colored vintage Wurlitzer jukebox cranks out a jaunty rendition of Ella Fitzgerald's "Cheek to Cheek." A decades-old song, preserved forever in this tinny recording. The jukebox's volume is set on nine. Reaching over my booth, I notch it up to ten and smile wryly into my arms.

Weird. I can remember the days of the week...and the capital of Arizona. Butter burns, margarine melts.

Mercury, Venus, Earth, Mars, Jupiter, Saturn, Uranus, Neptune.

I can remember plenty of stuff. But it's the missing chunks of C. Kyle that chill me the most. Nothing but wind whistling through those dark gaps.

Absently, I reach into my jacket pocket and fish out the plastic 8-ball keychain. Just like its larger toy counterpart, this 8-ball has a tiny window on it. I think I remember this toy from when I was a kid. You ask it a question, and some random answer appears the window, like a fortune teller's crystal ball. Of course, the answer you get is usually so vague it's hilarious.

Nevertheless, I cook up a question in my head.

What's my name?

I give the tiny 8-ball a shake, then flip it over. Nothing happens. The window remains inky black.

Okay, smarty-pants. Let's try a "yes-no" question.

Am I going to get eaten by a gargoyle today?

Genuinely curious about this one, I slowly turn over the 8-ball. Still nothing. Well, this thing is about as useful as a screen door on a submarine.

Why was C. Kyle hanging onto it in the first place?

I dunk my hands in my tumbler of ice water and splash it over my face, then grab the remains of my burger and slide out from the booth. Outside, the library clock tower heralds four o'clock. The sun has dipped lower, casting dazzling orange refractions that melt through the glass panes on the library's belfry.

I rip a bite off my burger and stand there chewing it. As the day grows later, the sycamore shadows are lengthening and the lone bat-faced gargoyle is getting hard to see. But it's still there. I can make out the shape of its folded wings. Hard to believe a creature like that is trolling around town right now. Alive, under a car somewhere, watching me... Or in the sky...

My burger feels like a brick in my stomach. The large-scale spook factor of this whole day is enough for me. Besides, I reckon I'd better start scouting out a place to stay the night while I figure things out.

I impale what's left of my burger on a prong of the black iron fence.

"Bon appétit," I mutter, giving the gargoyle a little salute. Then I turn on my heel, but I don't walk away. Because I'm staring at it again.

The water tower.

Looming sleepily on the horizon, it seems to stare back. What *is* it about that rusty old tank that prickles my guts so much? It wasn't something I'd heard, or read about. Something bad happened there. Happened to *me*.

Just can't remember what...

I want to bang my head against the diner's window box, but the purple pansies in it are so darn pretty I just can't bear putting a dent in it.

Concentrate, C. Kyle.

I narrow my eyes at the water tower. Fragments of memory, vaporous as wet tissue, sticking to the inside of my head like dregs in a sewer after a storm....

The smell of pine. Spicy smoke... My own sweat...

How long ago?

A few days? A few hours? I have no basis for measure. All I know is my pulse is racing...

No...

No, it isn't.

Why isn't my pulse racing?

By all rights, it should be. When I had startled to consciousness in that hospital room, by all human rights, adrenaline should have been surging through my veins and slamming against my ribcage.

And all of a sudden, the memory tumbles over me like a wave...

I hit the ground butt-first. A terrible way to land, and I know it, but I wasn't given the luxury of choice when we fell off the water tower. Jolts run up my spine and slam the air from my throat. He's sitting on me now, the black-eyed Irish freak, heavy on my chest despite his slight frame, his combat boots grinding my arms into the soil...

Even now, thinking back, I find I'm swallowing repeatedly, remembering how I'd struggled to push words out and keep the vomit down as I lay there in the dirt, beneath the shadow of that water tower. How I tried to keep calm, even though every bone might be broken and I was pretty sure that was blood pouring from my nose.

Then Irish freak reaches into the duffle bag slung over his back and pulls out some kind of brushed metal cylinder.

"What've you got there?" I ask him. I have to hand it to myself, I sound downright casual, despite my voice shaking like a baby bird.

He doesn't look at me.

"Ye seen those tubes at the bank drive-through window, right?"

He calmly screws a bulb into the top of the cylinder, attaches three wires like miniscule jumper cables. It's only when he's peeled down the neck of my shirt and I can feel the edges of the cylinder boring into the thin skin of my chest, a ring of tiny drills burrowing into the taut flesh over my breastbone – that's when his black eyes shift down to me.

I can't lift my knee. Can't snap my arms wide, or buck to throw him off balance...

So I do the only logical thing I have left.

I've just worked up a good mouthful of spit when he wags a warning finger at me.

"Shhh, easy, Doc." The son-of-a-hump is actually grinning. "Stop wigglin'. It'll be less than silky if ye tense up."

That open-mouthed leer. Like a shark, like night itself.

Like the gargoyle grinning down at me...

The canister releases a hiss. It's now air-tight against my tented skin, the smell of singed flesh stinging my eyes.

Here we go...

I brace my back against the soil and swear on all that is and ever was that he will not hear me utter a sound when it happens...

And suddenly I remember.

I *remember* what he stole from me, beneath Carnival Creeke's old water tower.

My fingers fly to my neck, pressing against the side of my throat to my jugular, searching for a pulse.

Nothing.

Where my heartbeat should have been, there is simply...nothing. There's enough adrenaline streaking through my system to light up the sky like the Fourth of July. But all my synapses are firing blanks, all at once, off into a canyon of nothingness. Nothing to receive them.

Although I know better, my fingers dart to my wrist, scrambling for a second opinion. No pulse. I try my other wrist, and, in a last-ditch effort, I find myself tearing away my jacket and pressing my palm flat against the stinging, circular scar that the metal canister left over my breastbone, one hand curled around the other as though I intend to do CPR on myself.

Nothing.

Silence.

Because my heart is gone.

ONE DOWN BY SUNDOWN

The human heart beats 100,000 times a day, tirelessly sending two-thousand liters of blood, oxygen and vital nutrients surging through your body, feeding every organ. By an average lifetime, the heart will beat 35-million times. It never sleeps. Never stops. Because when it stops, so do you.

Scientifically speaking, there is no frakking way that I should be alive. And yet here I am. I may not be ticking, but somehow, slapping physics in the face, I'm still tocking. Maybe I'm a zombie.

Or maybe I can't die.

A silver Chevy Tahoe is reeling into view, taking the street corner a little too fast. The calm of my mind is transcendent, like water. There's only one way to test my immortal zombie theory.

I plant my palms on the curb and cartwheel into the street.

It's an oddly random childhood memory that flashes into my head, vivid and warm: Ice cream bars melting in the hot picnic basket, our fingers sticky on the badminton rackets that we were using to swat at gnats down by the lake. We needed a ball, so somebody pulled out a hard-boiled egg. It's funny how I suddenly and perfectly remember every squishy detail of that egg colliding with the racket...

As the silver Tahoe smacks me through the air, I'm the egg.

Then I'm gasping on the asphalt like a beached whale.

I'm not immortal.

I feel like an idiot. People are running into the road, but not to crowd around me – they rush right past me. Apparently, the lunatic who just cartwheeled out in front of a truck takes second fiddle to the hulking gray shape slinking up onto the roof of the post office.

Enter the gargoyle.

Making awful burbling sounds, it ratchets up the shingles on gangly limbs, stone-flecked rib cage rising and falling rapidly. It turns its gaping mouth to the crowd below and they recoil at its face, a ghastly mash-up of ape and bat. The creature surveys them with wildly rolling eyeballs; a couple of folks pull out their cellphones to snap pictures. The reality of this creature being here is blowing their minds, but I can't say I'm paying too much attention at the moment because I'm still lying in the road trying to remember how to breathe.

The silver Tahoe that creamed me skids to a halt. A blonde teenager in a gray hoodie tumbles out of the driver's side, nearly strangling himself with his seatbelt until he remembers to unbuckle it. His glasses fall off and bounce under his truck.

"Were you trying to kill yourself?!" he gasps at me.

"No," I wince, peeling myself off the pavement and pretty likely leaving half my molecules smeared on it. "Well, sort of. It's complicated."

He puts his glasses back on and stares at me like I just turned into a giant squid.

"It's a science experiment," I offer weakly.

Actually, it's not *me* he's staring at, but my left arm. I look down. My arm is hanging at all sorts of creative angles. Pretty sure my shoulder is dislocated.

Tahoe Kid looks a little green. He nods at my arm.

"Uh... Was *that* supposed to happen?"

"Preferably not."

I go to slide my jacket off and pain stabs through my shoulder. Oh, spank me with a frying pan... I'm going to have to pop this stupid bone back into its socket. Lucky for me it's an anterior dislocation, which means I should be able to do the job myself without the help of Doctor Fairchild or any of his crew. But it also hints that this isn't the first time I've dislocated this shoulder.

C. Kyle, what have you been up to?

Exhaling all my breath out between my teeth, I rock back and forth on my butt cheeks until I've backed all the way up against the Tahoe's tire. I cradle my left arm limply in my lap, easing the elbow to a ninety-degree angle. Pain sinks its jaws into my entire upper body.

This is not going to be fun.

Slowly, steadily, I rotate my entire left arm and shoulder outward, and begin to press hard on my balled fist. I feel the shivers setting in; my whole body is convulsing and my skin is slippery. Tahoe Kid is running around behind me like a chicken trying to find ways to "make me more comfortable." Eventually he goes into his truck and turns the radio onto some kind of soothing jazz.

"I'm not giving birth here!" I try to holler, but it comes out more a sick croak. Anyway, I don't think he heard me. The drone of the gargoyle's crowd over at the post office has gotten pretty loud.

Tahoe Kid crouches beside me again, a rolled-up T-shirt in his hands. "Here, I thought this might, um, maybe you could, y'know..."

I jerk my head emphatically for him to scram, since my head is the only thing I can control right now and I really need to concentrate and it really looks like he's formulating some method of wedging that T-shirt behind my head like a pillow. Kid looks worse than I probably do. I think he might actually pass out in a second. Hope he doesn't hit his head on the pavement; I can't tend to him.

I inhale and push my fist hard.

Pop.

Searing pain explodes through my body as the ball joint of my shoulder scrapes back into its socket. For a moment, all I see is white.

And then I see *him*.

Across the street, black leather, standing motionless while the world spins around him. The only other pair of eyes not glued to the post office. Eyes black as burnt brisket, surveying the scene from a distance with dark interest.

Wonder if it's me or the gargoyle he's so engrossed in.

I curl up to my feet and start limping across the street toward him. A rising heat in my guts suffocates out all my other senses.

Tahoe calls out. "Whoa, hey, can I at least, uh, give you some money or something–" He trails off as pencils and granola bar wrappers and completely legal-looking electronic devices spill out of his messenger bag. But I can't stop, can't even acknowledge the pain I know I'm feeling in my shoulder.

I feel nothing, see nothing – nothing but the Irish creep's grin watching me approach.

"Hey!" I bark at him. "I think you've got something of mine!"

The black-eyed organ thief winks and slips lithely into a Chinese restaurant. I plunge through the swinging door after him, nearly knocking a brown take-out bag from the hands of a woman exiting. I immediately halt in the doorway, begging my eyes to hurry up and adjust to the dim red light.

Lau Chow's Bistro is all tassels and gold. Xian soldier figurines squat in front of miniature gongs on wooden stands between the red-curtained booths. A dinner buffet has been set out early, the table lined with metal hotplates and strewn with white Christmas lights.

No sign of the Irish creep. It's just me, the hefty Hawaiian waiter yawning behind the counter, and the sizzling buffet. Steamy air, thick with savory sesame oil and Kung Pow presence.

Ugh…no, can't think about food right now. My stomach starts churning. Feels like a somersaulting rhino trying to bust out…

I slide slowly into the booth nearest the counter, every hair on my body as tense as a razor. There's small glass dish of wrapped fortune cookies. These things just keep popping up today. Well, since I missed my chance earlier… I grab a fortune cookie and tuck it in the pocket of my jacket.

Big Kahuna eases over and hands me a menu. He's the size of a polar bear, a grease-stained red apron tied between his back rolls. His doughy face grimaces at the way I'm cradling my left shoulder.

"You want some ice for that?" he asks me. "We got a big freezer in the back–"

"Thanks, I'm okay."

I pretend to peruse today's specials, but my gaze hasn't stopped sweeping the room. Above the bar, a green-handled katana rests on a display stand above the liquor shelf.

I nod up at it. "You know your sword is Japanese?"

Big Kahuna shrugs non-confrontationally. "Dude, I'm from Connecticut."

"Ye look a bit worse fer the wear, Doc."

The sound of the soft voice snaps my head around so fast that I almost throw my arm out of socket again. The Irish freak is grinning at me from an adjacent dining booth, the tropical fish tank between us. His perfect face looks pallid, corpse-like even, in the fever-dream glow of the shimmering aquarium.

"Oh sorry, should I look better?" I hiss through the glass. "*I remember* what you did to me."

"Congrats." His feathery voice is like black satin.

"How am I even still alive?!" I snap.

"Take care'a yerself, doc." He studies me through his eyelashes. "Ye find yer a tad more...*delicate* now."

"More delicate than *what?*"

"Than ye were before."

"Before you stole my–" But I can't say it. The ridiculous words won't even form on my tongue.

Before you stole my heart.

"You–" His leather creaks as he traces my outline through the fish tank glass. "Only got six liters of blood in yer veins. An' it's doin' a fine job bein' recycled. But don't push it too far. A cigarette, a soda–" His voice lowers even softer. "All these could flat-line ye. If ye *could* flat-line, that is. But I think ye catch my drift."

I hate what I'm about to say. I hate the weakness I'm about to rip open and expose. And worst of all, I hate that I'm exposing it to *him*.

"Okay." I inhale slowly. "Listen. I ate a burger earlier. And onion rings... Not exactly health food. My stomach's been killing me ever since."

The black-eyed freak actually chuckles. "At the diner? Number two on the menu? Comes with a milkshake. Did ye order that, too?"

"You think this is funny?" I howl. "One meal and now I'm going to die, thanks to you! You could've warned me earlier! Could've troubled yourself to give me a health disclaimer when you made your little '*withdrawal*' from me."

"So that's a yes? Ye drank the milkshake, then?"

"Just tell me how long I've got, you–"

"Relax. Ye not gonna die." His boots scrape as he gets up. "Yer lactose intolerant. Skip the milkshakes from now on."

My mouth falls open. I snap it closed.

I'm not really relieved. Well, maybe a little. But mostly I'm furious. It's infuriating, him knowing this factoid about me when even *I* didn't know. To have information as intimate as my irritable bowels... Either this boy is a very close personal friend, or he's got serious dirt on me. And I don't need memories to know this creep is *not* a friend. Might as well have a flashing neon sign over his head blaring 'PSYCHO,' with the word 'psycho' circled, underlined, and highlighted in red.

He drops unceremoniously into my booth. My face burns. My eyes dart toward the restaurant exit, calculating the exact number of steps it would take to reach it if I had to make a dash for it.

"Aw, I know," he purrs smugly, leaning forward onto my table. "I scared ye just now, didn't I? What I said about ye bein' lactose intolerant? Ye questionin' how much info I got in here on ye." He taps his temple, a hint of a smirk playing at his mouth.

I'd love to set his hair on fire. See if he'll keep smirking.

But I force myself to smile back, saying, "You don't know anything about me that I don't know myself."

"Okay." He puts a cigarette between his lips without looking at me. "Then what's yer name?"

"...Kyle."

"Yer *first* name."

"How do you know that's *not* my first name?"

"This ain't the eighties. Kyle ain't yer first name." He cups one fingerless-gloved hand, lighting the end of the cigarette in his mouth. "But it don't really matter. There are more important things stewin'. Namely, a gargoyle on the loose."

"Oh, and I guess *your* name is much more public–"

"Holliday." He answers without skipping a beat. "Rascal Holliday. Careful now, mind ye, don't breathe the smoke." He waves one gloved hand in front of my face, gentleman that he is. Beneath the smoke, he smells like cherries.

"'Rascal,' huh?" I mutter. "Would've pegged you for the more mysterious nameless type."

He shrugs twitchily. "Call me whatever ye want. Like I said, there are more important things brewin'. What once was stone, now flesh an' bone. An' before the sun goes bye-bye tonight, ye gonna have to find a way to turn that monster *back* into stone."

He pulls out his old pocket watch. Glancing at it, he cocks one black eyebrow. "Better hustle, Doc."

"Excuse me? After what you *did* to me–" I can barely spit the words between my gritted teeth. "What makes you think I'm going to oblige and scamper off after some crazy-pants monster just because you appeared out of thin air and gave me an order?"

Whatever he said to convince me, I'll never know.

Because the next thing I know I'm suddenly standing alone by the fish tank, watching the little clown fish slide in and out of a plastic pirate. No sign of the jerk who just introduced himself as Rascal Holliday. Yet another thing to throw on my "unexplained" pile for today.

Weirdest of all, I'm surprisingly calm. Even my desire to wring Rascal Holliday's neck has cooled down. I'm inexplicably refocused on hunting down the stone monster I saw earlier, and putting it back where it belongs. Completing my mission is an urge as strong and real as the need to eat, or drink, or scratch an itch. All I know is I've got a job to do.

All I know is...*that gargoyle has it coming tonight.*

I slide down the bar counter on my butt and close my hand around the Japanese sword. I look over at Big Kahuna.

"Sorry, Connecticut. Mind if I borrow this for a sec?"

He puts both hands in the air. "Hey dude, do your thing."

I skid to a halt in the center of the street outside, sword in my hand. According to the clock tower on the library, it's just after four-thirty. That should be plenty of time...

If I knew what on earth I was supposed to do next.

Across the street, Hank from the auto parts shop and that Tahoe Kid are sitting at a little café table, trying to look inconspicuous. They've obviously been watching me, wary,

36

waiting for me to exit the Chinese restaurant. Not that I blame them. I'm new. Not exactly their typical small town two-scoops-of-vanilla entertainment.

I point at Tahoe, singling him out. Kid hit me with his truck; he owes me.

I yell, "Make my day and tell me how to kill a gargoyle, will you?"

It's a rhetorical question, of course. I'm just buying time while I'm thinking. Tahoe gives me a look I probably deserve, considering I'm pointing a sword at him. Then all of a sudden he snaps his fingers.

"Rock, paper, scissors!" he exclaims and takes off across the lawn toward the library. I'm in hot pursuit behind him, but I can't help feeling like I should be chasing something much more winged and monstrous and bitey.

"Anything you care to share?" I holler at his back.

"You remember that old game, right?" he shouts over his shoulder. "Well, what beats rock? I've got an idea, promise!"

Great. The fate of this cute little town and all its future pie-eating contests rest on the promise of a kid with a TRON patch sewn to the rear of his pants.

We take the library front steps two at a time, the lifeless silhouette of the gargoyle's harmless twin leering down at us from the overhang. The irony here does not escape me.

Using my good arm, we heave open the cherry wood doors together and plunge through the corridors faster than anyone should ever move in a library. Our footsteps echo through the high stone cathedral rafters. This place is a castle of aisles, a labyrinth of a million words. Fortunately, Tahoe is apparently a nerd and knows exactly where he's going. He disappears into the bowels of the labyrinth. I hear a rolling ladder across the floor, and the muffled thump of books being slid off their shelf.

I fold the sword across my body with my good arm and begin to pace. "Faster, please?"

Rainbow-colored paper kites rotate lazily from the light fixtures over my head.

"You know," Tahoe's voice carries from somewhere down the aisle. "You can actually win at rock-paper-scissors every time. What I'm saying is, the game isn't totally random. Because humans aren't really random. Living things tend to use some kind of pattern."

"That's very fascinating."

But I think I understand what he's getting at. He's saying you can play the game with a degree of skill by recognizing, and then exploiting, your opponent's non-random behavior.

Tahoe comes careening from the far aisle, not unlike how his truck did when we met in the street earlier.

"Here – here we go!" He almost loses his glasses again, trying to keep three books tucked under his elbows without losing certain pages. He dumps them all in a controlled spill and spreads them out onto the floor.

"Okay, check this out. Dead gargoyles."

I squat down on the floor and study the pages he's hovering his hands over.

They're illustrations. Old wood-carving plates transferred to ink, each picture depicting a hero – some holding spears, one with an English broadsword – and each brandishing the head of a dead stone monster.

"Does it mention how they killed them?"

"Well, not exactly... But they *did* it."

"Not overwhelming me with confidence, kid," I grumble. "Anything else helpful about these pictures?"

"Uh, they're all doing their little death-pose at night? Look, the moon appears in the background of each illustration. See?"

It's true. There's the moon, a crescent slice in a black sky, peeking through a fruit tree. And again, a full-on bright orb, high on a hilltop. All these gargoyles were slain at night. Which means...

A whole lot of nothing.

I rock back on my heels, hotly annoyed at the long-dead artists who penned these not-quite answers. I know it's childish, but if they're not going to offer anything useful to my current situation hundreds of years later, how dare these drawings even exist.

"I don't know," Tahoe rakes a hand through his sandy blond hair and starts flipping pages. "Maybe their gargoyles were stone in the daytime. Maybe they only came alive at night?"

"Well, that's not the case here. Mr. Cuddly out there is *very* much alive, and it's five in the afternoon."

"Yeah, I know." He squats beside me, defeated and confused. "Sorry. I thought for sure this wouldn't be totally useless. I mean, considering we're dealing with something that was fiction until an hour ago..." Then he turns and stares straight at me. He's wearing a curious expression. "You were sent here to help us... Weren't you?"

I don't know how to answer him.

The sudden bell clang makes us both jump out of our skins. I'm actually surprised I don't jump higher. C. Kyle is a rock. The clang – more like a sonic boom – is resounding through all the library rafters and rattling the volumes on the shelves. The rainbow kites spin wildly overhead. Either Carnival Creeke has the world's biggest bell up in that belfry, or a small planet just crash-landed on this library's roof.

We bolt out to the front lawn. I crane my head back, looking up.

It's like a scene from some Japanese monster flick. The gargoyle is slapping its way across the library's slanted roof, ripping off shingles and whipping its gaping monkey mouth back and forth. Panting out a horrid rasp, it drops off the side of the roof, landing in the graveyard. Several tombstones crumble like cheese as the creature scrambles in reverse, flattening the wrought iron gate with its gangly granite hide and then trying to tear the first car it collides with in half.

The clock on the library says 4:52. Not an even-hour, so I *know* that bell didn't just ring by itself. Some yahoo must be up in the belfry.

"Hey!" I shout up at the tower. A portly man with a face like a Windy City red hot peers down at me from the belfry like I just caught him in the cookie jar.

"I was thinking," he bawls feebly. "Perhaps the bell might scare it away?"

I have a headache.

I yell, "Well, perhaps you take a break from thinking and get your butt down from there, eh Quasimodo?"

The rest of the street crowd doesn't take much prompting, heeding my instructions and hightailing it to the nearest door that locks. Tucking its legs up, the gargoyle beats its bat wings and soars off against the sun. It doesn't stay up very long, tilting sharply and dropping onto a shingled roof in the distance.

"Looks like it's landed again," I observe. "What building is that?"

"Oh, man..." Tahoe grabs his hair in both hands and blows out a breath. "That's Tuscany Mill. An old grain depot they fancied up and made into a restaurant. It's kinda overpriced, but they've got this killer cheesy clam stuff–"

"Okay. You sure?"

He shrugs sheepishly. "I kinda work there."

*

The town's streets are laid out in a traditional grid pattern, taking me straight to the plaza where the Tuscany Mill restaurant is.

The old mill has been given a facelift for the twentieth century, but certain remnants have been left untouched for charm's sake. Wooden wine barrels, now housing begonias; a short stone wall encircling a cobbled patio has been roped off and set with iron tables for outdoor seating, its forest green patio umbrellas strung with white lights. A covered wagon, plucked straight out of the Old West, has been permanently parked at the entrance between two iron streetlamps. A heavy chain has been looped through the wagon's wooden wheel spokes, bolting it to the streetlamp as though someone might actually try to steal it.

I take the weathered wooden steps two at a time to reach the restaurant's balcony entrance.

"Welcome to Tuscany Mill!" chirps the blonde teen at the hostess podium. "Will you be having dinner tonight, or just dessert–" Her expression crumbles in horror at the sight of me tromping up, sword in hand.

Dinner or dessert? Both sound fabulous… Maybe later. Depending on how this goes.

The main dining area is upstairs. The bright, atrium-style room is filled with hanging plants, old iron pulleys and other antique mill equipment parts suspended decoratively from the ceiling timbers. Along the wooden walls are framed sepia-tone pictures featuring the original grain mill in the 1800s. Most of the dining room's east wall is observatory glass. Outside is a roof ledge covered in white pebbles, overlooking the broad expanse of the town.

I jog along the row of window-side tables until I've located the optimum exit nearest the ledge. An elderly couple looks on in horror as I mount their table, taking care not to knock over their breadbasket with my katana. There's really no point apologizing as I'm placing my boots carefully between their dinner plates, but I do anyway.

The glass window slides open easily. I cat-crawl out and drop onto the white pebbled ledge. Here the roof drops off sharply, and I can see the town spread out below like a miniature model.

In the distance is a black oval jogging track, flanked by rows of silver bleachers and floodlights that glint in the flame-colored sunset. That must be Carnival Creeke High School, the one having their homecoming game tomorrow night. A white square building, its roof marked with a faded red cross indicating the helicopter landing pad on the hospital; beyond it a vast patchwork quilt of farm fields blankets the horizon. Far on the opposite side of town I can make out the water tower, its domed head nestled in pine. It appears that Tuscany Mill is the tallest structure in Carnival Creeke.

I turn back to the ledge. An HVAC unit hums in the corner. There's a service ladder behind it, leading up to the top-most pinnacle of the roof. I quietly hoist myself up the rusty ladder rungs with my good arm, the katana tucked under my other. It's slow going, using just one arm – but if that gargoyle is still up here on this roof, I can't afford to blow my one vital advantage: Surprise.

I ease up onto the ledge of the precipice.

Surprise.

The abomination is sprawled out on the shingles like a dog in the sun. It takes up half the roof, its membranous wings stretched between its skeletal limbs, ribs heaving rapidly under the late-day bake. The creature's awful face is pointed away from me, so I can't tell whether the thing is sleeping or just resting. But it hasn't noticed me yet.

You know those moments when you know you'll be lying in bed later that night, completely saturated in whatever emotion you've earned, depending on whether you hit that one-in-a-million shot? Tonight, I'll either be lying in bed reliving whatever I do next...

Or I reckon I'll be too dead to care.

Tucking my useless left arm in an L-shape tightly against my body, I hook my fingers through the belt loop at my right hip. My right hand tilts the katana's tip upward, slowly squeezing my pinkie finger along the sword's woven handle. It was chilly down on the restaurant ledge, but up here on the roof the wind is gale-force freezing. It's all I can do to keep myself from becoming a human kite. I keep my eyes on the gargoyle. I'll only get one shot at this.

Here goes nothing.

I rocket into a bounding sprint across the roof, slicing the sword downward at the creature's bulging neck.

The blade snaps off with an anticlimactic clunk.

Stone.

It's not flesh – it's still *STONE.*

Rock beats scissors.

The monster flips its bulk, surprisingly nimble on its clawed feet. It whips its mutant monkey face my way, cavernous bat mouth swinging and spewing strings of spittle. It splits the air with a horrid scream that's unnervingly human.

I fling the sword handle as hard as I can at the gargoyle's gaping pie-hole, hoping it might fly down its throat and choke. But the creature just jerks its head aside and the sword handle bounces uselessly off its still-intact neck.

Okay, Plan B.

Run.

I spring backwards, and for a moment there's nothing but whistling air. I land hard onto the roof ledge below, pulling off an awkward sloppy tuck-and-roll. My right elbow crunches into the white pebbles and the sinews in my left shoulder ignite on fire; it hurts so badly that for a moment I can't tell which way is up. I halt in a crouch, shutting the lid on the pain. Frantically, I scan my surroundings. The roof ledge is enclosed on three sides, one side covered in the restaurant's glass windows which I crawled out. There's the ladder, and the humming AC unit.

The gargoyle thunders down onto ledge, spraying white pebbles and making guttural, wheezing barks at me. Acknowledging blind stupidity, I sprint straight toward the living statue as fast as I can – and for a split second, the creature balks in surprise. That's all the time I need to pull a Bo Duke slide across the AC unit and land on my knees behind it. I plunge all ten fingers into the panel-mount gauge and pull as hard as I can. The screws pop off, along with a few of my fingernails, and I hoist the gauge with both hands. It's incredibly heavy, like a cinder block stuffed into a fire extinguisher. Using all my might and all the centrifugal force, I swing toward the charging monster and I smash it in the face. The beast's head breaks off and rolls through the pebbles.

We both take a staggered step backwards.

Then the gargoyle crouches down, scoops up its head like a baby, and flies away.

For a moment, there's just wind whistling. Then the squeak of glass, and a muffled din behind me. I look back over my shoulder. Aghast faces are pressed against the restaurant's windows, all left their dinner to come watch my shenanigans.

I've got an audience. Super.

So much for keeping a low profile.

I raise my good arm in the air and belt out, "Try the cheesy clam stuff. Goodnight!"

Which was actually a stupid thing to do, because then I have to crawl back in through the window and limp across that dead-quiet dining room like a moron while they all stare at me.

*

I spend the next hour wandering the town streets, scouring the darkening sunset skies. Trudging along, I have a lot of time to think, and I'm only thinking about one thing. Something Tahoe said earlier. Something about rock-paper-scissors.

I can play this game with a degree of skill by recognizing, then exploiting, my opponent's non-random behavior.

My opponent is the gargoyle. Think, C. Kyle. What have you seen that creature do that's been non-random?

The last of the sun slips down and streetlights come on, casting evenly spaced circles of soft light along the sidewalk. Jack-o-lanterns grin and flicker in shop windowsills.

Getting chilly. I flick the collar of my bomber jacket up around my neck. My hands and feet are going slightly numb. I rub my fingers, scrubbing off the cold.

Cold?

That's it.

Earlier, the gargoyle had been stretched out on the restaurant roof, basking in the sun. Just like a lizard. Reptiles are endothermic, cold-blooded. With no means to regulate their own body heat, they rely on the sun for fuel. Without warmth, their energy is sapped, like a car running on fumes. If there's one non-random thing I can bet on, I'm betting that gargoyle is camped out right now in the hottest place in town.

Literally.

I've walked an entirely fruitless loop around town, now I'm right back in sight of the library on the street where Tahoe hit me. I frown up at the inky clusters of gray in the sky. It's gotten way too dark. Strips of deep blue dusted with stars begin to appear. If something was flying around up there, I'd never be able to see it. My only hope now is finding the warmest spot in Carnival Creeke.

I stop walking.

Lau Chow's is across the street. The Chinese restaurant sits in a dark pocket on the tree-lined sidewalk, spidery branches shadowing the pale circles cast by the streetlamps. Decorative lit torches are affixed on either side of the restaurant's gold-painted dragon sign, illuminating it by gaslight. And there, nestled tightly on the ledge above the sign, in the warm, flickering shadows, is the gargoyle.

How perfectly non-random.

No wonder all those old illustrations showed those guys slaying their gargoyles at night! Nighttime – when the creatures would have been sapped of warmth, deprived of their energy sources. Sluggish. Vulnerable.

"Tahoe, I could kiss you!" I hiss in a throaty, elated whisper.

Not so fast, Kyle. That monster will still be rock-hard, and you're acutely without a weapon...

Then it hits me. Something the Big Kahuna said earlier. It's a desperate shot in the dark...

But it's the only chance I've got left.

Squatting, I grab a rolled-up town gazette from the doorstep of a closed shop. For those who missed my cartwheel into the road earlier, I'm sure my barreling across the street narrowly missing becoming part of several people's bumpers will give them a fun story to talk about at the dinner table tonight. Gripping the rolled-up newspaper, I run under Lau Chow's ledge, jump as high as I can, and give the coiled gargoyle a good, hard whack. Just enough to wake it.

My roar for everyone in Lau Chow's to scram is enough to get their attention. Everyone clears out like the place is on fire. For all they know, it probably is. Now alone in the empty restaurant, I crouch behind the buffet table, gleaming in the Christmas lights.

Wait for it...

The headless gargoyle explodes into the restaurant, splintering the doorframe and sending up a flurry of menu brochures and coupons for the Pinkie Poochie Spa. The enraged beast fills the narrow aisle, its gangly limbs and heaving ribcage scraping the booth tables. I can't guess where it dropped its head, or how it's still moving toward me without any eyes, but who am I to question rules.

The gargoyle makes several attempts to spread its bat wings, but it doesn't have enough room; its wings thump the walls, toppling Xian soldier figurines from their stands in a hail of fortune cookies. The fish tank tips over and shatters, gushing neon-blue water. I'm just barely able to scoop the poor teeny clown fish off the glass-peppered rug into tea kettle before the gargoyle is back trying to give me a clawed hug of death.

After a fumbling just short of deadly, I manage to roll the heavy wooden cash register podium between my body and the lunging monster. It's by a frenzied hair's breadth that I'm managing to keep the podium between us. Like a strobe, the granite body flings itself at me again and again, lunging and colliding against the wooden podium with a mad and unearthly speed, each time knocking me a staggered step backward. Even without its head, the gargoyle's rage is overpowering – all it would take is one swipe of that stone talon, or the edge of a two-hundred-pound wing, and I'll be ground beef.

The cash register pops open with a musical *ching*. Rolls of quarters bounce off both of us. Crap, it hurts.

Suddenly there's no more room behind me, and my back slams against the wall. I roll over onto my stomach, scrambling through the swinging kitchen door. The rubber floor leaves an imprint on my hand as I sprint behind the metal food prep cart. Woks and pans clatter to the floor, signifying the gargoyle's arrival right behind me.

Didn't Kahuna say there was a big freezer back here? If he meant "small ice tray," I am about to die in the stupidest way possible. Then I spot it, behind a rack of soup cans. A huge, metal walk-in freezer.

A silver containment chamber of hope.

Skidding toward the freezer, I rip aside the strike latch and heave the door open, the kitchen floor booming behind me. I tumble in faster than the stinging cold air can get out, knocking over every box, every shelf, every vacuum-sealed pack of frozen meat, until I run out of things to throw and I've reached the back wall of the freezer.

I whirl around to face the gargoyle as it charges in after me. Shielding myself futilely with a gallon can of stewed tomatoes, I brace for impact. But the headless monster gets tripped up in the pile of shelves that I knocked over. It sways drunkenly on its gangly clawed legs, galumphing around in the cold chamber. Its movement grows slower, thick and confused. Then at last it collapses, dumping heavily into the pile of food containers. It doesn't move.

Not waiting for confirmation, I plunge in like a lumberjack, using the can of tomatoes to smash off as many pieces of the creature as I can – a leg, part of a wing, a whole lot of claws. I keep hammering until my knees buckle and I fall onto the stone body, my cheek smushing against the cold granite.

Stone-cold.

Past the walk-in freezer entrance, the kitchen door is wide open. I can see all the way out into the dining area. Red and blue police lights strobe outside, casting weird glimmers through the jagged, busted fish tank glass. I can't exit that way. Too many questions, and I don't think I could string three words together right now.

The numbness I'd felt earlier in my hands and feet has spread, now creeping up my arms and legs. I don't feel cold. More like my limbs have been chewed off at the shoulders and hips, replaced with the sensation of ants crawling around in my veins where my blood should be. And it's getting hard to breathe. Without my heart, I knew I shouldn't run myself too hard. Rascal Holliday warned me I had a limit. Apparently, I just crossed it.

I slink out the back kitchen door into an alley. No people, nothing but trash under a light bulb. Stumbling along the cold sidewalk, I lose my balance every few steps, pushing myself back upright with my good arm. My vision narrows like a tunnel. I'm doing my best to stay in hidden in shadows, but I keep staggering into the soft light circles cast by the streetlamps. A few people stop to stare at me, but I can't remember why I would care.

My throat and lungs feel like they've shrunk to the size of a drinking straw. Every breath is filled with broken glass. By the time I drag myself to the wrecked graveyard, I can't feel a thing and I collapse, gasping, on J. Robertson's cold tombstone. Funny how this day came full circle.

It's alright, Kyle…

Giving myself silent permission, my eyes slide closed.

"Well, well, Doc."

Even before I can wrench my eyelids open, I hear his gloved hands coming together in a slow clap.

Rascal Holliday is standing over me. I can't see the creep's face. He's silhouetted against the streetlamp, a faint halo outlining his shoulders and wild black hair. The only reason I know he's real is his breath coming in slow, smoky swirls, just like mine in the cold air. He doesn't offer congratulatory roses, or some futuristic serum to help me breathe. He doesn't even ask if I'm okay.

And ready or not, here comes his feathery Irish brogue.

"Remember today," he purrs. "Not that I have to tell ye to. Ye *will* remember. Startin' tomorrow, the day will repeat. Twenty-four hours, skippin' like a bad record. So don't bother buyin' a calendar. Oh, and not that I'm up in yer business, but ye may wanna choose wisely where ye hole up for beddy-bye tonight. 'Cause it's gonna get real familiar, real fast."

Holliday leans down so I can see his face. His lips pull back into one of those open-mouthed grins, only this time, I swear his teeth appear sharp and jagged, like a shark's.

But I blink, and they're just normal teeth.

"One more thing," he says. "Today was just a warm-up. Each day, there'll be somethin'...*different*. Like today, the gargoyle. A wildcard, if ye will. One day, it might be werewolves. The next day, everyone'll be inside-out. Ye gonna have to find the wildcard each day – and neutralize it – before the day resets. That's the game. Think of it as an Easter egg hunt where the eggs can kill ye. Here. Write it all down in this notebook."

He pulls a spiral-bound out of his leather jacket and hands it to me. With effort, I wiggle my numb hand and take it. On the notebook's cover is a bunch of doe-eyed kittens in a pink basket.

I frown. "It has kittens on it," I cough in a raspy whisper.

"And?"

"So I'm supposed to write about...*inside-out* people...in a book with kittens?"

"It'll make it easier to keep track of things if ye write it down. Ye can whine about the cover design later. Trust me, come sundown tomorrow, some Day-Glo kittens won't seem worth it."

Is this guy for real?

"Tomorrow?" I sputter hoarsely. "Look at me! What makes you think I'll even make it through the rest of tonight?"

"Oh, ye not gonna die tonight." He gnaws at his thumbnail, distracted, his black eyes trailing the people strolling by outside the cemetery fence, oblivious. "In fact, ye gonna wake up tomorrow feelin' right as rain."

"Is that a joke?"

Actually, my voice does sound better. The hoarseness is gone, my throat having gradually expanded from a drinking straw to a slightly larger drinking straw. And I can feel my pinky toes inside my boots.

"I'm not jokin' with ye, Doc. Sometimes the wildcard will be obvious. Sometimes, ye gonna have to hunt it down. And sometimes...it'll be hunting *you*. But ye gotta figure it out. 'Cause if ye don't use yer brain an' find a way to fix the wildcard before the day resets, it's gonna stick. Permanently. No more resets, no second chances. And no end."

A vicious edge creeps into his voice. "You, and everyone in this town, will be stuck in that same day. Forever."

"Like, everyone will *stay* inside-out?"

"Correct."

"Wow," I snort. "Sunscreen sales sure would go up…"

I think about this for a moment. How would you "fix" everyone getting turned inside-out, anyway?

"Oh, they won't actually be inside-out," Holliday coolly counters my thought. "That was just an example. But beyond that… No promisin'."

"Fine, okay." Glaring at him, I fold the kitten notebook in half and stuff it down the back pocket of my pants. "So let's say I do it. I zap the wildcard every day. How long am I stuck with this gig?"

"Till ye stop time from skippin'. Of course."

"Then you'll give my heart back?"

He just stares at me, amused, tracing a restless finger along his lip, back and forth.

"Time shall tell," he says finally.

"That's not an answer."

"That's all the answer ye gonna get." His shark-toothed grin startles me. "Reckon I can officially say it now. Welcome to the game, Doc!"

*

Later that night, I'm propped up on pillows on a rustic four-poster bed at the Red Rooster, a little bed-and-breakfast on the edge of Carnival Creeke. Ice wrapped to my shoulder with a rooster hand towel from the bathroom, two antacid wrappers on the dresser beside me. The pink kitten notebook sits draped across my lap.

They chained up the walk-in freezer with the gargoyle still in it, now harmless as a lawn gnome, then they wheeled the entire freezer out of Lau Chow's. Rumor has it, the stone creature is being held in some high-security military compound outside town. No doubt it's gotten heads and pens scratching all across the country.

I wrote it in the notebook. I wrote everything about today – but in my own tiny rebellion, I wrote it all in an acrostic shorthand code.

Figure that out, *Rascal*.

I smugly flap the notebook closed, then slide it under the box spring of my mattress.

There are a few things to attend to before I can sit still tonight. First, I unscrew the hallway light bulb from the fixture outside my room, crush it in another rooster towel, and sprinkle the glass shards on the hardwood floor just outside my door. The maid service likely won't be by to clean it up before tomorrow morning, and the crunch of the broken glass will alert me if anyone came to pay me an unexpected visit in the middle of the night.

I cleaned my fingernail stubs that got ripped off and wrap them with gauze and tape. I drank four bottled waters from the parlor downstairs (apparently having a limited blood supply makes you really, really thirsty). Then I did some calisthenics on the blue rug up in my room. Don't know why. It just felt right. Maybe this was part of C. Kyle's bedtime routine every night. My dislocated shoulder still burns like the dickens, limiting the exercises that I can do, but I muscle through. Crunches and V-ups are tolerable.

Heck, I even shave my legs. One less thing to think about once my indefinite tomorrow starts. Now, I'm splayed out on the four-poster bed under the gathered buttermilk canopy drapes. My whole body is aching, and what isn't aching is gasping on pins and needles. Obviously, I overdid it today. I'm learning so much about C. Kyle. Okay, so I'm having to re-learn everything. Especially with my new "condition."

Gingerly, I rub the stinging circle on my breastbone, remembering Holliday's last words to me in the graveyard earlier tonight:

"Carnival Creeke... This town don't have a clue. These people, they won't know the day's any different from any other. So try to give 'em a break, will ye?"

"Hey, Holliday."

I hated how my voice sounded like a child's. But I asked anyway.

*"Why me? Who decided it should be **me** stuck in this game?"*

He just grinned, a grin that would haunt my dreams for a long slice to come.

"Good luck, Doc. I'm bankin' on ye!"

Then he was gone.

It would've been so much easier if he had turned out to be a liar. But he didn't, and that's just something I'm going to have to deal with.

One day down. One day, and a drawer full of mementos:

A plastic 8-ball keychain.

A negative pregnancy test.

An empty hole in my ribcage.

And an unopened fortune cookie.

I peel it from the plastic wrapper and crush the cookie in my hand, sliding the paper slip out.

"Live for today – it's all you've got."

DAY 1: MOO

I'm awake.

Groggy as a toad, but awake.

I could've done with more sleep, what with my banged-up body and yesterday's shenanigans with the gargoyle – but someone's car alarm went off right outside my window at 6:11.

At least I'll have *that* to look forward to every morning.

A porcelain rooster is staring at me from the dresser. Rolling myself out of bed, I can tell right off the bat that my shoulder is feeling better. A lot better.

Freaky-inhuman kind of better.

I know that my body's new super-fast healing ability should be encouraging. But this, and the way I keep pressing my fingers into my neck, searching for a pulse... Guess I'm secretly hoping one time I'll find the comforting, steady tick of my heart just miraculously came back. I know it won't. But I keep checking. Like how you open the fridge for the umpteenth time, even though you know there still won't be any doggone lunch meat in there. It would help if I had some memory of who I was. But my brain is still shut up tight, like some old condemned building. Just glass and empty corners.

No past. No pulse.

I'm beginning to wonder if I'm even human anymore...

No time for thoughts like that, Kyle. File under "pity party" and move on. Let's get down to business.

Lacing my boots, I attempt to smooth the ridges in my brain's spinning gears. My primary objective for today is simple: Find the wildcard. Neutralize it before the day ends, and time resets.

Sure. Easy as pie.

*

Downstairs, Mrs. Moffatt, the tiny, middle-aged, Filipino proprietor of the Red Rooster, is bustling around the little dining parlor, laying out hotplates and baskets on crisp Chantilly lace. Her gunmetal-gray bob disappears around the corner as I slide down the banister to investigate the spread.

Breakfast looks like a country commercial. Fat fluffy waffles, ruffled with crusted drips around the edges from the hot press. Buttermilk biscuits, scrambled eggs, and plates piled high with sausage – ropes of good old-fashioned links, the kind you see in children's books. There's a tin of fruit and toast, with a little cup of whipped butter that smells like honey. Honey and wonderfulness.

Holliday's warning pops into my head, interrupting my tummy's revelry:

"A cigarette, a soda – all these could flat-line ye. If ye could flat-line, that is. But I think ye catch me drift."

I lean back and narrow my eyes, assessing the innocent-looking breakfast. I need to weigh my options here carefully. Don't want to eat the wrong thing and croak on my first day in this "game." Guess the sausage isn't my friend. I use my fork to scoot the links off my plate. But I'm still going to need protein, especially if last night's exhausting escapade was an accurate preview of what's in store for me each day. Eggs? What are they saying about eggs these days? I think health magazines had decided that eggs are choline-packed powerhouses, but for all I know, they could be the artery-clogging snot of demons again.

Oh, screw it. I have nothing to clog. I'm eating the eggs.

I wolf down my meticulously selected breakfast while the two ladies in the denim-cushioned chairs by the parlor window twitter on about purebred Corgis for longer than I ever thought humanly possible.

*

After breakfast, I set off walking into town. The Red Rooster sits on the outskirts of Carnival Creeke, the only other building alongside the Quik-Pump gas station. Two lone teeth in the old road's grin, greeting visitors and passersby.

To get into town, you cross a low covered bridge. The air is even cooler inside the timber-truss enclosure, a real-life Sleepy Hollow kind of feel. Glancing down at the chilly morning vapor coiled on the dark water below, I find myself half-expecting the Headless Horseman to come tromping up from that creek bank and introduce himself as my next wildcard.

But my walk is uneventful and nothing tries to kill me, so I'm free to take in all the scenery. Honestly, I don't give a flying fig about the locale right now – but my brain nonetheless takes snapshots of everything I see in town. One of the street lampposts is decorated with little painted wooden birdhouses. The "don't walk" sign flashes half a second before the light actually changes.

Minute details, filed for later.

A chilly autumn haze drapes the town sleepily. Over at the library, construction workers are sweeping up the damage caused by the gargoyle's rampage yesterday. Roof shingles and debris are scattered all over the cemetery, along with various unidentifiable metal Twizzlers of the car that the monster tried to rip in half. Hope that car's owner has one heck of an insurance plan. Then again, I don't really think there's any option for "acts of gargoyle" coverage.

Lau Chow's Chinese restaurant is a total wreck. They have the place taped off like a crime scene, a small sign is hung in the window: "Temporarily closed for repairs." Guess they couldn't hang it on the door, because the door is still lying somewhere on the dining room floor.

I can't help but feel a little guilty watching Carnival Creeke dust itself off. I mean, maybe if I'd been able to wrap things up quicker yesterday. Kept a clearer head, nailed down that gargoyle before it went completely hog-wild. I did a sloppy job, and that monster ripped the stuffing out of this cute little town.

One of the workmen up on the scaffolding shouts to another below, tossing a handful of debris down into the gravestones. If this day is really stuck on repeat, those poor yokels are going to be shuffling brooms around in that cemetery tomorrow, and the day after, and the day after, for...

Well, who knows how long?

But I've got a new kettle of fish today. In addition to finding the wildcard, I have another task on my mind. A secret secondary objective, hidden quietly on the back burner, where I can focus on doing it in my own timing: *Getting my heart back.*

Of course, that means finding Rascal Holliday. But I've got a plan for that part. Get the authorities involved. Get the police to keep an eye out for that Irish creep, should he ever slither back into town and show his pretty face. Then I can focus my attention on dealing with the wildcard.

I can describe Rascal Holliday to a T, right down to his gnawed-off fingernails and the brand of combat boots he was wearing. Same brand as mine, oddly enough.

I open my mouth and softly mumble, "What's up, Doc?"

Hot dog, I'm a pretty good parrot.

C. Kyle. must have been the life of the party.

The police station is as prim as a Swiss ski lodge. Judging from the meticulously scrubbed floors and gleaming lemon-scented wood surface, I'll bet the most action this town ever sees is who kissed Norma Sue behind the Dairy Queen last weekend. The station lobby is split in half by a long rectangular desk.

Against the wall near the door is a tall oak cabinet, displaying an antique rifle, an American flag, and a brass plaque listing the names of Carnival Creeke's honorable Moose Lodge elders. There's a small, no-frills jail cell in the far corner, containing nothing but the bare essentials – a steel toilet and a wooden slab of a bench built into the concrete wall.

The smell of coffee wafts from a small office in the back. The door is cracked open; inside I can see a boy, maybe fifteen or sixteen, slouched boredly in a plastic chair. He repeatedly tosses his shaggy bangs off his face despite them landing back in the exact same place, twirling the drawstrings of his black Slayer hoodie and chomping his bubblegum with unnecessarily loud pops.

I sidle up to the counter. Sheriff Gammell's nameplate looks like it's been moved around the desk a few times. The novelty drinking bird toy tells me he's got a cheeky side – the collection of Tasers says, "but not too cheeky." Guess the desk pulls double-duty, as right now it's occupied by a pencil-thin, silver-haired secretary with a button-up lace collar. Gladys, her crocheted nameplate says.

She ignores me, hammering mercilessly at a computer keyboard with her bony fingers. She's wearing festive blinking ghost earrings and a vulture-like scowl, one of those probably more befitting of her personality than the other.

I stuff my hands in my jacket pockets.

"Yeah, I'd like to file a report for stolen property," I say.

Gladys hands me a clipboard with paperwork attached and keeps typing. "And what was the nature of the stolen item?"

"Some Irish guy. He stole my–" I stop cold.

Oh. I get it.

Ha-ha.

"Forget it," I mutter, handing the clipboard back. "Never mind."

I didn't think this through very well. Since that creep Holliday turned me into a walking Valentine cliché, there's no way anyone in their right mind will take my story seriously.
Well, hunky-dory. This just forces me to concentrate on my mission. And as much as I hate to admit it, I've got an unsettling feeling that the wildcard is probably of more immediate importance than my poor little misplaced heart.

Besides, who knows? Maybe that Irish punk will actually make good and return my heart. Maybe once I've blasted enough wildcards and won his "game."

Yeah... I'm not holding my breath.

Alright. If I'm going to win this game, I'll need to get organized. I can't just dive in haphazardly with my tail feathers in the wind. The sun will go down, night will fall, and I'll be out of time. I need a plan. Establish the constant, the normal. Whatever today's wildcard turns out to be, it will be something *abnormal*. Abnormal always causes a ripple effect. So I just need to identify the normal then find the ripple. The problem is I have no clucking idea what's normal in this town.

Even as I'm opening the police station door to leave, I can hear an argument heating up in the back office. I'm not trying to eavesdrop, but with the door cracked, everyone in the station can hear every word between the Sheriff and Slayer Hoodie Kid. Something about him getting busted last night for cow-tipping.

Cow-tipping. Never understood that hobby, personally. I guess I just don't possess the level of higher genius it takes to appreciate the exhilaration of watching a cow fall over.

"But I didn't *do* nothin', Sheriff!" The kid's voice jumps an octave. "Why you always gotta make me out to be some criminal?"

"Oh, I don't know," a gravelly voice sighs wearily. "Because it's all that makes my cruel existence happy. Now Randy, let's pretend I don't give a hoot what you and your friends were doing out in Mr. Tannon's field last night. You said you saw a man out there. Can you describe him?"

"Uh." The boy deliberates for a moment. "Like normal height... Brown hair, I think. Pretty normal."

"And was there *anything* unusual about this very normal person?"

"Um, well... He had a tail."

I stop dead in my tracks.

Kyle, ripple. Ripple, Kyle.

Nice to meet you.

*

The police station sits right across the street from the
Tuscany Mill plaza. The dining tower where I engaged in my epic
battle last night stands against a cheery morning sun. I can see
the parking lot from here. I half wonder if a silver Chevy Tahoe is
parked among those cars.

Reckon I'd better start putting my allies into place.

The chirpy blonde isn't at her host post in the restaurant this
morning. I hadn't really expected her to be. She looked roughly
high-school age, and that would have been a turnaround shift for
the poor princess. Though I admit, it would have been funny to
see her reaction when I walked in again. At least I'm not carrying
a sword today.

I spot Tahoe. He's bussing away breakfast plates from a table
in the dining room. His sandy hair is raked up, his waiter's crisp
white button-down shirt untucked over black slacks.

He spots me from across the room, and nearly drops a water
glass. I put on a smile and wave. Tahoe sets his stack of dishes on
the nearest empty table and trots over to me.

"Hey," he grins, wrapping his arms awkwardly around his
upper chest. "Ah, so you're still alive, huh?"

"Looks like."

The gold name tag on his shirt says "Merrick."

"So your name's Merrick?"

"Oh, yeah. Merrick Cohen." He extracts a hand from his tangle
of arms. "Good to, um–"

"You can call me Kyle."

"Kyle?" He grins. "That whole 'guy's-name' thing, huh? I mean, it's kinda cute…"

I must not have much sunshine in my expression, because he clears his throat and quickly switches gears.

"So, how's the shoulder?" he asks.

"Been better, been worse."

I'm being a little cold to him, I guess – but I'm tired and hungry and lactose intolerant, and one of my vital organs is missing – so I don't think anyone would blame me for being a bit of a grouch. Customarily, I wouldn't be so rude.

Or maybe I would. I don't know.

"Listen Merrick," I begin. "I've got a business proposition for you."

He gets serious as I explain that I'm heading to the Tannon farm in search of some guy with a tail. Figure I might as well cut to the chase. The kid's held up relatively peachy so far. He displayed quick thinking last night with the gargoyle, and didn't puke or ask a bunch of stupid questions under the firestorm of weirdness. He might be a good asset to have in my back pocket.

Today, though, all I need is a ride.

"So what do you say?" I conclude evenly. "Do we have a deal?"

I even extend my hand. But he doesn't shake it. He just stands there, assessing me in silence for an awkward minute.

"If I take you to Tannon's farm," Merrick says slowly. "Will I see another monster?"

Oh, land sakes, he's actually serious.

"I'm going to level with you," I tell him. "I can't promise you anything. But whatever we find at Tannon's farm...odds are highly in favor of monsters."

I don't get why he isn't smiling like the TRON-patch kid from yesterday. Why the frick is he still staring at me? Do I have to pay him?

"Okay. Deal." Merrick takes my hand and shakes it once. "But for the record–" He pauses, unpinning his name tag from his shirt. "You could have just *asked* for a ride. I'd still have said yes."

Then he grins and trots off to tell his boss that he's taking off the rest of the day. Not that he has any idea what he just signed up for.

Not that *I* have any idea.

Gonna be one heck of a day, kid.

*

To reach the farms, you take a left at the General Store, where the road forks off into a Y. For a short drive, there's nothing but thick shade and chestnut trees, the gently-curving country road carpeted in yellow heart-shaped leaves. And then there's nothing but golden cornfields. I watch the fence posts fly by from the passenger seat of Merrick's Tahoe.

"So what's your story?" Merrick broaches light conversation from the wheel. "Avenging angel sent from another dimension? Secret government agent? C'mon, be honest. You've got our town in some manila folder marked 'X', don't you?"

I can't answer him.

Literally, I can't. Because I don't have a clue myself. All I know is what Holliday told me: This is some kind of game. A twisted game, where this day is cursed to repeat over and over, until I can get my ducks in a row and figure out how to stop the record from skipping.

Merrick is in college. Cute, too, in a nerdy sort of way – tall despite his passive slouch, matching set of dimples, sunny green eyes. He's probably got a major in school, a favorite song, a table his family all gathers around each year at Christmas. How would he react if I told him his life was the game board for somebody else's amusement?

How would *I* react?

When I don't respond, Merrick smiles. "It's okay, Kyle. I can tell you're not from around here. Kinda obvious, actually."

"How's that?"

"Well, for one, you don't know who Old Man Tannon is. *Everyone* in Carnival Creeke knows the guy. Crazy old dude, always yelling at birds from that Rambo Mobile on his lawn. But he also hosts the high school's homecoming bonfire. So, he channels some of his crazy for good. Everyone in town likes him despite. Kind of our own cuddly, whacked-out mascot."

"You've got a way with words, kid."

"Kid?" Merrick snorts a laugh. "You're like the same age as me. A year older, tops."

Am I? Hadn't really noticed.

Then why do I feel so much older?

Whump.

Merrick slams on the brakes and our seatbelts lock protectively around us, nearly popping our eyeballs from their sockets. The Tahoe skids to a dirty halt. We catch a glimpse of the cow he just hit. The Oreo-spotted animal totters off to our left and scrambles into the wall of cornstalks, obviously still alive, if not a little dazed. I crane my neck out the window. Beyond the tops of the cornstalks is a blue three-level farmhouse with a wrap-around porch. A brown police car is parked in the circular gravel drive. Looks like the Sheriff beat us here.

Merrick repeating over and over how he's never driving again, I battle for a minute to convince my seatbelt that I'm in no danger of flying out the windshield, coaxing the gray strap to ease up its anaconda grip on me. The taut belt is gnawing against the scabby scar on my chest. It itches.

I get out of the truck and zip my jacket. There's a gorgeous dent in the Tahoe's front grill, whether it's from me yesterday or the cow is anyone's guess. Either way, I decide to spare the kid an ulcer and not mention it.

"So," I call loudly, hoping to draw Merrick's attention toward the cornfield. "Where's this Tannon fellow? Would've expected a warm welcome, from the way you described him."

"Probably got spooked by the tail-guy," Merrick replies distractedly. He closes his driver's side door very gently, as though to avoid hurting the truck any further.

Most of the morning's fog has burned off, a few remnants lying in ribbons of vapor across the gullies of the field. The only sound is a steady orchestra of crickets and insects. Parked on the farmhouse lawn is a huge, weather-beaten WWII armored patrol vehicle. Its camo siding is rusted, tall shoots of grass growing up through its massive tires. "Rambo Mobile" is actually a pretty accurate description.

The Sheriff and his lanky, bowlegged deputy are standing over by Tannon's fence.

Sheriff Gammell is a solid man, not of spectacular height, but his barreled chest is broad under his ironed brown uniform, and his arms are strong. Steel-gray hairs have begun to streak his sideburns and pepper the dark, smartly trimmed mustache that covers his square jaw and craggy, weathered skin. His keen eyes are an old bulldog's, drained of their bark and injected with world-weary cynicism, softened by recent years of home-cooked spaghetti meals and full of a thousand stories I reckon I won't ever hear.

Right now Sheriff Gammell and his deputy both have their hands on their hips, kicking around a pile of beer cans and frowning off into the surrounding cornfield with dubious expressions.

Let them do what they like. My interest lies inside that farmhouse. That big piñata of secrets…

"Merrick," I say calmly. "I need you to go talk to Sheriff Gammell."

Merrick turns around, pushing his glasses up his nose. "Any particular subject?"

"Challenge him to a game of chess. Sing a song. Just keep him busy as long as you can."

"Huh? Where are you going?"

"Gonna check out Tannon's house."

"Why don't you just go ask Sheriff Gammell? He'd probably take you inside."

"I'm shy."

Merrick snorts. "And I'm tonight's homecoming queen."

"Whatever, your majesty, just keep it inconspicuous. I don't want to have Gammell's mug eyeing me every time I go into town for Pop Tarts."

"*Should* he be? Just what are you planning to do with these Pop Tarts?"

"Get out of here."

Merrick throws both hands in the air, conceding defeat. "Yay, I'm the Unabomber's errand boy." He starts off across the grass toward the Sheriff and his deputy.

I won't have much time.

I shoulder into the wall of crispy cornstalks and pop out a second later on Tannon's front lawn. On the other side of the strip of cornstalks, Merrick's footsteps are approaching behind the cops.

Showtime.

I unzip my jacket and start toward the front porch.

"Oh, hey, Sheriff!" I hear Merrick's voice, intentionally loud and clueless. "What's going on?"

"Who's your lady-friend, Merrick?"

I freeze. Instinctively, I hit the grass. Crouched here, I can see them through a slit in the cornstalks.

"Lady-friend?" Merrick is playing dumb. "I don't, uh, really have any of those…"

"Son, I saw somebody of the female variety get out of your truck just now."

"Aw…" Merrick drops his head into his hands. "Sorry, she *made* me bring her! She's some friend of my sister's. Said she heard Old Man Tannon's got himself a box of long-haired Dachshund puppies for sale. She saw a flyer in the diner, and wouldn't leave me alone about it. And her basket-weaving class isn't till nine, so she's all like, 'Oh, we've got time, Merrick, I've just gotta go have a look-see at those little darlin's!' She's over there now, checking for Old Man Tannon in his house. But if there's been a murder or something, we can leave."

Hot dang. Got to hand it to the kid, it's a pretty convincing cooked-up version of the truth.

The Sheriff looks at Merrick like he's wearing nothing but ketchup. "Puppies, Merrick?"

"They're so gosh-darn cute!" Merrick contributes helpfully.

"You're saying *Tannon* has *puppies* for sale."

Merrick lifts his shoulders and says mechanically, "So cute."

My boots crunch across the gravel driveway. The lawn is scattered with bizarre weathervane contraptions, pieced together entirely from found objects – scraps of aluminum and tin, stippled copper half-moons. Tiny spinning fans, their blades made of soda cans, are whirring and glimmering in the morning sunshine. Wind chimes, strung from dulled green and clear glass bottle shards, tinkle lightly on the porch.

The front door is open.

"Mr. Tannon?" I call in my throaty voice.

No answer.

I tap gently with my knuckle and the screen door creaks open.

There are cows in his house. One standing in the living room, staring at the TV as if waiting for it to turn on. Another animal is whuffling around some sort of vintage broad-wave radio equipment. Stacks and stacks of cassettes, no doubt packed with conspiracy whispers from the Oval Office, wobble precariously around on wooden shelves. A third cow is tromping around up on the second floor. I can see its cookies-and-cream rump at the top of the narrow staircase; heaven only knows how it got up there.

And someone is in the kitchen.

There's a drywall bucket by the door, holding a striped umbrella, a fishing pole, and an assortment of unopened newspapers. I slowly slide the umbrella from the bucket. Not that I really need to be quiet, what with the holy racket from all those cassettes crashing onto the floor. The cow in the living room turns its head and stares dumbly at me. I give it a covert nod and slink across the carpet. I press my back against the corner wall at the bottom of the stairs, tense as a bowstring. Then I spring into the kitchen.

It's Randy, the boy from the police station. He throws both hands in the air, abandoning the bowl of cereal he was helping himself to.

"Don't knife me!" he yelps.

He's saying this despite the fact that he's the one standing next to a drawer of knives, while I am holding an *umbrella*.

Am I really that scary?

"Really?" I sigh. "That's your first reaction?"

I herd Randy past the menagerie in the living room and out onto the front porch, using the umbrella. I give him a whack on the tush, just to show I mean business.

There's a terse little reunion as we join Sherriff Gammell, Merrick and the deputy out by the cornfields, so my presence is nicely overshadowed. I'm briefly introduced as Merrick's sister's whoever from Idaho, but for the most part, it's a whole lot of the Sheriff chewing out Randy. I innocently mention the cow infestation inside Tannon's house. Cue another squabble. Randy flies off the handle, hollering how he and his buddies don't know squat about those cows (his words, not mine). He swears they only snuck into Tannon's field last night because they saw some weird blue flash of light in the sky and they thought it was a UFO.

Because UFOs are *way* classier than cow-tipping. Way to boost your alibi, kiddo.

Sheriff Gammell grunts. "So, *that's* when you saw the man with the tail?"

Randy mumbles "yeah, whatever" and covers his face with his hood. Gammell pulls off his mirrored Ray-Bans, rubs his eyes, then replaces his sunglasses. A rust-colored cow is loitering around by their police car. The deputy squints at the animal thoughtfully.

The deputy looks a lot like the scarecrow from The Wizard of Oz. With his gangly bowed legs, orangey tan, and tendency to grimace in a way that causes his chin to wrinkle up like a feed sack, he really isn't doing himself any favors.

"Well, while we're here–" Deputy Scarecrow wipes his hands on his pants and squats down beside the cow. "Any'a you ever had fresh milk?"

"Oh, what the hey." Sheriff Gammell pulls a steel coffee mug off his belt. "Put some'a that in my cup here, would you, Joe? My wife's been wanting to make her cornbread, you know."

He pauses, the mug in mid-pass.

"Wait. Joe, why doncha hold up a sec." Then the Sheriff turns his gaze on me. "Seeing as Miss Kyle here came all the way from the Cohen's farm in Idaho... What say we let her do the honors? Reckon it'd help her feel more at home."

He swivels the coffee mug over to me, keeping those mirrored shades locked on my face like a terminator.

"That is, *if* she'd be game?"

For a fleeting moment, I wonder if I could take out all four of them with the umbrella before one of them shoots me.

"My pleasure, gentlemen!" I erupt in gooey delight. "Oh yeah, just like home."

I give Sheriff Gammell a wrinkle-nosed grin, maybe snatching the steel coffee mug from his hand with a hair too much gumption, then squatting over by the rust-colored cow. Its udder hangs there like an over-inflated latex glove.

I know they're all watching me. Waiting to see if Kyle can bust out the milking skills. Even the cow turns its head and stares at me serenely.

Ugh. This day had better pick up real soon...

"Hey," Randy sidles up to Merrick. "That man with the tail... You think...he was an alien?"

"Yes," Merrick replies solemnly. "A tail alien. A *tail-ien.*"

Randy's face blanches. I swear the entire foundation of his universe just collapsed.

"But what if–" he begins.

Whatever poetry was set to flow from his mouth is lost, as the still morning air is pierced by a screeching metallic sound that sets all our nose hairs on end. The cow rips its nipple out of my hand and goes galloping off into the corn. The snarling roar of a motor fills the field and rings off the trees nearly a mile out.

There's no delicate way to ask this.

"Sheriff, does Mr. Tannon have a chainsaw?"

*

The utility barn has a concrete tractor ramp up to the ten-foot shed style doors, which are shut tight. Aside from the small loft hatch above the doorway, the barn is a four walled lunchbox. One way in, one way out. And inside that barn, most likely, there's a nutty old man with a chainsaw.

What could possibly go wrong?

Sheriff Gammell puts his ear up to the barn's warm wooden siding. "Emmett, you in there?" He calls, gesturing for us to get behind him. "We're comin' in, friend."

On the count of three, we dart into the barn.

The thick smell of grass and gasoline hits us full in the face. Old Man Tannon is sitting in the far-left corner, half-shrouded in shadows. He's hunched over, clutching a bulky chainsaw in one hand, his long silvery head bowed as though deliberating what to do next. His overalls hang down around his knees.

And his tail is in his hand.

Long and thin, it resembles a lion's or cow's tail, ending with a silvery-white tuft of fur the same color as his hair.

"Holy crap!" Merrick coughs beside me, not that anyone can hear him. The rip-snarl of the chainsaw is deafening.

Tannon whips his head around to look at us. With his low-shelved brow knotted over a long, sharp beaked nose, he looks like a nervous vulture. His wild, deep-set eyes are set so far apart that he could probably look to his left and right simultaneously. His eyebrows are two angry white caterpillars, springing out from his face at absurd angles. This poor man probably looked a nutcase long before he discovered he'd sprouted a tail.

"Look what they done to me, Sheriff!" Tannon yowls. He holds his new appendage in the air, shaking it like a dead snake.

"Didn't I tell ya? It's the government! Squirtin' gas into our pipes! Bugs in our sandwiches!"

Yep, this man's cheese has obviously slid off his cracker.

If he ever had any cheese to begin with.

"Easy now, Emmett." Sheriff Gammell's gravelly voice is calm. He unbuttons his holster. The movement is so subtle, I don't think any of the others even notice. But Gammell doesn't draw his gun. He just keeps his gaze locked on Old Man Tannon. I watch Gammell curiously.

Trembling, Tannon slowly lays the chainsaw on the workbench. His eyes are mad as a hatter.

"Lock me up, Sheriff!" he shouts, spraying spittle. "Something's happenin' to this town! It's gonna be just like I always told ya!"

"Easy now, Emmett. Nothing's boiling in this town."

Actually he's right, I want to pipe up. Maybe Old Man Tannon always ranted about aliens making people grow tails. Talk about your "I told you so" moment.

But then Tannon grabs an axe from the wall and adds axe-swinging to his moment, escalating the situation from "Friday night weird" to "buck-wild bonkers."

*

About ten minutes later, they're tucking Old Man Tannon's unconscious feet into the squad car and Sheriff Gammell is tucking his Taser back into his belt.

"I'll walk back," I suggest quietly.

I'm hoping I can just slip away while they're all enjoying a victory pass-around of the coffee mug with the frothy fresh milk. When it's offered to me, I wave it off, admitting that I'm lactose intolerant. Which is possibly my first true statement of the day. What I need is some time to myself. Time to recalibrate. Figure out what I'm supposed to do next.

Merrick trots after me. "Hey, can I give you a lift?" A grin crosses his face. "I mean, aren't you afraid the tail-iens will get you on the road? And do tail-y things to you?"

"I'll be fine."

"It's a really long walk back into town. And, if I can just reiterate... *Tail-iens?*"

"Trust me, kid. I can take care of myself."

"Yeah, um, I don't doubt that. But–" He reaches into his back pocket and pulls out his cellphone. He holds it toward me.

"Here. At least hang onto this."

"Thanks, but not necessary."

Unless that is a nitro-powered phone that can remotely scatter peril with its magical anti-peril ringtones. And I don't need my 8-ball keychain to tell me the chances of that are slim.

"Yeah," Merrick adjusts his glasses. "But this way I'll be able to reach you if, say, I run into someone else in town with a tail."

He has a point.

I turn the sleek blue phone over in my hand and slide it into my jacket pocket as he climbs into his truck.

"Oh, hey...and Kyle?"

I stop walking and turn around.

Merrick frowns. "Please don't ask me to lie again for you. I'm not into the whole lying thing."

The Tahoe rolls down the arrow-straight road, leaving a slow cloud of dust that hangs out long after the truck has disappeared.

*

I don't follow them back to town. I probably should, but I don't. Instead, I turn around and start trudging the opposite direction, toward the outskirts of town. And the whole time, I think about today's wildcard.

Holliday said I'm supposed to fix it each day. That's the game. But how am I supposed to "fix" people having tails? Aside from Old Man Tannon's horrifying yet resourceful approach with the chainsaw...

I reach the Red Rooster and I still haven't come up with any solution, so I just keep on walking. Past the Red Rooster. Past the gas station. I come to a wooden sign with faded painted letters:

Carnival Creeke Town Limits.

What would happen if I refused to play Holliday's "game?"

Brimming with curiosity, I step past the sign and keep walking. But I don't get anywhere. It just keeps going and going, like the road is stretching, stretching like warm pulled taffy, the horizon planted at an unchanging distance ahead of me. Even when I break into a jog it's like running a treadmill, running in place, until I expect a giant sandworm to burst up from the ground and eat me to put me out of my misery.

After a few minutes of this ridiculousness, I concede and stomp back to the Red Rooster. I clomp up the stairs to my room. Looks like Mrs. Moffatt must have come and cleaned while I was out. The broken light bulb glass is gone from the floor outside my door.

I find an old record player on the shelf in the closet, a vintage machine covered in faded brown cloth. Even a handful of dusty records tucked behind it. I thumb through the music selection. Sinatra, Duke Ellington... Django Reinhardt, Coltrane...

Is this me refusing to play the game? Theoretically, I could. Just hide away in this closet here, drown it all out with old music. What difference would it make tomorrow? As long as the wildcard wasn't too unreasonable... People with cow tails wouldn't be so catastrophic. They'd all get used to them. Find them sexy. Come up with new, tail-accessorizing fashions. But then they – and I – would be stuck on this day for all eternity. And I can't even leave town.

I sit on the four-poster bed and let myself flop back onto the blue quilt, staring up at the ceiling.

What if I *can't* fix the wildcard?

What if I'm an appalling failure?

Maybe if I crash and burn on my first day, someone would come to knock me back into line. Maybe Rascal Holliday himself might even have to make another cameo appearance…

Just thinking about him, I realize I'm grinding my fingers into the corner of the record sleeve that I'm holding.

Muffled music startles me out of my thoughts. I frown at the empty record player. It takes me a second to figure out that the music is coming from inside my pocket.

Merrick's cell phone is ringing.

I slide it out, frowning. It's playing the Spider-Man theme song. That kid is a goof.

I press the button and raise the phone to my ear.

"Hello?"

"Hey. It's Merrick."

I can tell right off the bat that something is different in his voice. "So who's got a tail now, Merrick?"

"Well, um. That's kinda why I'm calling you."

That sits me up sharp and straight.

"Who's got a tail, Merrick?"

"Me." He takes a deep breath. *"I do. But I need to tell you something. It's not just a tail we're talking about here. I'm changing, Kyle. I know this is gonna sound crazy… But I think we're turning into cows."*

84

A TAIL OF TWO CITIES

I tell Merrick to meet me at the diner in thirty minutes.

So Old Man Tannon wasn't simply sprouting a tail earlier. He was *transforming into a cow.* As I'm jogging past the police station, a weird curiosity suddenly seizes me. Merrick grew a tail in just over an hour after we all split ways. This transformation is fast. Crazy fast. At this rate...

What does *Tannon* look like?

I lean against the police station door, cupping my face to the mesh-screened window. It's dark inside. Squinting through the wire mesh, I can't make out much. My view through the window is obscured by a poster for tonight's homecoming football game. But I know Tannon is in there. Gammell told us he was going to stash him in the jail cell for the night.

Morbid curiosity wins. Just a quick peek at Tannon. It'll only take five seconds...

Easing the door open, I slither inside.

"I've been to Idaho, you know."

The gravelly voice is right behind me. C. Kyle's built-in composure is the only thing that prevents me from yelping as I spin around. It takes my eyes a moment to adjust to the dark.

Sheriff Gammell is sitting in a chair at his desk, soldering wires on a gutted Taser. Looks like he's been waiting for me.

"Right, Idaho," I say quickly. "My home state."

I shrug and don a smile, even though I know better. We're way past chit-chat. He knows I'm not Merrick's sister's whatever, that much is plain as day. Now it's just me and Sheriff Gammell, all cards out on the table.

"Back at Tannon's farm," I say slowly. "You unbuttoned your holster. Testing to see if I'd try and swipe your gun?"

"Emmett Tannon is blind as a bat without his Coke bottles." Gammell clicks the casing back on the Taser and stands up. "If I really wanted to get his attention, all I'd have needed is a banana or my finger." He folds his arms, assessing me with frosty regard. "I...had to see what you'd do."

Remind me never to roll on first impressions. Gammell's country bumpkin status is diminishing by the minute. Unfortunately, so are Merrick's human features. Every cell in my body is screaming at me to turn now and run away, run to the diner, where Merrick is waiting for me. But I don't. Not yet. I decide to give Sheriff Gammell the benefit of the doubt.

And that's why he's able to toss me into his stupid jail cell.

I whip around furiously, grabbing the bars and pressing my forehead to the cold metal.

"Gammell, what in the–"

He avoids my eyes. "I'm sorry. But what I've got right now are *good folk* turning into *cows*. And I'm not blaming you for it. It's just..."

Inhaling slowly, he finally meets my gaze. "I think you'll agree, every manner of odd started happening here since you showed up."

He's right about that.

"You're right about that." I hold his gaze hard. "Something *is* happening in this town. But believe me when I tell you, I am the only person who can fix it. And *I can't* do it from this cell."

Gammell stares at me. His eyes narrow.

"Carnival Creeke is mine to protect. You understand?"

"Yeah. That's why you need to let me out of here, Sheriff. Right now."

Something ignites in me, whooshing up like a flame in a gas stove. Something urgent, full and fierce. This town isn't his. It's *mine*. And this man is standing in my way.

My town is in your hands, Sheriff.

And I don't know a thing about your hands.

"Let me out, Gammell." If he thinks I'm pleading, he's not wrong. "All you have to do is unlock this cell door, then go take a walk. Please. Let me go."

Sheriff Gammell straightens, glancing over at the bench behind me in the cell, where Old Man Tannon's lumpy form is lying under the blanket. Then Gammell looks at me, his gaze flickering finally to the floor.

"I can't do that."

He grabs his jacket and leaves the police station. I hear the door lock behind him, and all the lights go off with a click.

My situation has been drastically spun on its head. Just a peek, I said. And now I'm stuck in a drunk tank with…

My breath catches.

There's an awful lot of snorting and whuffling coming from behind me. I turn around. Slowly, the body in the corner sits up. The blanket slides off his shoulders, and Old Man Tannon stands upright. He sways slightly.

Sweet heaven, he looks like a minotaur.

He still has his clothes on, thank goodness, but his baggy shirt and overalls are hanging off him at odd angles. It's as though parts of his body are changing faster than others. I can tell something is going on with his legs, the way he's lurching from side to side, making his long arms swing around like pendulums. And he has a cow head.

For real. The guy has a *cow head.*

His silvery ears fan the air, nostrils quivering, glistening with wetness around the rims. But instead of big sweet Bessie eyes, I see Tannon's wild, shell-shocked human eyes staring at me from this animal's face.

"SWEET HEAVEN, HE LOOKS LIKE A MINOTAUR..."

I scoot back slowly, until my heels hit the corner of the cell, like a gymnast preparing to unleash a crazy sequence of flips. Looks like it's you and me, Tannon. An inevitable stand-off, a climactic clash between fates. Man versus cow, a brawl to the death from which only one of us will walk away.

Well... Maybe if I had time. But I *don't* have time.

And neither does Merrick.

"Tannon," I clear my throat and raise both hands. "I don't know if you can understand me... But I don't want to fight you. I'm going to give you the benefit of the doubt."

So naturally he comes charging at me. I catch his arm and whirl him around, punching him square in the cow kisser before he can even let out a moo. Minotaur Tannon collapses onto the concrete in a heap. I go to check his pulse, but I can hear him whistling melodiously through his nose, so I don't bother. He's breathing.

Well, that's it for me. I'm done giving people the benefit of the doubt.

"*You hear me*, Carnival Creeke?!" I shout out the vented window. "No more benefit of the doubt!"

For the next few minutes I pace around the jail cell, doing nothing useful and burning the walls with my fury. Stupid trusting corndog... Would C. Kyle have let herself get tossed in here? Probably not.

Focus. Get focused.

I stop pacing and start scanning my surroundings. The holding cell is a square room, ten-by-ten. Flawless concrete. The stainless-steel toilet is bolted to the floor, a sink basin built into its top. The smooth wooden bench that Minotaur-Tannon was snoozing on, also bolted to the wall. Tamper-proof fluorescent lights affixed to the ceiling. And the window. Small and square, more of a vent than a window, covered by a metal grate fastened by concrete nails.

C'mon, Kyle. Bring the pieces together, and they'll click into the shape of an escape.

I drag the unconscious Minotaur-Tannon over to the wall beneath the vent. He's really heavy. Being a cow must make you denser. Using Tannon as my step stool, I'm just able to reach the vent. Using the motherboard from Merrick's cell phone as a wedge, I eventually manage to jimmy the metal grating off from the vent. I feel a little bad, desecrating Merrick's phone like this, but somehow I think he might have had the same idea.

Plus, I'm standing on Tannon. I feel bad for that, too, for the record. But I rationalize that if I don't spring myself out of this lunchbox – and fast – this whole town will have a whole lot more to moo about than cell replacement plans.

The vent grating clatters to the floor and cool October air pours in through the open square in the wall. I test the width. My head could squeeze through…but that's all. They say if a hamster's head can fit through an opening, its whole body can fit through. Too bad I'm not a hamster.

91

On the other hand... I *am* a fast healer.

Just yesterday, I dislocated my shoulder. Shouldn't take much to pop it out again. And now that I know I'll heal up like a freak... Theoretically, I'll be good as new again tomorrow. I smirk. Gotta hand it to you, Holliday. I may have no heart, but I'm tough. He said a cup of coffee could potentially knock me flat. But if I can just eek by, as long as it doesn't kill me, my body will always bounce back, revved and raring to go. I'm a glass supergirl.

What a warped balance to strike.

I slide off my jacket. Placing Merrick's cell phone between my clenched teeth, I loop my left arm through the cell bars, grasping my shoulder and applying counter pressure. I take a deep breath. Then I give my arm an almighty twist to one side. Familiar fire explodes through my upper body as my shoulder's humeral head slips obediently from its socket. I feel all the surrounding ligaments snap.

Once I've kicked the wall about thirty times, I spit out Merrick's cell phone and wriggle myself through the scrapingly-tight vent. Sidenote: I'm flexible. The sort of flexible that would have required daily stretching. Maybe C. Kyle was in a circus. Sweating, I enjoy a private chuckle at the notion. I hope I was a carnie. That's just cool.

My boots hit the concrete outside, sending lightning bolts of pain through my shoulder. Hopefully Merrick is still at the diner. It's been over an hour...

Tucking my busted arm tight against my body, I take off at a flat sprint up the street. Everything that I zombie-shuffled past earlier today flies by me now in double-speed. By the time I plunge through the diner's old-fashioned fifties-style door, my ears are aching from the cold. The grill's heat feels like a furnace on my flushed face. Or maybe it's some other emotion that I'm feeling because I know I'm so late, and it's my own stupid fault.

I scan the booths. Couple of families, eating their dinner. No sign of Merrick.

But I don't see a cow in here either, so that's good news.

I find Merrick in the men's restroom. He's in the last stall, curled up on the back of the toilet, his knees drawn up to his chest like he's afraid somebody might see his feet. I try not to let my eyes wander over him. I can't spot anything cow-like at first glance, so I'm trying to keep calm. But he's sweating bullets.

"Kyle?" Merrick pulls off his glasses and squints up at me from the stall. "How'd you know I was in here?"

I shrug my good shoulder, trying to look nonchalant for his sake. "There's only one place I'd go if I were transforming into a member of the animal kingdom."

"Sorry," Merrick laughs awkwardly. "I waited in a booth for a while. But I had to get out of there. Things were, uh, changing. And I didn't want to scare the kids." He glances at the way I'm cradling my arm. His face knots with concern. "You...jacked up your shoulder again?"

"Must've bumped it on the door on my way in," I answer carelessly.

Holy Toledo, there's his tail. I just noticed it. Merrick must have noticed me noticing, because his face turns an impressive shade of red. He mumbles, "It's freaky, I know."

"Pfff. I've seen worse."

Bet you I'm not lying, either.

"Humans and cows really aren't that different," Merrick remarks as I help him to his feet. "I mean, we share ninety percent of our DNA. They've created a cow-human embryo, they've even bred cows that give human milk. If something were to re-write my DNA, make it say 'cow' instead of 'human'…"

He coughs, pulling off his glasses again to wipe his face. "Well, it wouldn't take much. It wouldn't be all that crazy. I mean, *yeah*, it's *crazy*… But not impossible." He adds hesitantly, "You think it was that milk from this morning?"

"Makes sense," I say. "I didn't drink any, and I'm not a cow."

"Wait." Merrick frowns suddenly. "Old Man Tannon doesn't even own any cows."

I follow where he's going with this, even though I really don't want to.

"You mean those cows we saw at his farm–"

"Must've been Randy's buddies. Yep." Merrick shudders soberly. "That's pretty messed up."

So why did that one cow let me try to milk it?

Mental note: Once I fix this and those boys turn human again, I'm going to find that little Pervasaurus and nail him to a telephone pole.

*

I drive Merrick to the bed-and-breakfast in his Tahoe. By the time we get there, I'm practically dragging him up the carpeted stairs, his arm around my neck, me clutching his belt loop with my good hand. It's not my first choice, revealing which room I'm staying in. But if I can successfully pull this off, the day will reset, good as new, and nobody is going to remember me dragging this kid into room four. Besides, I don't think Merrick is taking notes right now.

I set him on the floor, his back against my four-poster bed.

"So you've got the antidote, right?" he jokes weakly. "In your company's X file?"

I don't answer.

Merrick drops his head into his hands. "Oh, man…oh, man." When he looks up again, his expression has changed completely. "Then listen, Kyle. Because I need you to do *exactly* what I tell you… Remember what I said earlier, about human and cow DNA?"

"Sure."

"Well," he takes a deep breath. "I think somehow ours got rewritten. From 'human' to 'cow.' So all we have to do is change it back, right?"

"You say that like you've got a plan."

"Uh, not exactly. But if we can make a nucleic acid inhibitor–"

"In English?"

"Sorry, think of it like switching our DNA's train tracks."

He gestures for paper. I hand him the flower-shaped pad and pen from the dresser, and he starts scrawling stuff down.

"Okay, Kyle." Merrick rips off the top page. "Here's a list of ingredients. You'll have to track these down."

I nod, because something is different in his voice. I know that tone. Maybe I even respect it.

I pause in the doorway.

"Hey," I say. "Are you a rocket scientist or something?"

Merrick shrugs, smiling weakly. "Bio-chemistry student. B-plus average."

*

Armed with a plastic Batman thermos, I sprint through Carnival Creeke. The sun is just beginning to sink, a buttery glow to warm the sidewalks for another hour before the October night's chill sets in.

I've located most of the ingredients on Merrick's list. Mostly cooking and cleaning supplies. Merrick explained how we'll mix it into a sort of hormone disruptor, but I'll just call it "anti-cow juice." That's good enough for me. All *I* need to know is that this wicked little cocktail might reverse the transformation in everyone's DNA...if we're lucky.

Now all I need is a liquid to carry the compound.

Downstairs, Mrs. Moffatt is flitting back and forth between the kitchen and the parlor, laying out silverware for dinner. Baked chicken and wild rice, from the aroma. Rummaging around in the mini fridge in the parlor, I locate a carton of orange juice. Perfect. The acidity should actually help break down our anti-cow antidote... Theoretically.

*

Merrick looks up from the floor as I walk in, casting a feeble smile at the Batman thermos in my hands. The kid is as pallid as ash and sweating up a storm. His ears have begun to take on a pointed shape, giving him the appearance of a very sick elf. But other than that – and his tail, which he's sitting on, probably on purpose – he could still pass as a human.

I twist the top off of the thermos and hold it to his lips.

"This probably won't taste too good," I warn him. "Just don't barf it up."

He heaves a strained chuckle. "Ah, it's okay. I've got two stomachs now, right?"

"That's the spirit."

"Thanks, doc."

What's up, Doc? Merrick's innocent response causes Holliday's smug, silky voice to come crashing into my brain. It triggers a surge of sour bile in my throat. I mutter, "Do me a favor and don't call me that, okay?"

After a few tries, it's pretty clear that Merrick can't swallow the liquid. The bones in his facial structure have started to transform, elongating into a snout. Which I have to admit, is pretty freaky to see – especially since it happened within the time it took for me to run downstairs and grab the orange juice. Like Tannon, it appears that certain parts of him are turning into a cow at a much faster rate than the rest of him.

But the real problem is Merrick's tongue. It started to swell, and now it's pretty much filled his entire mouth. It's like it's not even a part of him anymore. Must be pretty scary for Merrick. He's masking it well, playing it cool. But that doesn't change the fact that he still can't swallow this antidote.

Time to improvise.

I bolt down the carpeted steps, hopping the banister. In the kitchen, there's a first aid kit. By stroke of luck, it contains a length of tourniquet tubing and a bottle of rubbing alcohol, both of which I grab before Mrs. Moffatt can ask any questions. Back upstairs, I uncoil the tubing and scrub it in the bathroom sink with the alcohol, sterilizing it. Not that I really need to. Getting an infection from a rubber tube is really the least of Merrick's worries right now.

I ask him to sit up beside the bed and take off his glasses. Then I place one end of the tube behind his ear lobe.

"Hold that there for me," I instruct.

Obediently Merrick presses a finger to it, as if simply assisting me with tying a ribbon on a Christmas present. With a funny look he watches me draw the tube to his nose, measuring the distance down to his stomach. Just a funny look, though. He doesn't ask me what the heck I'm getting ready to do to him. Maybe he's already got an idea. Or maybe his tongue is just too messed up to talk.

Using the pen, I make a little mark on the tube where it ends at his stomach. That should be about the length of tubing that I'll need.

Guess I should warn him.

"Merrick," I say. "I've got to get this anti-cow juice in you. But it's not going to be too terribly comfortable. Ready?"

He nods once.

Gently as I can, I start threading the tube down through his nostril. His body stiffens under me. That's okay. If he starts wheezing or bucking around, it'll mean the tube may have accidentally entered his lungs instead of his stomach. There's a little resistance, but I keep on feeding the tube all the way down until I get to the mark, indicating that it's reached his stomach.

Doing things delicately doesn't come naturally to me, but I've learned. Once when I was a kid, I accidentally exploded a bird's stomach attempting to give it mouth-to-mouth after it slammed into a window and knocked itself out cold.

Hey, look at that. I actually remembered something.

"You know," Merrick mumbles thickly. "It's times like this that life would be so much better with a soundtrack."

Well, if he's talking, at least he's not dying.

I smile. "So what would be playing right now?"

"Freddy Freeloader. Or Flight of the Bumblebee. I dunno, maybe Yakety Sax." He swallows with some difficulty. "They're all pretty riveting compositions."

"Riveting compositions," I agree woodenly.

That's the last time he's able to speak to me. Sitting here on the floor, holding a tube down his throat, I think I figured something out. Why he stood there this morning, staring me down, as I offered him a golden ticket to run alongside me and see monsters or turn inside-out or goodness knows what else. Merrick wasn't checking me out, or weighing what was in it for him, or whether he'd be back in time to watch Star Trek that night.

He's simply not an idiot.

*

Merrick eventually falls asleep, his pointed elf-like ears and strange elongated nose already reverting back to human form. Once I'm satisfied that he's not going to puke up the anti-cow cocktail in his sleep, I quietly pull the door shut then make a beeline back to the police station.

Merrick was a good guinea pig. At least we know our antidote works. Now all I've got to do is make enough to fix...every...single...affected person in town.

That's a lot.

Wasn't there only supposed to be *one* wildcard? This is super unfair. Of course, Holliday never said each day would be a repeat of the gargoyle.

And he sure never said it would be fair.

I get to the police station to find all the lights off. Only the soft, gold glow of a gooseneck lamp cuts the shadows. Sheriff Gammell is sitting alone, slumped in a chair. The steel coffee mug hangs from his fingers. There are two cows snuffling around in the jail cell behind him. One is silvery-white – that's Old Man Tannon, I presume. The other cow is cinnamon-hued, scrawny, and gangly. A stifled whistle escapes my lips when I realize that must be Deputy Scarecrow. Honestly, neither animal looks too stressed about their situation, chomping contentedly at a stack of donuts from a paper plate in the cell.

Even without looking up from his coffee mug, Gammell seems to know it's me.

"Annabelle's...sick," he mutters. "My wife. I think she's changing too. I...need your help."

"I know you do." I tell him gently. "That's why I need you to do exactly as I say."

*

I've never seen people move so fast. Sheriff Gammell rounds up a motley crew of townsfolk, including Kindly Mustache Man from the General Store, Gladys, and Hank, the Jamaican fellow with the auto parts shop. Then we scrape together a faction of other willing spirits who still have feet, as opposed to hooves. Each of them clutching Merrick's list of anti-cow ingredients on a chili pepper recipe card, the group scatters out into town like a swarm of bees, on what I'm sure will be the weirdest mass scavenger hunt never recorded in history. Now we just need a way to gather everyone in town.

Then around six o'clock, the noise begins outside. Softly at first, muffled by street corners and brick siding; a rattling crack of snare drums, growing louder as it nears. A marching band. The homecoming parade is starting.

Bingo.

*

From the street corner, I watch from a distance as Sheriff Gammell mounts a truck riser on a parked homecoming float, a bullhorn in his hand. He addresses the crowd, a good many of whom are hiding under blankets to mask their cow-like features. At least they showed up.

Every float in the parade has been halted. Hay wagons and flatbed trucks have been lovingly transformed into various Halloween themes – a cemetery scene, complete with foam tombstones; an eight-foot-tall Grim Reaper made of chicken wire and tattered strips of black cheesecloth, all decked out with streamers and clusters of maroon and orange balloons. An enormous wolverine, presumably the high school's mascot, looms imposingly over the street in all its paper mâché glory. It's actually pretty impressive. When Carnival Creeke does a thing, they do it with all their small-town hearts.

And today, that's a very, very good thing.

I watch them unfold a long metal table on one of the risers and pass out Dixie cups of Merrick's anti-cow O.J. to the masses.

The sunset dances, glistening off the surface of the orange liquid in those hundred cups. I recognize Mrs. Moffatt from the Red Rooster, handing out cups and helping those who can't swallow or hold their cups with their hooves under their blankets. A group of fully transformed cows are slurping antidote cocktail from an aluminum ice bucket.

It's all surprisingly well-organized. You'd think it was just another one of their pie-eating contests. Now we just wait and see if this takes care of *every* wildcard. There's no way to be sure, and that makes my palms sweaty. For one panicked split second, I have an awful thought. What if there's one person off in a closet somewhere, being antisocial and turning into a cow all by their lonesome? That would be horrible...

That one jerk would totally ruin my wildcard tally.

And then what? Crazy cow disease would spread? All the milk-drinkers of the world would slowly join us in becoming part of the bovine community?

But the people of Carnival Creeke seem to be good team players, and when Gladys checks off the town census, it looks like the whole town turned out tonight.

We did it.

*

After dark, I'm sitting on the roof of Lau Chow's. Camped out on the ledge above the restaurant's sign, same place where I found the gargoyle snoozing, my feet dangling by the torches.

Sheriff Gammell is sitting beside me. Below us the town is all aglow, one big party. No cows in attendance.

"We'll dive right into an official investigation," Gammell mutters. "Reckon they'll seal it off, quarantine us all here. Gonna be eerie, seeing this town all wrapped up in those plastic hazmat tunnels."

I'll let him have his plans. It's too complicated to explain, so I don't. I don't tell him that, come tomorrow, there won't be a need for any investigation. There's no culprit here, no mastermind with an axe to grind against the dairy community.

So I just nod.

Then Gammell does something I don't expect. He turns to me, and in his growly bear voice, he says, "I won't forget what you did for our town."

My throat locks. Feels like I'm supposed to say something. Something encouraging or profound, some junk like that.

"Buck up, Sheriff." I shrug brightly. "Your wife's going to be fine."

I rise, clapping him on the back with my good arm. He returns it with a deep nod. Something beyond gratitude. Something I'm not sure what to do with.

*

Merrick found the old record player in my closet while I was gone. So when I return he's waltzing around the room like a nutcase, singing along with the scratchy recording.

"*Blue Moo-o-o-o-n!*" (He purposely holds the note, accentuating the "moo.") "*You saw me standing alone...*"

He looks so plumb ridiculous that I almost laugh, because he's actually got a pretty decent singing voice.

I remark, "Feeling better, I see?"

He just sings louder. I shake my head.

"Oh, hey Merrick? Remember you almost turned into a cow today?"

"That's kinda funny."

"No, it's not."

"A little, yeah."

He takes my good arm and tries to twirl me. I root myself grumpily to the floor.

"I *will* shoot you, boy."

Merrick lets go of my hand, waltzing off and belting, "*Kyle's gonna shooooot me, without a dream in my heart...*"

It's actually a little sad, considering he won't remember a lick of this tomorrow.

"Hey," Merrick grins, pulling on his gray hoodie. "Wherever you're from...good work today. You, um, going to be around town tomorrow?"

I don't know why, but I suddenly think of the 8-ball keychain.

"Yeah." I smile quietly. "All signs point to yes."

*

So here I am, propped up on the four-poster bed again tonight, the pink kitten notebook on my lap, a rooster towel of ice slung across my re-injured shoulder. Déjà vu. Only tonight, it's different.

Today, I was part of something.

Across the room on the record player, Sinatra's swanky voice is crooning through the scratchy vinyl.

Who knows? I might feel different tomorrow. But at this moment, in the stillness of this night, there's this inimitable sense of peace that's radiating from knowing that right now, I'm exactly where I should be – doing exactly what I'm supposed to be doing.

Today, I got it right.

DAY 2: COUGH

I didn't sleep well.

I kept finding myself watching the little tin clock on the bedside dresser, burning a hole through it with my eyes because I wanted to see what time the day would reset itself. But I guess I was more wiped than I realized, because I still kept dozing off.

I didn't catch what time the day reset. All I accomplished was tossing and turning like an apple fritter, finally jolting awake when that stupid car alarm trumpeted outside my window at 6:11.

If you open the window in my room and look straight down, you'll see a sweet little fenced-in tea garden, with a wrought iron table and lattice-work chairs. A horseshoe of Japanese maples completes the charming scene. Let your eyes wander beyond the garden, and you're treated to a less picturesque view of the tire-stacked garage behind the gas station. So I usually just stick to looking at the garden.

I decide to gather all my belongings and take them with me today. Except for the pink kitten journal, of course – *that* little trove of secrets will stay firmly tucked under the mattress box spring. So that leaves four items: A wad of cash, the clothes on my back, my "live for today" fortune, and the little plastic 8-ball keychain.

Ah, the 8-ball keychain. Still haven't figured that one out yet. But it's coming with me. Who knows? It might just save my life. I'm not taking anything for granted today.

Yawning, I shrug into my red leather jacket. My dislocated-relocated shoulder has knitted itself back together again nicely. A little lingering stiffness, and I'm sure I've got a nice glob of scar tissue around the joint now.

But I'm alive.

More than alive. Even on a crappy night's sleep, I'm tapping my boots like a racehorse jigging in the starting gate. My body is fizzing with eager anticipation, knowing there's a wildcard out there with my name on it.

I had no idea at the time, but my new mantra was born this morning:

My arms move. My legs move.
The wildcard is just the kind of challenge I like.
Today is my day.

*

After breakfast, I set off walking into town. It's a long walk, and long walks allow your mind to wander. One question in particular keeps flitting around in my head like a bird in a hardware store. What if *I* had taken a swig of that milk back at Tannon's field? Would *I* have sprouted a tail and an udder, too? Maybe. Or maybe...

108

Here's another option I must consider.

Maybe I'm immune.

Maybe that freak Holliday injected me with something. Or put some sort of force field around me, something to grant me immunity to the effects of the wildcard. Something to ensure I would stay fit to play this "game." I guess it would make sense.

Am I really talking about things making sense in Carnival Creeke?

*

By the time I reach town, the morning fog has burned off. The clean-up construction crew is hammering away on their scaffolding in the graveyard by the library.

I don't know what kind of wildcard will greet me today. All I know is it probably won't shake hands and play nice. I'll have to be prepared for anything. Literally. Which means I'll need a few basic provisions.

On my way to the General Store, I pass by a shop with "Antique Weapon Replicas" in Old English lettering on its window. I stop walking.

Oh, hello. Did someone say weapons?

The shop is dark inside. A little cardboard hand-written sign is taped to the door. It says they open at nine o'clock. I check my watch. 7:23. Cupping my hands over the glass, I peer through the window and check out their selection. A couple of Civil War-era rifles, some Klingon blades, a ruby-eyed, snake-handled dagger. One particular beauty catches my eye – a battle axe, probably solid steel, from what I can see. Pressing my nose against the glass, I admire the sultry symmetrical curve of the two-headed blade, like steel butterfly wings. Bet that thing could do some serious damage. It would sure be more helpful than Lau Chow's incredibly breakable katana.

At the General Store, the wooden chief on the pumpkin-lined porch greets me with his customary scowl. Today he has a Cubs baseball cap on his head.

The cowbells clatter as I walk in, prompting Kindly Mustache Man to look up from the counter, where he's arranging huge pink-and-yellow spiral gourmet lollipops into small holes in an upright wooden log next to the cash register.

"Well, howdy-day, young lady!"

He snuffles into a handkerchief then tucks it into his apron pocket, beaming at me. I rustle up a little collection of random sundry survival essentials – a small utility knife, a lighter, earplugs, dental floss. Kindly Mustache Man cheerfully scans my items. His smile crinkles the corners of his eyes, as though his face were sprouting wings.

"So, if I may ask…" He pauses covertly. His voice lowers to a whisper. "Do we have a bun in the oven?"

Huh?

Oh, that's right. Last time he saw me, I was in here buying a pregnancy test.

"Ah." I shrug awkwardly. "No buns in my future, apparently."

"Well." He pats my hand. "When the time is right, I'm sure."

When the "time is right?" Let's examine the irony in that statement. "Time" in Carnival Creeke is about as far from "right" as I am from being a stegosaurus. Besides, could you imagine *me* with a kid?

Hold on, sweetie, mommy needs to go turn all the cow-people back into people again before time resets.

I look up and catch Kindly Mustache Man sneaking a lollipop into my bag. I frown.

"I don't need any special gifts."

"Who's special?" He gives me a wink. "We give 'em to all the kids free on Fridays."

For a moment, I'm just plain not sure how to respond.

"You don't even know me," I finally say.

Ugh. Why does everything that comes out of my mouth make me sound like a grade-A jerk? Luckily Kindly Mustache Man makes it easy on me, dissolving into a barrumphing fit of coughs before our conversation can train-wreck any further. He excuses himself through his handkerchief and shuffles back to the restroom.

That's one thing different about Carnival Creeke. They seem to genuinely give a hoot. Everywhere else, people are so quick with an excuse and an exit strategy. They won't get too close because they're sick; they "don't want to hold you up" because they know "you're busy." I mean, I'm guilty of it.

But Kindly Mustache Man has a cough. And a store to run. And yet, with nothing to gain, instead of kicking me out the door and getting back to whatever he was doing, this man showed a genuine interest in my oven buns and even slipped me a free lollipop for the heck of it. It's like joy is the default human emotion here.

I slink out the door and transfer the contents of my bag into various pockets on my cargo pants. I stare at the swirly pink lollipop, nestled at the bottom of the brown paper bag. *I'm not a kid.* That's what I should have said to him, when he nailed me with this uninvited guilt trip on a stick. Either that or "thank you."

I clear my throat and stuff the rolled-up bag in my pocket. Stupid lollipop is still in there, pummeled me with its searing guilt.

"Okay, fine!" I hiss at nobody in particular. *Fine.* I'll play nice. I'll go back and check on Kindly Mustache Man. It shouldn't take but a minute, if I don't fart around.

The counter is unoccupied when I reenter the General Store. Kindly Mustache Man must still be in the restroom. I meander around the aisles like I've got a purpose for being there, strolling my way to the back of the store. Sure enough, the restroom door is shut. Hanging on the door is a little, wooden, heart-shaped sign that says: *"How long a minute is depends on which side of the bathroom you're on."*

Cute.

I knock on the door with my knuckles. "Hello?"

No response. Feeling a little like a creeper, I cup my ear to the door. A muffled coughing sound can be made out.

Okie-doke. Well, at least I know he's still alive in there. I guess it wouldn't kill my day to hang out for a few more minutes. I could keep an eye on the counter for Kindly Mustache Man until he gets back. Besides, there's been no hint of the wildcard so far.

I make my way back up to the front of the store, leaning on an ice cream freezer chest and gazing idly out the window.

It's interesting how you can still hear a person's voice in their cough. A cough, an involuntary reflex – and yet they still sound like themselves. I guess a lot of what we do is like that. Mundane, automatic, subconscious acts. We're still us. Whether we mean to be or not.

Curiously, I stretch out my finger and write my name in the condensation on the windowpane.

Kyle, C

My handwriting is a new wonder to me. Scratchy, like Japanese characters, but less graceful.

But then a jolt runs through me. After writing "C," another letter flows from my finger; automatic, as natural as breathing, like it's always been there. Stepping back, I assess the new letter in shock and awe.

Kyle, Cl

But it ends there. I can't make myself remember the next letter, no matter how long I stand there with my finger out. I even trace the "CL" a couple times. Whatever part of me had momentarily surfaced, it's gone. Run off again. But it's something.

Kyle, Cl

I'm in there somewhere.

*

Time passes like a slug. I wander the aisles of the store, straightening the tins of shoe polish. Still no sign of Kindly Mustache Man. There's a bag of fun-size Snickers lying on the floor; I scoop it up and return it to the cardboard display of Halloween candy setup by the entrance. A lady carrying a wiener dog in a pumpkin costume comes in to buy some chewing gum and a lottery ticket. Luckily, the cash register is older than dirt and it springs open for me automatically after I punch in the total. I shut the register drawer. That was oddly satisfying. I'm starting to feel all sweet and helpful and warm inside, then I return to my senses.

I glance at my watch. This is starting to get annoying. It's now half-past ten and Kindly Mustache Man has yet to emerge from that restroom.

What's he *doing* in there? Building a house?

Impatience creeps up my back. I can't an't help feeling that I would be better out there looking for today's wildcard. Of course, I *could* just *leave*... But then I think of his stupid free lollipop and inexplicably resolve to give him five more minutes. So I count the cans of beef-a-roni (there's eight, by the way), straighten the sodas, and alphabetize the cereals. Eventually I end up just pacing in front of the counter like a hyena. As soon as Kindly Mustache Man finishes coughing his lungs out, I'm seriously going to kick his butt, lollipop or no lollipop.

Click.

The restroom door opens. I stop pacing and look up.

He looks fine. He's not coughing or hacking – in fact, he's smiling. A cheese-eating grin is stretched across his face.

"Feeling better?" I laugh. "I was ready to call in the National Guard."

Wordlessly, Kindly Mustache Man brushes right by me and takes his post behind the checkout counter. And that's it. He literally just stands there. Grinning like a Cheshire cat. Very slowly, I lean across the counter and snap my fingers in front of his nose.

"Hello?"

He's staring straight at me – but not really *at* me. Kind of through me, as if I'm not even here, with his teeth gritted together, frozen in a creepy, carnival barker grin. I'll admit, it's a little unnerving. Given how his eyes so recently twinkled at me, this hollow and vacant stare feels like a completely different person.

A chill of excitement ripples through me.

This has "wildcard" written all over it.

I grin and mutter, "Kyle, you lucky son-of-a-gun!"

I could potentially knock out today's wildcard, bada-bing, and still have time to spare for lunch. Catch a nap, maybe even take a tour of Carnival Creeke on one of those little buses that look like trollies.

Now, if I could just figure out what I'm supposed to do.

I hook my thumbs in my back pockets and start pacing again, keeping my narrowed eyes trained on Kindly Mustache Zombie. Nothing I do gets a reaction out of him – not when I jump up onto the counter, or even when I grab all the cream sodas from the fridge and start chucking them out into the street one by one. Shoot, I even try telling him I'm pregnant. He doesn't even blink.

This is enormously frustrating. I'm one hundred percent sure this guy is my wildcard. But I have *no clue* what to do with him.

Slapping twenty bucks on the counter (for all those cream sodas that I demolished), I finally resort to just leaving the store. I lock the door behind me. Through the glass, Grinning Mustache Zombie watches me the whole time, unmoved from his cash register counter.

Now I'm just irritated. I guarantee that Irish creep Holliday is enjoying this. And why not? He's given me nothing to work with. A puzzle, with no pieces.

But I've got a plan.

I shimmy up the fire escape and climb over to my roof perch atop Lau Chow's marquee sign. A few folk below stop walking, tilting their heads up at me curiously. I'm calling unnecessary attention to myself. Sure. But I don't care. Let them think I'm up here waiting for King Kong to come scoop me up. It's not *their* attention I'm hoping to catch.

What I'm about to shout from this rooftop is so brilliant, Rascal Holliday will have no choice but to show himself. For the first time, I feel in control. Powerful, invincible.

I clear my throat. Twice.

Stupid tickle. Feels like I've got a caterpillar in my throat...

The cough seizes me without warning. Ducking down like a moron, I crawl off the sign anticlimactically and fumble my way across the rooftop, coughing so hard my body is shaking like a jackhammer. I can't stop. It's like my lungs are rejecting air.

This is no ordinary cough.

I can feel myself becoming incapacitated, vulnerable. I need to get out of sight, and fast.

Grasping the roof's gutter, I swing clumsily down onto the fire escape with a clatter, horking and hacking. One of the apartment windows is open. I tumble through the windowsill and stumble into a living room, doubled over coughing, barking like a sea lion. A cute little girl, about four years old, looks up from the TV, watching me curiously with round eyes shining in her lovely dark face. Now she's thrusting her pack of Twinkies at me, but I can't help her open her tasty little cakes because I'm in the throes of the most evil and violent cough the world has surely ever witnessed. Okay, perhaps I was a tad premature getting so ticked off at Kindly Mustache Man earlier. This is awful.

And that's when I feel the lump in my throat. I try to swallow, but it's like a sandcastle in a tidal wave. With each cough, the lump keeps squirming (do lumps squirm?), up my throat, higher, higher, to the base of my tongue...

Tripping over a basket of laundry, I lurch toward the soft caramel shower-curtain-glow of this family's bathroom, managing to slam up the toilet lid in the nick of time.

Then I cough up my lung.

No... It's not my lung. Because I'm fairly sure my lung doesn't look like *that*.

A pudgy, flesh-colored ball, about the size of a Clementine orange, is sitting in the toilet bowl. For a moment, all I can do is stare at it. I'm reaching for a Dixie cup from the toothbrush stand when the ball wriggles and rolls down the toilet drain.

My mouth drops open.

"I didn't sign up for this!" I shout.

Come to think of it, I didn't sign up at all.

Or did I?

I really don't want to entertain the notion that I willfully agreed to this carousel of weirdness before I lost my memory. But I don't have time to muse on it, because Twinkie Girl's dad just burst into the bathroom doorway, screaming like a crazed Louisville Slugger and waving a baseball bat at me.

On the plus side, my cough seems to have vanished completely. I feel right as rain.

Except for the baseball bat swinging at my head.

OUT OF THE FRYING PAN...

Once I'm sure I've put a healthy bit of distance between my head and Twinkie Dad's baseball bat, I stop running and I start thinking. Needless to say, I don't feel invincible anymore. Now I just feel like a goober. Well, at least I've learned one thing. Now I know I'm not immune. The wildcard can suck me into its spinning blades of freakiness and infect me, just like anyone else.

I think of that fleshy ball that I coughed up into the toilet, and a shudder runs through me.

Where do these toilet drainpipes go? A water treatment plant, most likely. If that's where my little alien tangerine slithered off to, then that's where I need to head.

But I'll need a ride.

*

I jog up to the Tuscany Mill dining room without stopping at the host podium.

"I'm looking for Merrick Cohen," I announce breathlessly to whoever is listening. Which is pretty much everyone in the room, at the moment. I didn't use my indoor voice.

"Merrick?" Chirpy Podium Blonde shrugs. "He just went on his lunch break."

"Did he say if he was going home?"

"He usually grabs lunch at Merle's diner."

I wave thanks and turn on my heel. Right as I grab the door handle, the blonde girl calls out behind me. "Hey! Is Merrick in some kind of trouble?"

I pause before answering.

"If I catch up with him..." I shoot her a wry grin. "Yeah. Trouble is pretty much a guarantee."

*

My cough is gone, but I still keep clearing my throat. I can't help it. The nasty, slimy sensation of that alien tangerine keeps haunting me. I tug at my jacket zipper, even though it's already zipped all the way up to my chin. Feels like everyone is staring at me, their eyes catching on me like hooks. I've already got an empty canyon where my heart should be. And now, thanks to whatever that Evil Cough of Zeus dislodged from me... What *else* am I missing?

What *WAS* that wriggly lump?

I shove down that thought and clamp a lid on it, throwing a mental brick over the lid. Just concentrate on finding Merrick. More importantly, his Tahoe. Sure, I could probably stick out my thumb and hitchhike, snag a ride from someone else in town. They're nice. Someone would pick me up. But I can't deny that Merrick was handy to have around yesterday. I know whatever I ask him, he'll do it. He said so himself.

Plus, there's something else about Merrick. Something about him feels safe. Almost...familiar. Maybe he reminds me of someone. Someone Cl. Kyle used to know. Maybe that's why I see potential in the boy. Like there's more to him than the glasses that always seem to be falling off his face. But I guess time will tell.

*

Merle's Diner is buzzing with their lunch crowd, jingling conversation mingling with the clatter of plates and the steady scrape of a spatula on a grill. I spot Merrick sitting on a stool at the counter, his nose buried in a book. He's changed out of his work clothes, now sporting jeans and a gray hoodie.

I clear my throat and plop down beside him. Merrick looks up with a mouthful of turkey on rye. When he sees it's me, he chokes so hard he almost loses his glasses.

"Hey," is my dashing opener.

"Hey!" Merrick swallows and rescues his glasses. "Uh, so you're still alive, huh?"

"Looks like."

His Tuscany Mill waiter's shirt is folded into his open messenger bag, and I can conveniently see his gold name tag pin. I decide to play clueless, nodding down at the name tag.

"So your name's Merrick?"

"Oh, yeah," He wipes his hand and extends it awkwardly. "Merrick Cohen."

"Call me Kyle."

This feels so weird. I mean, I prepared myself. I knew the kid wouldn't remember that we've already introduced ourselves, or that he grew a tail, or that he essentially saved the whole town yesterday. But it's still weird.

"So, how's the shoulder?" Merrick grins sheepishly.

"Been better, been worse."

Is it bad that I'm wishing we could just jump to the "him trusting me" stage? Because the clock is ticking, and all I can think about is that gross alien tangerine that I coughed up. Out there somewhere, slithering through the sewer pipes...

I'm calculating how much chitchat it will take to convince Merrick into lending me a ride in his Tahoe when a shrill laugh suddenly breaks my thought. The chubby, balding businessman on the stool beside me is holding his belly, giggling like a donkey. I turn and stare at him. What is this corndog laughing at? Merle, the beefy lumberjack in the white apron behind the counter, just brought him a second slice of rhubarb pie.

Why is that funny, you ask?

See, Baldy hadn't finished his first slice. With an absent expression, Merle had plunked the new plate right on top of the man's first pie, smushing the half-eaten dessert, his fork still hovering in mid-bite.

Baldy wipes his eyes and continues to hee-haw as Merle shuffles to the other end of the counter, presumably for some napkins.

I kind of feel sorry for the big guy. Even in an apron, Merle has this fresh-out-of-prison look, partly thanks to an unfortunate thick scar running through the meat of his cheek. Then there's the tattoos and oil-slicked black hitman hair, gentled by the first streak of grey, giving him the appearance of someone you wouldn't really want to sit next to on a plane. But he's not a bad guy. It's not like we've exchanged BFF bracelets or anything. Yet Merle brought me my burger and milkshake that first day, when I was feeling really crappy and confused. Gave me my shake on the house, too. Because I've got kind eyes, Merle had said. Okay, so he obviously doesn't know me very well. But he's decent.

"Um, are you hungry?" Merrick offers brightly. "Can I buy you something?"

"No thanks. Don't worry about it."

"I seriously almost made roadkill out of you yesterday. C'mon, it's the least I can do. Want my pickle?"

He reddens and drops his face into one hand.

Merrick Cohen, ladies and gentlemen.

About six seconds later, Merle tromps over with a third plate of pie. And then returns with a *fourth* slice. Diner patrons pause to watch in amusement as proceeds to plop each new plate on top of the stack. The precarious tower o' plates wobbles. Baldy has stopped laughing, less amused now as he wipes his rhubarb-splattered shirt with a napkin.

"Wow, what's up with the free pie today?" Merrick snickers under his breath.

People around the diner are also starting to giggle, but I'm focused on Merle. Because I recognize that hollow funhouse grin plastered across his face.

Same exact grin that Kindly Mustache Man was wearing earlier...

Did I mention that Merle is a big guy? And right now, all seven feet of him are standing across the counter, sawing blankly at the empty pie stand with his knife, as though trying to cut another slice. But he doesn't seem to notice. Mindlessly, he's going through the motions. Something is wrong. Very wrong...

Something in this diner is getting ready to explode.

And if I can't prevent the explosion, maybe I *can* control *who* it explodes on.

I hop off my stool. "Mercy me," I announce brightly. "There's a fly in my chowder!"

Merle turns his head and looks at me. He never stops grinning.

Then he goes berserk.

I duck as his fist comes flying at me – good thing, because there's a knife in it. Unfortunately, I'm not so lucky dodging his second punch. I'm flung backward like a sack of potatoes, bouncing off the jukebox and crashing into a dish cart, knocking a cascade of rolled silverware into a nearby family's soup. The chalkboard announcing today's specials clatters to the floor. The jukebox cranks to life, auto-selecting "Crazy Dreams" by Conway Twitty and blasting it at full volume. Everyone snatches their jackets and purses, dashing for the door. Everyone except Merrick – and Baldy, who stands there gaping at me like he's about to pee himself.

"Just *run*, will you?" I shout at him, rolling off the table. "Go! Work off that pie!"

Merle pivots slowly, grinning like a goon, this time turning toward Merrick. He raises the knife, seemingly deciding that Merrick needs less limbs and more holes in his body.

Merrick throws both hands in the air. "Whoa, Merle! It's me! It's Merrick!"

"Don't bother," I mutter, remembering Kindly Mustache Man's vacant stare. But of course Merrick can't hear me; I'm drowned out by Conway Twitty's nasally twang blasting from the jukebox.

Merrick helpfully trips over backwards. Then he abruptly grows a pair, snatching the still-brewing pot of coffee off the hotplate, shaking his head apologetically at Merle before smashing the pot across his face.

Good boy, I applaud.

But Merle doesn't drop the knife. Doesn't react.

Might as well have blown a dandelion in his face.

I slide across the floor, grabbing the chalkboard and flinging it frisbee-style at Merle's burly form. It shatters all over his back and suddenly I've got Merle's attention again. He lumbers toward me, his gritted teeth reflecting in that fine stainless-steel blade. I spring behind the counter, scanning the shelves for anything that might be used as a weapon. Rolls of napkins, a bunch of ketchup and mustard in squeeze bottles... I grab a sauce bottle labeled "XX Volcano Juice."

125

Swinging around, I aim the bottle and squirt Merle square in the eyes. He doesn't even blink.

This *is* hot sauce, right?

Crouching with my back behind the counter, I flip the bottle and squeeze a few drops onto my tongue. Vinegary fire blasts through my mouth. Definitely hot.

I look up just in time to see Grinning Zombie Merle bend over the stove. His beefy hand closes around the handle of a cast-iron skillet, causing all the sausages to roll off. I wince. That's a hot pan. I mean, I can *smell* his flesh searing. But no reaction. He's swinging that thing like it's a tennis racket.

Now it makes sense.

"Merrick, he can't feel pain!" I scream over the ridiculously loud jukebox.

Wow, my sinuses are super-clear thanks to the hot sauce.

Merle reels toward the sound of my voice, windmilling at me like a grinning T-Rex.

"Heads-up!"

I duck as Merrick charges by, swinging a stool. Seizing the opportunity, I roll under Merle's feet and kick his knees out from behind. By the time the big guy goes timber, I've ripped the orange and black Halloween tinsel from the heavy cream fridge and hogtied his hands and feet with the spooky garland. Of course, Merle instantly snaps it like a shoestring.

There's no blocking his arm as it swings at me. It hits me like a battering ram into my stomach. I topple back into something solid that breaks apart; judging from the sweet taste of the splatter, I'm guessing that I just demolished the lemonade machine. Two quick electric whoops sound outside, followed by a flash of red and blue. Looks like the cavalry's here. Smearing the syrupy lemon goodness off my face, I peel myself up from the sticky floor as Sheriff Gammell and Deputy Scarecrow burst through the diner doors.

Good. Let Carnival Creeke's finest handle Merle. I have a more important mystery to solve. Namely, what is causing the good people of Carnival Creeke to suddenly go ape-nuts crazy.

Sheriff Gammell is embroiled in a knock-down, drag-out wrestling match with Zombie Merle. I'll hand it the sheriff, he's actually got some good moves, and he seems to almost be holding his own against the knife-wielding lumberjack in the apron. Deputy Scarecrow is standing in front of me, watching the scuffle with his hands balled into enthusiastic fists. I guess I should stop calling him Scarecrow, seeing as I found out yesterday that his name is Joe, but it would be so tragic to give up such a perfect nickname.

My eyes slide down to the shiny set of handcuffs hanging from the deputy's belt.

On our way out, Gammell glances at me – but only because I'm a new face in his town. There's no warmth in his eyes, no memory of yesterday's cow-curing, town-saving escapade.

As Deputy Joe-crow passes, I quickly unhook the handcuffs and key from his belt and return his civil nod, no one the wiser of my artful dodging.

*

We file outside. Merrick grabs his knees and looks like he's having an asthma attack. I crouch on the pavement beside him.

"Merrick, this is very important. Before Merle flipped out, did he have a cough?"

Merrick stops gasping long enough to look at me like I'm nuts. "I didn't notice anything," he shakes his head. "But I know he was coughing earlier."

"How do you know?"

"I heard some lady complain. She was afraid Merle coughed on her toasted cheese, got phlegm on it. Why?"

"So he *was* coughing?" I stare him down hard. "You're *absolutely* sure?"

Merrick raises his eyebrows, curiously baffled by my insistence. "Pretty sure!"

Great. So first comes the cough, then they go fruit loops crazy. Maybe we're coughing up pieces of our brains. Lobotomizing ourselves. But if that's true... How long have *I* got? An hour? Less?

I still *feel* like myself...

It hit Kindly Mustache Man relatively fast. About an hour. Maybe he coughed up a larger chunk of brain. As for Merle...

Well, I have no idea how long before he became Michael Myers. Somehow, I think it all hinges on finding my alien tangerine.

"Hey, Merrick." I press my fingers to the bridge of my nose. "Is there a water treatment plant in Carnival Creeke?"

"Yeah, on the north edge of town. Why?"

"I need you to drive me there."

He looks a little uncomfortable, like I just pulled a gun on him or something. So I soften my approach.

"Listen," I begin. "I think the town's water supply might be contaminated. But I won't know until I've run some tests, alright? I'll pay you gas money for your truck. So what do you say?"

I extend my hand, although I know he won't take it yet. Because I know Merrick. He has to ask me his question first.

"If I take you," Merrick says slowly. "Will I see a monster?"

"Monsters galore. I promise."

"Okay." He takes my hand and shakes it once, grinning. "Deal."

See, relationships aren't really all that complex. Just push the right buttons, and bam. Just like a jukebox.

I'm not sure why, but I suddenly feel like somebody just dumped a big glass of guilt over my head.

*

Leaning my elbows on the metal railing, I squint out across the row of four swimming pool-sized sewage treatment tanks. The water's surface is murky and serene as glass. The reflection of the afternoon sun gleams a darkish putrid green. Even if I could isolate the right tank, finding something the size of a tangerine in there would still be tricky. A needle in a freaking haystack.

"So what's your story?" Merrick asks behind me. "Avenging angel sent from another dimension? Secret government warehouse? C'mon, be honest. You've got our town in some manila folder marked 'X', don't you?"

Listen to this kid, making the same joke as yesterday. It's almost cute. Maybe if I hadn't just horked up a brain ball, I might've even chuckled.

Then Merrick asks another question.

"So where's your equipment?"

I turn around. He's sitting cross-legged on the concrete, eating a granola bar and watching me through distinctly suspicious eyes. I know that look. Same exact look Sheriff Gammell gave me before he threw me to the wolves and ordered me to milk that stupid cow at Tannon's field.

"What do you mean?" I say, turning back to the railing.

"You said you're here to test our water." Merrick waves a hand toward the tanks. "Sooo...where's your equipment?"

Yeah, I didn't really expect that story to go over his head.

"You're looking for something in the water, aren't you?" Merrick cringes. "You...think it's another gargoyle?"

I wish.

The gargoyle was relatively straightforward. This is a whole different ball game. I don't even know what this wildcard looks like. I don't know *what* I'm dealing with. One thing that I'm sure of – that alien tangerine is *alive*. It slithered down the toilet drain, all by its proficient little self. It's enough to give anyone the heebie-jeebies.

I walk over and plop down beside Merrick. The concrete is warm. Maybe it's the peaceful silence or the toasty sun that's got me feeling all truthful, or maybe it's because I have nothing else to do – but I decide to level with him.

"Okay, Merrick." I sigh. "You want the truth? Nothing is wrong with your water. This morning, I coughed up what I suspect might be a piece of my brain and watched it slither down the drain. So now I'm here with you because this seems like the most logical place to start looking for it."

"Aha," Merrick says finally. This time he's wearing a tentative smile. "Thanks," he says after a beat. "For being honest. I'm not really into the whole lying thing."

With a grin, he breaks off a piece of his granola bar and offers it to me.

This kid is so weird.

Returning his grin, I take the granola chunk and pop it into my mouth. Oatmeal raisin. For a blissfully uneventful moment, we just sit in the sunshine, chewing.

"So," Merrick says after a moment. "What are you gonna do if you find that piece of your brain?"

"Shove it back in my head."

That's code for "I have no clue."

Merrick looks at me. "You think you'll end up like Merle?"

"I don't know."

I hold out my hands and examine them. Still steady. Still able to be clenched into a strong fist.

But for how long?

Will I be like Kindly Mustache Man, docile and comatose? Or like Merle, a violent berserker? Guess it depends on what the original person was like. The person underneath. But I have no idea what kind of person "Cl Kyle" was...

I promised Merrick he would see a monster. What a grisly little twist of fate if that monster turns out to be me. Ain't that a kick in the head.

I can't deal with this.

I can't deal with losing my mind.

So I make some excuse and slip away from Merrick, and I head to the one place in Carnival Creeke that's familiar – the only place I can link to a specific event in Cl Kyle's life. The place I should have gone right off the bat when this whole thing began.

*

The water tower has never stopped watching me. And I guess, in a way, I've always kept it in the corner of my eye. Something tethers us together, like an invisible fishing line.

Time to revisit.

I point myself toward the structure and start walking. The water tower is located in a field behind an elementary school, near a red dirt baseball diamond surrounded by a thick semicircle of Virginia Pine. I linger like a ghost at the edge of the baseball field, nervously poking at second base with my toe.

At about thirty feet tall, this water tower is more of an elevated water tank. Not nearly as monstrous as those towering, big-city steel giants, but more than sufficient for the double-digit population like Carnival Creeke. I'm close enough to make out thin veins of rust feathering the edge of the mint-green paint on the bolted steel tank. Part of me expects the structure to come alive, rise up onto those spindly hydraulic legs, creaking, and go crashing off into the woods. I'm actually a little disappointed when it doesn't.

No, both the tower and I hold very still. And gazing up at its belly, I remember…

Nothing.

That's it, folks. No great revelation, no black-and-white flashback of me and Rascal Holliday engaged in some horrible blood-and-guts mêlée, or whatever happened leading up to that moment in the mud here when he jammed that canister over my chest and sucked out my heart.

I glance around, a weird shiver pricking my back. This was a stupid waste of time. I'm infected. Not only are my precious twenty-four hours counting down, but likely my remaining time as a sane person is also rapidly pouring down the drain. With a frustrated growl, I start to pace back and forth, forcefully raking my hands through my hair. I haven't bothered to brush it, and now it's a marvelous rat's nest of copper tendrils.

Gargoyles in freezers. People turning into cows. Even getting my heart sucked out... I can cope with all that.

But losing my mind?

How do I deal with that?

I don't know jack about myself to begin with. So I'm afraid I won't recognize the signs, when the madness starts. I might not be able to act rational. Or even know the difference.

Reaching around decisively, I pull out Deputy Scarecrow's handcuffs. Then I fish out a bobby pin from my jacket pocket. Leaning back against one of the water tower's support legs, I insert the pin into the keyhole on the handcuffs and bend one end of the pin into an L-shape. Then I wiggle it the other way, until I've bent the pin into a nice Z-shaped crook.

My hand bumps Merrick's cell phone in my pocket. He made me take it. He insisted – just like he did yesterday – so he'd have a way to reach me. Transferring the phone into my pants pocket, I slip off my jacket and toss it over by a tree. About eighteen feet up, a thin catwalk with a handrail encircles the water tank. I throw my bent bobby pin straight up. It takes a few tries before it lands on the catwalk without bouncing off.

Then I go over to the nearest support leg, give it a hug, and handcuff myself to the pole.

There we go.

My makeshift bobby pin key is eighteen feet above me with no ladder in reach. *If* I decide to free myself, it should be possible to climb up and retrieve the key, but still being tricky enough to require a truckload of focus – focus that *I won't have* if I turn into a grinning zombie nutcase. And if that happens, well... At least I'll be chained here like a dog and won't be able to run around town gnawing anyone's arm off.

Unless...

Would I gnaw off my *own* arm to escape?

The afternoon sun is high in the sky. An airplane glides by overhead, painting a white streak across the sky. Getting chilly. I'm beginning to regret tossing my jacket aside. But that's not all I'm regretting.

This was a terrible idea.

Like a pendulum, the reality of this decision has swung back to nail me in the face. Crazy or not, handcuffing myself to a pole was the most terrible of terrible ideas. Each passing moment I feel frantically positive that dealing with the wildcard far outweighs any mischief I might commit when I become a zombie. *I'm* the only one who can fix this... So what if I attack someone and bite off a few fingers? Fingers will reappear tomorrow. Just like new. I'll just have to try and keep myself together. Utilize whatever clout I have and fix this wildcard while I'm still sane.

I'll have to trust myself.

Determined, I brace my weight against the handcuffs and start shimmying up the support column toward the bobby pin, making an unholy clatter of metal scraping metal, and trying to ignore the cuffs grinding into my wrists.

Suddenly I realize I'm not alone.

Someone else has entered the clearing below me. On the other side of the water tower, nine o'clock to my six o'clock.

Has Holliday also decided to return to the scene of his crime?

I freeze, anticipation fluttering in my belly. But the person down there is buck-naked – and most definitely not male. Her copper hair is wet, hanging in stringy ribbons down her bare shoulders.

Then I realize who I'm looking at.

Because it isn't Holliday who's returned to the scene.

It's *me*.

My, how you've grown since the toilet.

HATCHLING

I cling to the pole like a koala, holding my breath. It's taking every ounce of control to keep my muscles rigid, because I had to freeze in the most awkward, scrunched-up position. I wasn't really prepared.

Then again, who *would* be prepared to come face-to-face with the twin they coughed up an hour ago?

The thing that looks like me is creeping into the clearing like a feral cat, moving until she's directly beneath the water tower. She's darting her head back and forth, but she hasn't looked up yet. Would I look up?

Heck yeah, I would.

But I don't know how much like me she is. From my overhead view, she certainly *looks* like me. Skin like strawberry milk, same messy, wavy copper hair. Same deltoids, even though she probably hasn't done a single push-up in her two-hour life.

An exact copy of me.

A sudden, fierce curiosity seizes me. More desperate than anything I've felt or wanted since this whole thing began.

I need to know...

Slowly straightening my legs, I push off the pole onto my toes, as quietly as I can muster, craning my neck until I'm looking down at her from just the right angle.

There's no scar on her chest. No circular hatch. But there on her pale freckled skin is something else. Something is written on her chest, like a tattoo. A word.

I crane just a little farther, trying to read it.

GOLEM.

What on earth is that supposed to mean?

She just spotted my jacket on the ground.

Crap.

My calf is twitching, the handcuffs are digging so deep into my wrists I swear they've scraped bone. Every muscle is on fire. And my palms are getting extremely sweaty and slippery. Whether she looks up or not, it doesn't matter. In mere moments, my grip will slip and I will tumble down this pole like a happy Christmas elf, and then I have absolutely no earthly idea what will happen next.

She squats down to inspect my jacket, still jerking her head back and forth, rummaging through the red leather pockets. Then she grabs the jacket and dashes off.

For a moment, I consider that I've gone nuts already. Maybe my psychotic breakdown has begun, and I'm hallucinating. But my missing jacket is evidence enough. She exists.

We didn't cough up our brains.

We coughed up our doppelgangers.

"AN EXACT COPY..."

*

Escaping my self-made captivity proved successfully annoying. After shimmying the rest of the way up the water tower support leg, I was able to retrieve my bobby pin key by doing some mad-crazy handcuffed ninja moves, kicking out and stepping on the pin with my boot, then scooting it closer until I could grab it with my mouth. On the bright side, after I finally got the pin, it took me only ten seconds to pick the lock and the handcuffs sprung open easily. I hit the ground and sprint off.

One thing is clear. If my doppelganger decided to pay a visit to this water tower, it would seem that she – *it* – is aware that something significant happening here. And if that *thing* can remember...

A jolt sizzles through me, tailbone to neck.

What *else* can she remember that I can't?

*

My first destination is the General Store. The place is wrapped in yellow police tape. The glass on the door is shattered, hanging off in jagged angles. Looks like Sheriff Gammell paid a visit after I left.

Carefully slipping my hand between the broken glass, I close my fist around the cowbells so they won't clatter as I open the door. The cardboard Halloween candy display is lying on the floor, but otherwise the place is as empty and untouched as when I left. Glancing over my shoulder, I trot down the far aisle to the back of the store. The restroom door is still locked. Using a propane gas canister, I bust off the knob then kick the door off its hinges.

Sure enough, Kindly Mustache Man is inside. His grinning twin must have stolen his clothes, because the poor man is curled up on the floor tiles wearing nothing but his skivvies. He reeks of menthol cherry cough drops, clutching an empty Ricola bag and shivering like a leaf. The restroom's tiny box window is permanently propped open, so the closet-sized room is freezing by now.

"C'mon, mister." I extend a hand.

Kindly Mustache Man squints up at me like I have light beaming out of my nostrils.

"Are you an angel?"

Jeez, that's the second time today somebody's asked me that.

I fill a Styrofoam cup with hot cocoa from the dispenser, which he accepts gratefully.

"Oh," I nod down at the Ricola bag in his hands. "And you can lay off the lozenges. Your cough isn't coming back."

Digging into my pants pocket for a five to pay for his cocoa, I stop. My 8-ball keychain is gone. It must have fallen out of my pocket at the diner during my tussle with Merle.

It shouldn't bother me. But if that little trinket was important enough for Cl. Kyle to grab at the hospital, then I'd better do myself a favor. I need to go find the stupid thing.

*

The empty diner is also twirled in yellow crime scene tape. We're really doing a number on this town today. Lifting the tape, I duck under and squeeze quietly in the door.

The diner is trashed. Looks like someone threw a square-dance for a herd of wildebeest. Who knows? Maybe that's what we looked like, a bunch of square-dancing wildebeest. I don't know. I was busy trying not to die.

"Crazy Dreams" is still playing on the jukebox. Either someone inserted a fortune of quarters, or my butt hit it just right and it's stuck on repeat.

Now that I'm standing still, I'm really starting to feel it. Not just my sore butt. The exhaustion. Really wish I could have gotten a good night's sleep. I spot a half-full cup of coffee sitting on the nearest booth. Guess its owner ditched it before finishing. What the heck? I'm not going to get through the next hour, much less this entire day, without some caffeinated assistance.

Grabbing the cup, I chug down the contents in one gulp, and keep moving.

Around the corner near the restrooms, there's a pile of something on the floor. Dark and wet and meaty. I have no idea if it used to be human, or who that mess could have been. It looks like barbecue ribs. A chill runs up my spine. There's no way Merle's doppelganger could have done *this*.

Still in a crouch, I step gingerly over the pile on the floor. Ugh. I'll never be able to eat barbecue ribs again... Not that I even still could. I'm pretty sure the spicy barbecue sauce would mess with my delicate pansy stomach. Now that I'm up close, I catch a whiff of the messy pile, and it does bear the distinct smell of sweet spicy hickory. Yup, it's definitely barbecue. Oh, thank goodness. I just can't stomach the notion that Merle was capable of something so grisly, even as his zombie twin.

I spot my 8-ball keychain. Over on the floor, rolled under the metal utility dish sink. I slink over and drop to my belly, stretching my out hand. The keychain is wedged nicely between the rubber floor mat and a pipe. My fingertips run on the 8-ball for a minute, like two little legs on a treadmill – then I've got it. Straightening triumphantly, I slip the troublesome little trinket into my pocket. There. Now the planets can realign, birds can sing, and all is well.

I blink, suddenly a little woozy. My eye sockets start buzzing. Maybe I stood up too fast...

I blink hard. My head is swimming. Grasping the rim of the utility sink, I pull myself up to my feet. Almost immediately the room tips and I lurch to one side.

*What on earth was **in** that coffee?*

Gripping the counter, I tilt-a-whirl my way over to the coffee machine, tripping over a waffle press lying on the checkered tile floor. I snatch the coffee pot to examine it, spilling dark coffee grounds out of the paper filter. It says French roast. Normal, robust cup of Joe. But it ain't decaf.

There's nothing wrong with this coffee.

It's *me.*

The buzzing behind my eyeballs hums louder, all my veins swelling, bloating like they need to pulse, but simply can't. Not without a heart.

The caffeine. Holliday warned me; looks like he was right. Man, I hope he's not watching me right now. Smug satisfaction dancing in those reflectionless black eyes...

I press my fists against my temples. On the jukebox, Conway Twitty's twangy voice cuts in and out, or maybe it's just my lack of pulse trying to drum up a desperate beat.

That's my last thought before a sharp electric jolt fries the back of my neck, my spine goes rigid, and everything goes black.

*

I wake on cold concrete. There's absolutely nothing graceful about the way I'm swinging my fists at the air. I catch somebody's wrist. It's Merle. He's crouched over me, grinning and digging through my pockets.

"No touching!" I bark sharply. I'm still dazed out of my aching brain and my loud shout startles me as much as it does him. Zombie Merle backs away like a scolded puppy, shuffling off into a corner, a glazed grin still plastered across his scarred mug.

Slowly, I roll upright to a sitting position. This concrete floor feels awfully familiar. Stainless steel sink in the corner, those fluorescent lights overhead... *Oh, son-of-a-monkey!* I'm in the jail cell again. Seriously, am I going to end up in here every day?

My head stops vibrating and I notice I've got an audience. Sheriff Gammell, Deputy Scarecrow and that mousy old secretary

Gladys are standing side by side outside the cage, surveying me, grim-lipped and arms crossed. I feel like I should offer them popcorn.

Kindly Mustache Man is in the cell with me, too. Not the real one that I rescued from the General Store restroom – it's his grinning zombie clone. And at the moment he looks happy as a clam, wiping at a stain on the concrete wall, over and over. I keep waiting for Zombie Merle to recognize me and try to pulverize me into jelly. But he doesn't. Aside from an obvious new curiosity over the contents of my pockets, Zombie Merle doesn't seem too interested in a rematch. Good thing – right now, my limbs are stiffer than that wooden chief on the General Store porch.

Then I spot the Taser on Sheriff Gammell's belt.

My face flares.

"Gammell, you *Tasered* me?!"

I'm hollering at him, but I know it's my own dang fault. I'm the one who fudged up my reflexes with that stupid coffee. I made myself weak...vulnerable.

I am *never* doing that again.

"Sheriff Gammell," I say slowly. "Look at them. They're zombies. You really think I'm one of them?"

Deputy Scarecrow and Gladys exchange a tight look. Sheriff Gammell slowly walks toward the cell, arms still crossed. He studies me thoughtfully through the bars.

"Never seen anyone pass out cold from a low Taser zap."

I shrug. "I've got low blood sugar."

"Yesterday, you dislocated your arm. And suddenly, today, you're trading punches like Sugar Ray down at the diner with Merle?"

"I'm a fast healer."

He raises an eyebrow and turns away without a word.

I grab the cell bars. "Listen to me, Gammell. Listen to my voice. I'm lucid. My *name* is Kyle. I'm human, the original Kyle."

"Alright, Miss Original Kyle." Sheriff Gammell leans back in a chair. "Tell you what. Unless someone is going to walk in that door and vouch for you... Well, I'm afraid you're just going to have to get cozy in that cell for the night."

I press my mouth shut and glare through the bars.

I could convince him.

I could tell Gammell how I know he spent Thanksgiving with Merrick's family in Idaho one year. Or that he's got a wife named Annabelle, who apparently makes fantastic cornbread. But I'm not supposed to know any of that stuff.

I let go of the bars. My eyes flicker past my zombie cellmates up to the small window vent. Of course, this time I don't have Tannon's unconscious head to use as a stepstool. And honestly, I'm *really* not looking forward to dislocating my shoulder again. But lucky for me, I don't have to. Because that's when the police station door swings open.

It's Merrick.

I watch him cross the room, pleading silently for him to recognize all the things he knew about me from a yesterday that never happened. Now he's asking the Sheriff something. They lead him over to Gladys' desk. Merrick picks up the phone and starts dialing.

Suddenly, I know what he's doing.

Plunging into my pocket, I grab out Merrick's cell and thrust it in the air like it's the victory trophy of my life. Across the room, Merrick can't help but grin. Then he hangs up the phone without bothering to dial.

This kid must really trust me.

*

Fast forward five minutes. We're all standing shoulder to shoulder with our arms crossed, this time with me on the outside, watching the two Deadheads shuffle around the cell.

Deadheads. That's what we're calling them.

They've given me a bottled spring water (Fact: Getting Tasered apparently gives you cottonmouth), and I'm nursing it like a fish. Small, steady sips with my eyes glued to that cell.

Finally Deputy Scarecrow speaks up.

"Look at 'em," he whistles in disbelief. "Land sakes, Frank! You ever seen anything like this before?"

"Yeah," Merrick snorts. "Invasion of the Body Snatchers."

"That's a movie, Merrick." Sheriff Gammell replies humorlessly. "We're talking real life here. Anyone seen this before?"

He's looking straight at me, of course. The odd duck.

Quack, quack.

Deputy Scarecrow's high-pitched voice cracks. "W-well, I reckon we're just gonna have to get rid of 'em." He clears his throat, trying to draw himself up like he just casually suggested we all go get pancakes. But his voice is still shaking. "I reckon we still got some'a that rat poison in the pantry."

"Why, yes," Gladys chimes in, pursing her lips. "I could bake it into something they'll eat. Brownies, perhaps."

"You're kidding, right?" Merrick laughs. "They're alive! Thinking, moving... I mean, they have beating hearts, for heaven's sake!"

I choke gracelessly on my water. Composing myself, I mentally establish a "no coughing" rule. Coughing is what got me into this mess in the first place.

Sheriff Gammell rubs his chin, his gravelly growl muffled through his fingers. "Merrick's got a point. They do seem to retain some memory of human function."

Deputy Scarecrow raises a finger excitedly. "When we picked up that fake Sam at the store, he was sweepin' the floor. Just sweepin' away with that broom! Just, well, doin' what he does."

"Doing what they do," Gammell echoes in a low voice. "So it's safe to assume these Deadheads got memories from their original person?"

The image of my naked doppelganger prowling around the water tower pops to mind.

"Yep," I mutter. "Safe to assume."

Then I remember something else. That tattoo, on Deadhead Kyle's chest.

"What's a golem?" I ask.

Everyone looks at me. Then we all look at Merrick.

"What, because I'm a Cohen?" He sighs. "Yeah, let's all make my grandma say I told you so. Anyway, the Golem was some Jewish legend. An anthropomorphic being – basically a husk, a misshapen hunk of clay. According to the legend, some wise-guy decided to knead it into the shape of a man and bring it to life. The copy could do pretty much anything its original counterpart could do…except talk."

"Okay," Sheriff Gammell grumbles, rubbing his eyes. "So how did they get rid of it, Merrick?"

"Um, well… According to the legend, the only thing keeping the golem alive was a word. Inscribed somewhere on its body. Erase the word, and… Adios."

I stop pacing.

Bingo.

*

Since I'm the only one with an evil clone running around, I'm unanimously voted "Brave Eraser of Magic Words on Deadheads."

I walk into the jail cell and Sheriff Gammell slides the cell door shut behind me. I hear the lock clank.

"If you feel threatened at any time–" he begins.

"I'll scream like a girl," I reply brightly, shooting him a thumbs-up. Gammell just shakes his head. He's still eyeing me like I'm a cyborg.

I choose Kindly Mustache Deadhead first. He's least likely to put up a fight, although he might try to give me a lollipop. Poor goon is still wiping that same spot on the wall. I edge closer, as though approaching a coiled rattlesnake.

"Hey there, er–" I glance back at Merrick.

"*Sam*," Merrick and my whole peanut gallery whisper in unison.

I nod. "Hey there, Sam. Remember me? Turkey jerky, cream sodas?" I stretch out my hand, testing. The Deadhead just stands there, grinning indifferently. Slowly, one by one, I peel apart the buttons of his flannel shirt, just enough to get a peek at his chest. Sam is as hairy as a Wookie, but I see it – on his chest, faint, like a faded tattoo.

GOLEM.

I gesture for a tool. Deputy Scarecrow flounders in a desk drawer, emerging with a bottle of White-Out. I grimace.

"Something a tad bigger, maybe?"

Merrick tosses a fat black marker to Sheriff Gammell, who feeds it through the bars to me. I pop off the cap. The poor zombie sap just grins as I scribble out the word on his chest. Then I spring back, waiting for the magic.

Nothing happens.

Then, under his fluffy mustache, the Deadhead's skin goes black as tar. There's a crackling sound, like leather tightening in the sun – then abruptly he explodes with a stifled pop, dumping to the floor a heap of ash.

Well, that was ridiculously easy.

We gawk in silence at the dusty mound. Deadhead Merle is next, and he also puts up no fight as I reduce him into a nice little pile on the floor. I stifle a cough. *Bleh.* I got some Merle dust in my mouth.

Sheriff Gammell grunts blearily. "We sure that's all of 'em?"

"No further calls or reports, sir."

"So there's just one more Deadhead left."

He's eyeing me again.

"Yeah," I nod, swishing my mouth with my water bottle. "Just Deadhead Me."

"Piece of cake!" Merrick hoots. "Kyle's marker is mightier than the sword!"

I laugh rowdily along with their optimism, pumping my fist in the air, hamming it up and plunging the black marker into my pocket as though sheathing a sword.

But I know better.

Somehow, I know Deadhead Kyle is not going down quite as easily as the others. This one's going to raise Cain.

But first I have to find her.

I pace the floor, slapping my palm against the flat bottom of my empty plastic bottle. Deadhead Kyle could be anywhere in Carnival Creeke. Screw it all, she doesn't make any sense.

Suddenly I stop walking and slapping.

Essentially, she's me. Out of everyone, she makes the most sense in the world. So where would *I* go if *I* wanted to hide away from the world? My room at the Red Rooster, most likely.

But I'm the only one with a key to room four.

*

Mrs. Moffatt stops me in the foyer on the way in. I lean coolly on the check-in desk, trying my gosh-darndest to look innocent and human. Merrick hangs off in the corner, gently spinning an old Victorian navigator's globe on a curio shelf.

Mrs. Moffatt gives me a dodgy, demure look. She forces a tight smile, knitting her delicate, doll-like fingers together.

"Hold on, honey." She's looking at the floor. "I am, uh...renovating the locks on all the room doors. Need to get you another key. Wait here, okay please?"

I watch her all the way until her gunmetal bob has slipped out the doorway into the parlor. Her body language is strange. She's as nervous as a long-tailed cat in a room full of rocking chairs. I wipe my palms on my shirt and suddenly it hits me.

I've been asking the wrong question.

Not "*where*" – but "*what.*"

Kindly Mustache Man tended his General Store, swept the floor. Merle served pie. And that's what their Deadheads did. Doing what they do.

*So what do **I** do?*

My goal is pretty singular. I hunt wildcards. That's all I know right now. Other than maybe finding that punk Holliday and wringing his neck, the wildcard is my only objective. And if that Deadhead out there thinks *she's* Kyle, then logically, in her brain...

I *am* the wildcard.

There's only one place she'd be going.

And that is to kill me.

On the reception desk, a piece of paper catches my eye. A note scrawled on a piece of flowered stationary. I discreetly slide it closer.

Attn: Proprietor of the Red Rooster B&B
Beware the wolf in sheep's clothing
KYLE, Room #4
If she should return to the premise, call this number
immediately:
(703) 555-1012
Note: Local authorities will not be able to contain
this person
Consider her a paramount danger to yourself
and your patrons!

My guts go cold.

Glancing at the parlor doorway, I swipe a pen from the holder. I flip the paper over and quickly write:

Beware the wolf in sheep's clothing

It's my handwriting.

I slap the pen down, snatching up the note. "Merrick," I whisper urgently. "We have to leave. Right now."

"Huh?" He looks up from the globe. "What's up? But nobody in town knows you're here, unless–" He frowns suddenly at the note in my hand. "Hey, that's my cell number!"

Yanking his cell phone from my pocket like it's on fire, I wrench off the battery flap. Sure enough – a tiny device is attached to the phone's battery, like a little alien crab. A small detonator snaked in wires.

"Is that what I *think* it is?" Merrick swallows.

"This," I state grimly. "Is you and me and probably everyone in a half-mile radius splattered all over the carpet."

I pinch the wire between my fingers then hesitate. This could be a messy mistake. But something inside me knows better. This device is simple, familiar... Somehow, I know it only will trigger when it receives an outside call.

Or maybe I'm wrong...

Ripping the detonator from his phone, I stuff it into my pocket then hand the phone back to Merrick. He gingerly accepts it like it's a dead rat.

Deadhead Kyle knew I would have that cell phone. So she knew I would be with Merrick – or, if I tried to slink off alone, like

154

I tend to do, she knew he'd insist on giving me his phone, predictable gentleman that he is. Mrs. Moffatt is probably trying to call that number right now. No way she could know it will blow us all sky-high, probably blasting the Red Rooster into a crater, thanks to the gas station next door.

But when did Deadhead Kyle do it? She never had access to Merrick's phone. Never an opportunity to attach the detonator.

Unless...

Zombie Merle!

When I woke up in the jail cell, I caught Jerko rooting through my pockets. He probably planted the detonator in the phone while I was passed out. The detonator Deadhead Kyle gave him. He was just following orders. Doing what he does.

I tell you, once I manage to fix this wildcard, I'll be hunky-dory with kissing this day goodbye.

*

Merrick pulls over into the grass and parks his Tahoe by the covered bridge, under the late-day sun. My mind is whirring.

Okay, so what do I know about myself?

I empty the contents of my cargo pockets. Aside from my "live for today" fortune, I have my usual sundry provisions from the General Store – the small utility knife, a lighter, earplugs, dental floss. Merrick picks up the floss with a grin.

"For those emergency strawberry seed situations?"

"Or tying off a severed artery."

He shivers. "Yeesh, okay, I get the picture, Sarah Connor."

I know he's just trying to lighten me up, but I wish he wouldn't. Not when my survival depends on the one thing I know nothing about: Me stinkin' I. And the longer I stare at this stupid little pile of stuff, waiting for the gears in my broken brain to magically start cranking... Frankly, it feels like squirting lemon juice into your eyeball. Painful and pointless.

I wish she hadn't stolen my jacket. I like that jacket. I mean, I know tomorrow morning it'll reappear on the dresser in my room, so no skin off my back. But that's not the point.

It was *my* jacket.

"Hey Kyle, what's this?"

I glance over. Merrick is holding my 8-ball keychain.

"Nothing," I say distractedly. "Just something I had on me at the hospital."

Merrick smiles fondly, turning the little 8-ball over in his hand. He speaks into it like a microphone, asking a question ("Did Han really shoot first?"), then he flips it over. The window remains empty.

"Huh," he says. "Interesting. It won't react to me. Here, catch." He tosses it to me. "Your turn. Go ahead, ask it a question."

"Already tried that."

"And?"

"And nothing happened, Merrick. Let's stay focused, okay?"

"Well, did you ask it out loud?"

I stare at him. I swear, sometimes I don't know what galaxy the kid is from. But now that I think about it... Back in the diner, did I speak to the 8-ball out loud? No. I just thought up some questions in my head. You know, like any sane person would do. A sane person who didn't want to seen alone in a diner booth talking to a plastic keychain.

Well, what the heck.

I frown and say, "Hey, keychain, can you actually do something helpful?"

Lo and behold, the inky window fills with tiny white words that read: "**SOURCES SAY YES.**"

There's a muffled grinding sound and the little keychain vibrates against my hand. Then the 8-ball splits into perfect halves, like a walnut, leaking inky water all over me. But something else slid out into the dark puddle in my palm.

A tiny silver key.

Merrick pounces over on hands and knees, like a kid on his birthday.

"Woo, baby! Yeah, just like I suspected – a biometric identification system!"

"Translation, professor?"

"Sorry, I mean somebody programmed this thing to open for your voice. And *only* your voice. Probably your fingerprints, too. A double security lock. See these sensor pads?"

I lean forward and look where he's pointing. Sure enough, the 8-ball is textured, covered in tiny pinholes.

I shake my head in wonder. "Merrick, you are an amazing human being."

"That's what they all say. Now I just want to see what that key opens. I mean, somebody left it for you, right?"

"Looks that way," I say.

I peer closely at my new key. It looks like the kind that opens a safety deposit box.

This day just keeps getting weirder.

*

There's only one bank in Carnival Creeke, so that narrows it down nice and simple for us.

A flamboyant fellow wearing a pink blazer and checkered hipster pants leads us to the vault. My deposit receipt says "*Thursday, Oct. 19.*" So whoever made this mysterious deposit did it yesterday. Or as I like to call it, "Gargoyle Day."

Pink Peacock escorts us down a carpeted hallway to a claustrophobic room with two walls of gleaming safety deposit drawers on either side. Using my silver key, he unlocks and pulls open my drawer, revealing an extremely unremarkable box inside. With a curt little smile, Pink Peacock struts off and Merrick and I are left alone in the room.

We stare at the box.

"You think it's a bazooka?" Merrick chimes hopefully.

My guts are in knots. I keep telling myself this shouldn't be making me so doggone nervous. But the contents of this box might as well be the whole of my existence. A puzzle piece, one that I obviously felt direly necessary to protect.

But what if it's not *my* deposit box? I didn't consider that until now.

What if Holliday...

What if it's my heart in that box? How would I explain *that* grim little surprise to Merrick?

I consider asking him to wait outside, but then I decide to quit noodling around like a coward. I wipe my palms on my pants, take a deep breath, and open the box.

Inside is a block of wood, about six inches long. Old and weathered, it looks like it fell off someone's log cabin.

The whole of my existence...*is some old block of wood?*

I pick it up gently, like it's a baby bird. It appears to be made of several segments, like puzzle pieces, interlocked tightly together. There's a small button on the underside. I rub my thumb over it. Feels familiar...

I press the button. The wooden device springs open like a mousetrap, almost eagerly, unfolding and reassembling like a Transformer right there in my hand. Merrick hollers and jumps back. My face breaks into a slow grin when I realize what I'm now holding.

"It's a shotgun," Merrick remarks.

I raise my eyebrows. "A Mare's Leg Winchester Model 1892, to be exact."

Someone has removed the stock and hacked off the barrel, shaving the weapon down to a mere nine inches and making it light enough to wield with just one hand. Under the vault's fluorescent lights, I can see that this puppy has obviously seen a few rodeos. It's covered with nicks and scuffs, and the walnut forestock is peppered with deep grooves. Every scuff is etched with a story, I'm sure of it. I think it might be the most gorgeous thing I've seen in my three-day life.

Affixed to the top of the shotgun's barrel is a small, bronze, fan-shaped display screen, a steampunk-Metropolis bit of flair that automatically popped open like an umbrella when I pressed the button and the weapon assembled itself. Two gray dots appear on the screen, motionless. With mystified admiration, I realize what I'm looking at. This screen is a wildcard detector. And those two gray dots must be Deadhead Sam and Deadhead Merle. No longer active.

But another dot just entered the screen. A red dot. And it's moving steadily toward the center of the display...

Toward *us*.

Merrick shifts uneasily. "Uh, what's the red dot, Kyle?"

I'm about to answer, but I just noticed the security monitor in the corner of the ceiling. On it, a grainy gray image shows an overhead view of the bank lobby. There's a stir among the crowd, then all the people turn in unison to look at something.

It's too late.

She's here.

NIGHT OF THE LIVING DEADHEAD

In the grainy image on the screen, the people in the bank lobby part like the Red Sea. Not that anyone could have stopped her. She walks just like me when I've got a purpose.

But what's that in her hands? The light catches it, and it glints. Something large and metal... All at once I remember something that I saw in the window of the Antique Weapon Replicas shop, and suddenly the four-foot steel-reinforced concrete walls don't seem like enough protection between us.

I slam the drawer shut.

"Merrick, listen to me, I want you to *run* out of here now. But don't go through the main lobby, take a left at the desk – remember the restrooms we passed? You should see the fire exit. Go."

He's frozen. "Kyle, what's going on?"

"Just do it, okay?"

I quickly run my finger along the cocking lever of the shotgun, feeling for the trigger.

There is no trigger.

A ripple of panic runs through me.

No trigger. How am I supposed to use this?

161

Flipping the weapon, I scour it for some to clue how to activate it, while still keeping one eye on the grainy surveillance monitor. I can't see Deadhead Kyle on the screen anymore. Of course not, because she's passed through the lobby. The red dot on the shotgun's screen continues to move toward us. She's approaching the entrance to the vault hallway, and if I correctly estimate the number of steps, that would put her about thirty seconds from us...

"Kyle, please just tell me why–"

"*'Cause I'm about to kill you with a battle axe, that's why!*"

Merrick cocks his head with strange admiration. "That was really specific," he remarks.

Not the reaction I wanted.

"JUST *RUN!!*"

I shove him hard on his chest and he stumbles out into the hallway. Clutching the useless mystery weapon against my ribs, I slide my little utility knife from my boot then edge out into the hallway after him.

No sign of Merrick. Man, I hope that boy listened and ran.

I know I waited too long to tell him to run, so really, I may have just sent him straight into the lion's mouth. Did I actually believe he would miraculously dodge her and escape? Or was I just sending him out like a rabbit, a distraction, to buy *myself* time? That notion makes me a little sick. I can't shut out the image of what that axe could do to him. She'll hack him into red ribbons, if it means getting to me...

Would I really do that to Merrick? Am I capable of...?

Pausing at the vault entrance, I glance at the shotgun's screen. The red dot is right in the center of the screen. It's not moving.

I peer around the corner, my back pressed against the wall.

It's nighttime. The bank lobby is empty and dark, dimly illuminated by the sparse glow of after-hour green desk lamps at the teller stations. A car passes outside, its headlights momentarily cut through the glass doors opposite the lobby and gleam like a flash down the marble floor, then everything is dark again.

It's too quiet.

I dash quickly around the lip of the vault and immediately slam smack into Deadhead Kyle. I ram my elbow across her neck, and she does the same to me; my small knife and triggerless gun feel like plastic toys in my hands compared to the majestic, razor-sharp, double-bladed axe in hers.

In the Jell-O-green lamp light, motionless, we survey each other for the first time.

Sweet mother of grace, it's *me*.

She's wearing my jacket, over a tan mechanic's jumpsuit with the name "Hank" sewn into the pocket. I wonder what grisly fate beheld the poor guy. She has my face – except she looks stripped and hollow, sick-looking under that curtain of damp hair. But it's the grin that chills me.

Me, grinning back at myself.

Lord, I've seen some weirdy weirdness here in Carnival Creeke, but this takes the cake.

We press each other's throats, refusing to budge. With panicked curiosity, I jerk my head to one side. She mirrors me, the grin never leaving her face. I rear back for a skull-blow and feel her do the same. Abruptly we both abort the attack and shove away from each other, both staggering backwards. She bounces off a Plexiglas partition and I hit a desk, knocking over a mug of ballpoint pens. Hitting my knees in a somersault, I feel her heavy axe slice through the air above me, just missing my forehead. The quick sting tells me that I got nicked, but my head is still attached.

Diving on my belly underneath the desk, I'm momentarily hidden in shadows. She's looking for me; I see her pass by the desk I'm under, her bare feet smacking on the floor.

I ready my little knife and draw a deep breath.

Rolling over, I stab my knife in the direction of her feet, the little blade sinking solidly into its target. She jerks away and my knife goes with her, yanking out of my hand. Scrambling out from the other side of the desk, I sprint all the way back toward the vault, throwing myself between two teller stations. I crouch there, holding my breath until it hurts.

How the heck did she find me, anyway?

The 8-ball. Of course. She knew that key would eventually lead me to this bank.

So did *she* come here looking for the shotgun, too?

"SWEET MOTHER OF GRACE...IT'S ME."

I look down at the strange weapon in my hands. If she wants this thing so badly, I'm definitely clinging to it like white on rice. She'll have to pry it off my corpse.

Which may happen sooner rather than later.

A movement startles me. I twist my head and look. A person is crouching across the aisle, making wild gestures at me.

Merrick! All his insides still inside, thankfully.

I utter a silent exhale of relief and clunk my head back against the wood panel. From somewhere outside the bank, a distant rhythm floats to my ears; a popping crack of snare drums and grunting tubas. *Six o'clock.* The homecoming parade must be starting. The windows near us are reflecting a red and blue flash. Sheriff Gammell and his crew have this bank surrounded. But he hasn't made a move yet – meaning that he's giving me a chance to handle this before things get really messy. This realization fuels me with an odd surge.

I won't fail him.

Holding my breath, I dare a peek around the corner.

I can see her. The thing that looks like me is stalking around the perimeter of the lobby, the battle axe in one hand. She's not even bothering to guard herself. She's *that* sure. Intentionally avoiding the windows and glass doors, so Gammell won't ever get a clean shot at her.

I need a distraction. There's a Halloween dish of candy corn on the desk above me. Scooping a handful, I hurl it at the wall behind Deadhead Kyle. Her head jerks momentarily toward the clattering sound. Then she turns straight in my direction, looking for the source of the flung candy.

Yeah...that wouldn't have fooled me, either.

Rolling over, I mouth to Merrick, *Give me your phone.* Reaching into his pocket, he slides his cell phone across the slick marble floor to me. With mostly steady hands, I re-attach the alien crab device into the phone's battery.

Time to up the stakes.

Looking straight at Merrick, I jerk my head up at the office phone on the desk by him. Then I put my pinky to my lips and my thumb to my ear, mimicking a phone call. He looks pretty freaked out, but I make sure that I see him nod before I run off.

Hunkered down, I slink along the row of teller stations, crouching directly behind the frontmost desk, and hoping against all hope that Deadhead Kyle keeps heading down her current trajectory. Quickly, I reach up and lay Merrick's cell phone on the desk.

Please call now, Merrick.

Then I jet the heck out of there.

Behind me, I hear about two seconds of the Spider-Man theme song before the bank lobby is blown to smithereens.

I don't wait. Leaping through a snow of deposit slips and a mouthful of dust, I burst through the debris into the night air, squinting against the assaulting flashes of blue and red lights. The entire Carnival Creeke police department has us barricaded in a semi-circle, laying across their car hoods with guns trained on me from every direction.

Even though every fiber of my being is telling me to run after my doppelganger, I thrust my hands in the air, making sure the shotgun is fully visible in my fist.

"Gammell, give me more time!" I bellow, pleading. "She's still out here!"

The homecoming parade is rolling full blast through the street now, and the sidewalks are milling with people. Many have donned Halloween costumes. Clowns, a tinfoil astronaut, a scarecrow holding hands with a pigtailed Dorothy in a blue gingham jumper, their three kids dressed up like winged monkeys. A cluster of zombie football players wearing blood-splattered shoulder pads bustles past, laughing loudly. The marching band thumps and blares.

Too much commotion. Between the festivities and my dazzling explosion, of course nobody would see one Deadhead slip out into the night.

A snatch of movement catches my eye. Tilting my head up, I see the red dot moving across my weapon's screen. I scan beyond the crowds. Through a cluster of maroon and orange balloons, I spot her. Under the glow of the clock tower, she disappears into the library.

I can't wait for the O.K. from Gammell.

I plunge off the bank's front steps and bolt across the library's lawn and through the heavy double doors.

All the lights are shut off. In the dark, the library seems more cavernous than I remember. Dwarfed by the pillars of the long, shadowy aisles, I feel like I've stepped into ancient catacombs. Every corner is blind, every obscured shelf a tomb reserved for Cl. Kyle. I just wonder which one.

Something wet rolls down my nose. I slap at it, and when I pull my hand away, it's smeared with bright red.

Oh no.

Quickly I scramble over to the nearest computer station and assess my reflection in a computer's dark screen. My fear is confirmed. That sting on my forehead was more than a scratch. Anywhere else on my body, I could probably deal – but the human skull, with its rich surrounding network of blood vessels, will always bleed like the dickens, even if the cut isn't all that deep. And I'm a waterfall. Dripping all over the computer keyboard. Under normal circumstances, this might be small potatoes for me. But now, at this moment, Holliday's words are pounding me with icy caveat: *"Ye only got six liters of juice in yer veins. An' it's doin' a fine job bein' recycled. But don't push it too far..."*

I vault over the computer and sprint across the library. There's a nurse's station, but the room is dark, the door locked. Along the wall is a cubby cabinet with a clear plastic tub of paper mâché supplies; I rummage feverishly through the dark contents, snatching a roll of cheesecloth and darting back behind the computer stations. Holding the shotgun awkwardly between my knees, I rip off a length of cheesecloth with my teeth and wrap it tightly round my head, securing it with a hasty field knot. I press hard against my head, trying to will my blood to clot. I conjure the image of corking a bottle of wine.

And it *looks* like wine. Thick, deep red, the precious liquid seeps through the cheesecloth, drooling persistently down my face.

The red dot hangs a sharp left, making a beeline for the center of the screen. Straight toward me. I throw a quick glance back over the computer desk, because I know she'll be there.

And she is – emerging from a dinosaur display shelf.

She won't stop. She just keeps tromping after me like a demon butcher from the farthest reaches of Hades.

And it's in that moment I realize I am afraid.

The truth is, I've been rattled ever since the water treatment plant this afternoon. I didn't want to see *it*. And now she's right over there, and she's terrifying...but not because she looks like a monster. Because she looks like me.

My breath comes quicker, then slows.

Maybe I'm fighting a losing battle. She has a heart. In a sense, this Deadhead is more complete than me. Perhaps more human.

Then a memory hits me unexpectedly, from nowhere. Just a seemingly random fragment, like a firefly that I wasn't even trying to catch, landing in my hand on its own accord. One time, when I was a kid, I found two toys in the bottom of a Crackerjack box. A random bonus. Not quite extraordinary... But it was *me*.

"*Crackerjack*," I repeat, as if suddenly this validates me. "Two toys... Crackerjack."

I have a right to keep breathing.

And I have an idea.

If I could somehow lure her up into the bell tower, I might be able to trigger the bell as she arrives. It's loud. *Really* loud. I remember the earth-shaking ruckus that day with the gargoyle, loud even when Merrick and I were on the bottom floor of this library. But if you were actually *inside* the tower, right *next* to that bell when it rang... At that proximity, the decibels would rip the legs off a grasshopper. And then, with my Deadhead temporarily incapacitated – just maybe – I might still have a fighting chance against her.

That is, if I can make it up these stairs. I'm dragging myself up the narrow wooden staircase leading up to the bell tower and it's getting hard to breathe. I'm doing my best to press on, but my laundry list of ailments has gotten mortally long. My limited supply of blood, which is rapidly pouring from my head. I'm freezing without my jacket. And now that I'm likely a few cups low on blood, nothing is going to keep me warm.

This fricking shotgun feels heavier with each step. I consider just ditching it, saving what shred of strength I have left, but instead I clutch the thing tighter against my ribs. Gripping the banister, I heave myself up one step at a time. I can see the dark bloody smears that I'm painting on the wood. Ordinarily I would try to prevent leaving a blood trail, but not now. I *want* her to follow me.

I'm *counting* on it.

Hope I can figure out how to ring the bell. Many of these renovated clock towers rely on programmable computers, rather than a simple Quasimodo pulling a rope.

Almost to the top of the stairs. Better get my earplugs in now...

Hoisting the shotgun up to the final stair, legs burning, I use my free hand to dig the packet of earplugs from my pocket, stuffing the little marshmallowy buds into both ears as I use the banister to pull myself upright. The sight of the dark bell chamber renews me with a momentary burst of hope. There's no switchboard, just an old-fashioned rope and pulley system set on a massive network of gears, suspended over a bottomless pit. A mug of cold coffee sits forgotten on the wooden railing, likely from whoever last helmed the ringer. The enormous bell is housed up in the tower's spire, almost completely recessed in shadow. But I know it's there. I can see the rope dangling down, just over the railing.

I start limping toward it.

BONG.

The bell rings.

My head explodes.

No... I'm grabbing my head all over and my brains are definitely still intact. But it might as well have exploded. Even with the earplugs, I was unprepared and the reverberation of the huge bell screams into a thousand places in my skull.

She had the same idea.

Of course, Deadhead Kyle had the *exact flippin' idea.* I should have known.

And now it's *me* crumpled helplessly on the floorboards.

She strides over to me and lifts the battle axe. With nothing left, I raise the shotgun and point it at her, as though I actually intend to shoot it.

Then it fires.

It doesn't hit her, and it's not a bullet. A pulse of blue explodes from the shotgun's barrel and zips across the small chamber, colliding with the coffee mug sitting on the rail.

We both jump back, shocked out of our wits. The mug rolls off the railing and shatters on the floor, sizzling, its contents rolling out – no longer coffee, but one solid brown concealed chunk of jelly. We jerk our heads back toward each other's throats. She's not grinning anymore. But maybe that's because of the shotgun barrel I've got pointed between her eyes.

Now it's my turn to grin.

"Ah, this weapon is what you've been looking for, isn't it?"

Deadhead Kyle's eye twitches in response.

Thanks, I note, with smug triumph. *For just confirming it's worth all the trouble.*

Of course, what I'm not saying – and what has my brain spinning frantically – is this: I have no earthly clue how I just fired the gun. This leaves me with only one option.

"Catch."

I drop the shotgun straight onto my boot, kicking it as hard as I can at her. Even with the gun twirling toward her head she doesn't drop the battle axe, but rather stretches it up like an umbrella, welcoming the precious weapon into her arms.

That's when I slam into her belly like a battering ram. There are no glass panes on the bell chamber's side windows, so nothing stops us from tumbling out. The cold night air hits us a second before the roof does, but the roof hurts a whole lot more. The weatherproofing sands the skin off my elbows as we roll in an unstoppable tangle off the edge of the gutter, splintering through what I can only guess was the scaffolding left by the workers cleaning up the gargoyle's mess. Then there is nothing but dark, whistling air as we fall.

The ground comes hard. I roll over and stagger to my feet.

We're in the cemetery. Under the thick tangled tree cover, the night is pierced by the bright duo of the moon and the artificial glow spilling off the library's clock above our heads. I should feel busted, or at least cold. But all I feel is venom. Pain is absent, temporarily replaced by adrenaline.

Without warning I'm jerked to my feet, jostled roughly by my shirt collar. A nightmare version of myself is dragging me through the gravestones, out the wrought-iron gate and into the street. There's nothing in her hands – nothing but me. She must have lost both the axe and the shotgun when we fell. I can't see either weapon anywhere on the ground nearby; heaven only knows where they landed.

Alright. Guess we're going to do this the old-fashioned way.

Still being dragged across the ground, I throw my arms up backward and catch the Deadhead around the throat, yanking her down on top of me and clamping every limb I have around her in a chokehold. Unfortunately, I'm weak – all my strength bled out, smeared up those clock tower steps. I can't hold her for long. Like synchronized swimmers, we roll apart and leap to our feet, facing each other in the ghostly glow of the streetlight. Puffy and bloodied, she grins at me through a beaded curtain of red. I bet I look just like her right now.

Enough hokey pokey. Only one Kyle will survive tonight, and I think we both know good and well that we're about to find out which one.

Then, out of the blue, I remember something. I glance up at the library clock. Last night, when I was walking back to the bed-and-breakfast...yes, I was crossing this same section of the street, right about this time of night...

I lean over and prop my hands on my knees, signaling defeat.

"You're a piece of work," I blurt hoarsely. "Yeah, I admit, you kicked my tail pretty good."

I need her to move backward.

Grinding upright, I take a labored step toward her. As if I could even squash a bug right now. But I know myself, so I drag my feet across the asphalt and take another step forward. It unsettles her. She's questioning my confidence. Questioning her safety.

My grinning Deadhead takes a wary step backward.

"You've still got your heart, don't you?" I press on. "Hey, bonus points for you. You can probably remember our first name...and our parents' names...and our favorite food. And it's a stinking shame because you probably won't tell me, ever."

Now the adrenaline is really flowing. I'm lit up like a firecracker.

"But here's something you *don't* know." I glance at the clock again, then look her straight in the eye. "Merrick isn't the only one who takes this street corner too fast."

The headlights veer into view half a second before a shiny black Hummer SUV smacks Deadhead Kyle out from under my nose. She rolls up the hood, busting the windshield and sailing airborne over the moving car before landing in a tangled, dirty tumble in the street, facedown and unmoving. The Hummer screeches to a halt, the bright moonlight illuminating the massive SUV's rear license plate. 'LUV-MNY,' the license plate reads.

Geez, what a chump.

Pulling the black marker from my pocket, I start plodding limply toward the Deadhead's inert form. A young yuppie with a prematurely receding hairline and a sports jacket has jumped out of the rumbling Hummer. He's jabbering some kind of panicked claptrap, but I'm not really in an explaining sort of mood. My focus is like a tunnel, solely on that facedown body in the street. The one that looks like me.

The one that just twitched under the eerie light.

I freeze on my clay feet. I can do nothing but watch as she crawls to hands and knees, then inelegantly drags herself to her feet. My mouth and my stomach drop. The marker in my hand seems suddenly such a mockingly flimsy weapon.

She's a mess. Her jumpsuit is filthy, hanging off her body in shredded tan ribbons. She turns her wet red head and grins, white teeth shining in hamburger meat. Then she starts to amble toward me.

"*Hey, Kyle!*"

We both jerk our heads toward the voice.

It's Merrick. Standing on the sidewalk across the street, the mystery shotgun in his hand.

"Smile for my boomstick."

Then he fires it.

The blue pulse momentarily lights up the whole street, hitting the Deadhead square-on and slamming her back against a blue postal mailbox. She pitches violently and flops, like a seizure on a merry-go-round, hurling herself sideways and flailing around before going completely rigid in a sitting position, her back slumped against the mailbox. I remember the congealed coffee up in the bell tower, and my mind fills with images of what her insides must look like.

Merrick gasps out a laugh, almost apologizing. "Wow, I can't believe I just said that out loud."

He hands the shotgun to me. And he actually looks none too sorry to pass off that hot potato, all traces of boomstick-weilding bad-Ashery gone, plain sweet Merrick returned again.

I gawk at the weapon then look at him.

"How did you shoot it?"

He shrugs sheepishly. "Oh, this lever here." He taps the cocking lever. "Works like a gear throttle. You squeeze it first, aim, then let go and – bwah! It fires. Pretty sweet, huh?" Merrick clears his throat. "But, uh, how about I leave all the shooting stuff to you, if that's cool."

I smile admiringly at him and say nothing.

"Will someone *please* tell me *what the heck just happened?!*"

Merrick and I turn. It's the guy from the Hummer. Oops. I forgot about him. Mr. Luv-Money is trying to restart his SUV, but it seems it ran out of gas. He groans, then he faints in the driver's seat. He faints. Seriously.

I'll happily let Merrick tend to that knucklehead. I've got bigger fish to fry.

Because the dot on my shotgun's screen is still bright red.

It's a little shocking to see Deadhead Kyle's eyes still rolling around, watching me approach. She's practically ground beef by now – and she appears to be paralyzed. The skin on her face and neck is laced with a lattice of bluish veins.

I squat down beside her, gently touching my finger to a trickle of blood on her chin. It's rock-hard. Just like the coffee. How is she still alive? That word on her chest must be the only thing keeping her ticking. Blood all gummed up like that, stiff as ice… She probably doesn't even have a heartbeat anymore.

Guess we have that in common now.

I pop off the marker's cap with my teeth and let it fall in the street behind me. "Sorry kiddo," I mutter, unzipping her jumpsuit. "Really… I am."

I don't look at her as I scribble out the word over her heart. I guess you could say it feels like a waste, watching all my memories, my name, my stupidity and my brilliance, all disintegrate into a pile of ash on the pavement. A lifetime's worth of files, irreparably recorded in a language that can never be spoken, a seal that could never be broken. Guess this is what it feels like watching your house burn down.

I consult my screen. Gray dot.

Scooping up my red leather jacket off the pavement, I dust it off and slip it on. My head just started bleeding again. But the adrenaline has all drained away, and now I feel it. The crushing exhaustion. Just like gargoyle night; ants crawling under my skin, a slow creeping numbness, my burning limbs turning to glass. I know this sensation. I know I pushed myself past my limit again tonight.

Merrick reaches to help me into his Tahoe.

"I can do it," I croak belligerently.

Merrick puts up both hands in resignation. He waits patiently until I've crawled in and dragged all my numb limbs behind me before closing the door, then he hops into the driver's side. Starting the ignition, he cranks the heat and hits the seat warmers. It actually feels really good. Like hot chocolate on my tush.

He's staring at me.

"Um, you should probably go to the hospital. But I'm guessing you probably won't go. Right?"

I swallow. "Tell him what he's won, Bob."

Merrick grins, flashing those impossible dimples.

"Okay, tell you what. There's a twenty-four-hour taco place just around the corner there." He points out the window and I pretend I see what he's pointing at.

He nods at me. "I'm going to run over there and get us some tacos, okay? Stay right here for me...okay?"

"Okay." I smile softly. "Go get us some tacos."

He pushes his glasses up and lingers in the window before throwing up his hood and jogging across the street. I wait until he's out of sight before I open the door and pour myself out onto the grass.

"Sorry, Merrick." I whisper.

I don't know why. Don't know what my problem is. Maybe I'm like those cats, the ones that go off alone to die. Is that what I'm doing?

After everything, I go and get myself bled to death from some little nick on the forehead. Super annoying.

Dragging myself across the cold library lawn, I curl up behind a stone memorial commemorating the library's grand opening in 1869. I can see the dark shape of the gargoyle, the one that didn't come alive and try to eat me, hunkered on the roof in the moonlight.

Drawing my knees to my chest, I think of my warm bed at the Red Rooster. I should write down all of today's adventures, but I don't have my pink kitten notebook. And anyway, I don't have a pen.

The ornate clock's face glows brightly above me. Two seconds to midnight.

Closing my eyes, I brace myself for the day to reset.

But it doesn't.

I frown. I know I've iced the wildcards. The three gray dots on the weapon's screen in my lap confirm that much. Okay, so maybe the day doesn't reset at midnight? Guess I just assumed. You know, Cinderella, and all that...

My toes are so cold without my glass slippers.

Hugging the futuristic shotgun to my empty chest, an hour goes by, and I know I'm going to make it. It will be better tomorrow. Because I *get* a tomorrow. Because I'll *make it* better.

Two seconds to one o'clock...

I smile.

Crackerjack.

DAY 3: ICED

I'm awake, but only because I accidentally just slapped myself in the face with my limp arm. I was sleeping hard. Really rock-hard.

Too hard.

My eyes snap open. The clock on the bedside table says... Hold on... The numbers somersault and float around, arranging themselves into a shape that my sleep-hazed brain can compute.

9:27.

I jerk upright, knocking my frilly pillow off the bed. How the heck could it be 9:27? That car alarm must not have gone off at six-too-early o'clock. I don't care *how* tuckered I was, the notion that I snoozed my way through that blasted honking outside my window is impossible. The car alarm didn't go off. It's the only possible explanation. But that means...

A tingle runs up my spine.

...Did I do it?

Did I somehow fix time? Inadvertently stopped Carnival Creeke's twisted record from skipping?

Game over, I win?

A surge of hope tumbles me out of bed, the coolness of the hardwood floor on my feet gloriously affirming that I'm not dreaming. But then I feel it.

A draft.

A chill, abnormally cold, coming from the window...

I edge slowly across the room toward the glowing yellow window box, and tentatively peel back the gingham curtain.

The world is covered in ice.

Below my window, the sweet little tea garden looks like someone took a blowtorch to it – only instead of flame, it's been blasted with ice. Gleaming winter shapes indicate where the wrought iron table and lattice-work chairs stand, the Japanese maples surrounding them in a glistening wall of diamond. The Quik-Pump gas station that my window overlooks is completely buried. Even the underside of the rusted tin overhang is coated with ice, its two self-serve gas pumps wrapped in white. Beyond is a frozen tundra, stretching as far as the eye can see in every direction.

Behind the gas station, tucked in the garage, I can make out a car-shaped lump. Most likely the culprit of that stupid alarm that honks me awake every morning. But not today. Under that block of ice, the car still sleeps, undisturbed.

Standing there at the window in my undies, two things are abundantly clear. One: The car alarm definitely never went off. And two: I didn't fix a dang thing. Time is still skipping.

Today's wildcard has come right up to my window to say hello.

8-ball keychain dangling from my teeth, I pull on my pants and jacket just as I'm cracking open my room door. A blast of cold prickles the skin on my face. The entire upstairs hallway is a tunnel of ice.

I back into my room and gently pull the door shut again.

No, it's not just my imagination. It's warmer in my room. A good thirty degrees warmer. Like the eye of a hurricane, my room appears to be – so far – the only thing *not* covered in ice. A veritable pocket of toasty normal.

I ease back out into the hallway, careful to lock the door behind me. Something tells me letting the townsfolk catch wind of my mysteriously cozy room would only result in a barrage of unpleasant questions, most likely ending with me in Gammell's handcuffs. And probably a set of handcuffs that I won't be able to ninja my way out of this time.

Getting down the slick staircase is interesting. I can't really grip the banister because it's coated in a tube of ice. So I just resort to sliding down the steps on my butt, sprawling like a cat into the dining parlor below.

I feel like Dorothy stepping into the Oz ornament room. Only here, everything is silvery-white glass. The fat waffles, the fruit, the beautiful coils of breakfast sausage – it all looks like some skillfully-carved ice sculpture arranged atop frosted Chantilly lace, frozen in its drape.

There's Mrs. Moffatt. She's frozen solid in place. A delicate ice sculpture, her slight Filipino stature bent motionless over the buffet table, still in the process of clearing away breakfast.

"Mrs. Moffatt?" My husky voice breaks the silence.

No answer. Not that I was expecting one.

Crouching over, I venture a peek at the tiny woman's face. This poor woman isn't *made* of ice – she's actually *encased* in ice. A gray-bobbed pixie, preserved in a gleaming shell.

"Can you hear me in there?" I ask.

I have no idea how she's breathing. Or if she is at all. I make my way into the kitchen. The faucet and its knobs are all frozen solid. I suavely pull the cupboard door off its frozen hinges. There's a box of matches under the stove, but it's a solid block of ice that shatters in my hand when I smack it against the counter. Okay, so much for matches.

The ice-coated rooster clock above the microwave seems to have stopped at 9:27. The exact same time that I woke up.

Interesting.

Examining all of the other clocks – the parlor, the mantle, even the grandfather clock in the foyer by the check-in desk – they all tell me the same story. 9:27.

My stomach growls. I allow my gaze to linger longingly on the stack of ice-encased waffles on the breakfast table. I attempt a little nibble on a shard of "bacon," but it's like chewing on cubic zirconium jerky. Water bottles sit on the table, set up in a neat triangle, like bowling pins. I snap one off of the frozen tray and hold it up to the light, examining it. I give it a shake. No sloshing inside. Frozen solid. That means gasoline, lighter fluid, cream soda – all those things are officially scratched off my list of resources. If I want anything *not* frozen, it's going to have to come from my room. Besides, something tells me that once I make that long trek into town, I probably won't be coming back here again. Better play it safe.

Let's loot my room.

From the closet I grab two wire coat hangers, then rip out a few sheets from my pink kitten notebook and a pen from my bedside table, pocketing them with my über-important 8-ball keychain. Rummaging through the tiny bathroom, I find a little plastic cup stuffed with cotton swabs. There are no scissors or razors anywhere, nothing I might use as a blade. The decorative porcelain rooster from the dresser echoes dully as I smash it on the floor. No blade? No problem. This jagged rooster shard will work in a pinch.

Glancing at the frozen hot water faucet, a creepy thought occurs to me. My heart is gone. Nothing pumping my blood around in my pipes... Nothing to circulate warmth. People with poor circulation and narrowed arteries are more susceptible to hypothermia. I'm a stagnant tank. What would otherwise be a nice brisk winter day to the average Joe is going to affect me and my no-pulse zombie body much worse.

How much worse...

Well, I reckon I'll find out soon.

I pull off my boots, grabbing some rooster washcloths and plopping down on the rim of the claw-foot bathtub. Carefully, I wrap my socked feet with the downy washcloths (good and tight, the way ballerinas bind their tootsies), then I cram my fluffy wrapped feet back into my boots. Using a towel, I wrap my chest and torso, squeezing back into my jacket and zipping it up tight. Sure, I look silly, like an overstuffed marshmallow dressed for a spacewalk – but all this extra padding should provide adequate warmth. Now I'm a little better prepped for whatever awaits me outside that front door.

Drawing a deep breath, I give my hands a brisk shake and rock my head from side to side.

My arms move. My legs move.

The wildcard is just the kind of challenge I like.

Bring it on, baby.

I step outside.

*

My walk into town takes a bit longer than usual. And by "a bit," I mean three hours. I have to concentrate on each step that I take, carefully walking like a flat-footed penguin to avoid slipping on the slick frozen tundra that once was the road. It's a slow trek. And I look a little ridiculous. I seriously should have a narrator.

Or maybe Holliday *is* narrating...?

I picture him watching me, somewhere out there, warm and smug, having a chuckle at my expense. Scowling as I plod, I wrap my arms across my towel-padded chest and gather every shred of my dignity into a mental reminder to kill him a whole lot. In the meantime, I use my long walk to prepare my game plan.

Establish my priorities.

Priority one: Food and water. From where? No clue. But keeping hydrated and nourished is vital. I don't want to pass out from exhaustion like a goober.

Priority two: The weird shotgun.

I definitely need to get it from the bank vault. Just one day with that cunning little weapon in my hand, and already I feel blind and naked without it. The wildcard detector screen was worth its weight in gold. I need to know what's waiting for me in the trenches out there. No more searching, I can run straight to the wildcard and knock it out – boom. But the shotgun is in a safety deposit box. In the bank vault. Likely under a wall of ice.

Well, I'll think up some way to get it.

My stomach rumbles, reminding me that I missed the most important meal of the day. As if I could forget. But I can hang. What I *really* need to find is some water.

Tilting my head to one side, I squint up at the bright sky. Something tells me even a steady noon sun won't be melting a speck of *this* ice anytime soon.

Because I know this isn't your typical cold snap.

This is a wildcard. An enchanted enigma, a logic-defying puzzle. And all my potential tools are buried under ice. Not entirely fair.

I really need to quit using that phrase.

*

The town is an iced wonderland. Cocooned cars sit motionless in the street. The Carnival Creeke homecoming banner is still stretched across the street, sagging slightly under its new weight and forming a wintry archway between two frosty lamp posts. Blocky white shapes of benches and mailboxes sit slouched outside the post office. A dog is frozen with his leg still lifted. Along the historic district row, every Redbud tree glitters, their silvery branches coated from trunk to tip.

And everywhere you look – everywhere – are people.

Pushing strollers, buttoning jackets, reaching for their car doors – all frozen *in situ*. Unmoving quartzite statues, just like Mrs. Moffatt. They don't look too concerned. Heck, some are even still smiling. All clues that indicate they didn't see it coming. This monster flash-freeze hit them *hard* and *fast*. And probably at 9:27. The instant I woke up.

Yes, I owe everyone an apology. But just consider me saving this whole town over and over, and we'll call it even.

My ears keep straining for noise, but there is none. I mean nada. Zippo.

Resounding, echoing silence.

It's all a bit post-apocalyptic, but not in a grim, terrifying, "oh-no" kind of way. More like the stillness following the mother of all snowstorms; like someone calmly hit the pause button. Mid-step, mid-bite, mid-breath. An entire town preserved like glass. Eerily beautiful.

"AN ICED WONDERLAND"

Plus, there's an added bonus to this frosty pause button: Breathing room. No cars, no milling crowds with faces to process, no peripheral chatter stealing my subconscious attention. Nothing but silence. Lots of it. It's kind of peaceful.

I trudge past various scenes of paused life. Morning coffee sippers, fused in mid-sip to their ice-coated iron patio chairs outside the café. Along the curb, the Carnival Creeke High School cheerleading squad has frozen jogging in a single-file line, their swaying ponytails solidified into gravity-defying, freeze-framed peacock plumes. I wonder how conscious they are. Maybe they're all in some sort of suspended cryogenic sleep. Or maybe they're awake, fully aware that they're garden statues, but unable to do a doggone thing about it.

Can they see me? Are they watching me right now, wondering why the heck this strange chick is strolling freely around their town all the while they're stuck in giant cocktail cubes? What would Sheriff Gammell do? Probably try and burn me at stake as a witch.

Let them try, I chuckle wryly. *That fire would feel pretty good right now.*

I pull my chilly hands out of my pockets, examining them. My already-pale skin is chalky white, mottled with blotchy patches of red and yellow. Sort of itches. Just the early stages of frostnip. No need to panic yet, but...

I frown at my hands. It's not like I'm tromping around in sub-zero temps here. These symptoms should take days to show up, not hours. This cold is kicking my butt faster than I'd expected.

There are documented cases of elderly folk, sitting in their own homes, developing hypothermia when the temperature dipped below sixty degrees. Poor souls didn't even realize it. Their bodies just lose heat. I may not be elderly, but at least they've got a pulse. I'm in permanent cardiac arrest.

Delicate, fragile... Like it or not, that's my category now. And yet, take a crowbar and bash me in the kneecap, give me an hour, and I'll be good as new. I admit, I'm still baffled by it. This weird balance of frailty and super-girl regeneration. Maybe I respect it a little. But it doesn't mean I like it. And I would spit poison drywall nails before I'd give Holliday a nod of regard.

Rascal Holliday, my author.

Holliday...

You've made me so much more than I ever could have been. Someday, I'll be dang sure to "thank" you for it.

*

I trudge on through town. I could really use a pair of gloves. But since no gloves come falling from the sky, I improvise by peeling off my socks and pulling them over my blotchy hands like mittens. The rooster washcloths should be enough to protect my feet. Push comes to shove, I'd rather lose a few piggies and *keep* my fingers. I need fingers.

193

But if I don't find some water soon (the non-frozen drinkable kind), this cold is going to dry up my bones like salt on a slug.

The pumpkins lining the General Store's slick wooden porch gleam in the early afternoon sun. The door is frozen shut. It won't budge, fused clean to the doorframe. I make use of a heavy frozen pumpkin to bust out the glass, then leisurely cat-burgle my way in.

The lady with the wiener dog in the ghost costume stands at the cashier counter. Kindly Mustache Man (I mean *Sam*) is behind the register, frozen handing her a lotto ticket and a pack of gum. It's a bit Twilight Zone-y. I remember this scene. I rang up Wiener Dog Lady yesterday, while Kindly Mustache Sam was busy in the restroom coughing up his grinning doppelganger.

Poor guy. This is the second day in a row that he's ended up with a grin frozen on his face. Only this time, it's literally frosted to his thick mustache.

I mosey up to the counter beside Weiner Dog Lady. Leaning in closer, I peek at her gum flavor. Wintergreen. Mmm, minty fresh...and ironic.

Winter? Suddenly, a big "what if" pops into my head.

The wildcard could be *anything*...right?

I pull the sock off my hand. Buzzing with curiosity, I wrap my fingers around the frozen pack of gum and give it a little tug. It doesn't budge. It's fused to Sam's long fingers.

Determined, I peel off my other sock-mitten. Using both hands, I give the gum another good yank – only this time my grip slips off, causing my elbow to bump squarely into Weiner Dog Lady. The titular frozen dog squirts out from under her arm and hits the floor, immediately shattering into kibbles and bits.

I stare with my mouth open.

Well, *that's* something I can never un-see.

On hands and knees, I'm able to rescue most of the pieces that slid off across the floor under the chip rack. I spend a few futile minutes trying reassemble poor Humpty Doggy back into the shape of...well, anything. I end up fetching a Styrofoam cooler from the back of the store and stashing the frozen dog chunks into it, all the while musing that perhaps this is not the sanest thing to be doing. With a whitewashed grimace, I give the cooler an apologetic little pat and slide it over against the far wall. I consider leaving the lady an apology note, or a frozen card or something. What's the etiquette for disintegrating someone's dog? Flowers wouldn't be enough.

So I just slink off into the aisles, secretly relieved to escape from any eye witnesses to my mini-massacre. Never mind that now.

Time to go shopping.

I scour the shelves with a scrupulous eye. I probably won't get the luxury of another meal (or flavor). My stomach growls again. I'm sorely missing Mrs. Moffatt's heavenly fluffy waffles right now.

I try to crack open a pre-made deli sandwich, but the ice seems to have made everything extremely brittle. A granola bar, a banana – even the slightest tap causes them to shatter all over the floor. Apparently, you can't break the outer ice-shell without smashing whatever's inside along with it. Good thing I didn't try busting Mrs. Moffatt out. I think of that poor wiener dog sitting in pieces in the Styrofoam cooler, and I'm hit with a fresh wave of guilt.

I consider chowing some frozen Snickers pieces – but gazing grimly over the scattered chunks, it's nearly impossible to distinguish the edible candy from the wrapper. And besides, eating frozen food would only lower my body temperature even more. Can't afford to speed up what's already happening. No, I'll need to thaw this food.

Righty-o. How do you start a fire with nothing but ice?

On a shelf I spot a stack of ant traps, and that gives me an idea. Remember those creepy kids who used to fry ants under a magnifying glass because they had nothing better to do? I just need to make a magnifying glass.

Finding a good clear chunk of ice doesn't take too long. Sitting on the porch steps outside, I use the porcelain rooster shard to whittle the chunk into a globe shape, then smooth it with my bare hands until I've achieved a polished, glass-like finish.

From the porch, the wooden chief watches me with a criticizing scowl.

"What?" I scowl back at him. "Don't look at me like that. I know what I'm doing."

Actually, something about this *does* feel familiar. Thanks for the skills, Kyle-of-the-past. Whoever the heck you were...

Cuddling that ice made my hands hurt. They've quit itching, now they sting like the dickens. Pretty sure my fingertips are frozen, judging from the angry fluid-filled blisters, and the way I can't feel the little flakes of skin peeling off. Whatever. Second-degree frostbite, tops. I'm not worried. I'm shivering. It's when the shivering stops that you *really* have to worry. This is just discomfort. Just a temporary thing. Tomorrow after I've wiped out the wildcard, I'll be feeling fit as a fiddle. I just need to focus on the task at hand and try not to think about my fingers shriveling off.

I carefully prop my newly made ice lens against the base of the General Store's steps. Tilting the lens a hairsbreadth at a time, I angle it until it's exactly perpendicular to the sun. Through the convex curve of the ice, the sun's glare shines a bright little bead of light on the wadded-up piece of notebook paper, which I'm using as my fire-starter.

Stuffing my hands in my pockets, I plop down cross-legged on the step. And I wait.

I stare and stare at the paper, trying to will hot lasers from my eyes. I adjust the ice lens a bit.

More waiting.

"C'mon, you little diva." I mutter. "C'mon. *Burn*."

Maybe it needs something more flammable to ignite. I pluck a few coppery stands of my hair and pile them onto the wadded-up paper, where the beam of light is shining. Wait some more. Standing, I poke my head around each side of the store, sweeping a glance up the street. Nothing but white ice in both directions.

When I return, a curl of smoke has appeared on the paper. Elated, I drop to my knees and cup my hands desperately around the tiny smoke thread, blowing gently, coaxing it into a delicately glowing red ember.

"Come on... Please... That's it!"

Eventually I'm able to get a fire going. It's enough to melt some water and a bit of electrolyte sports drink, which I catch in my little cotton swab cup, gulping each saccharine prized mouthful as it trickles into the cup.

Now for lunch. I select the biggest family-size jar of peanut butter I can find and crack it open, thawing the frozen chunks over my little fire and gorging myself until my stomach is ready to bust at the seams.

At last, I can pour all my attention onto what's really important. The wildcard.

Next stop: Let's go break into a bank.

COLD-HEARTED

With every passing moment, I find myself craving that shotgun in my hand. Lucky for me, a lady has frozen while exiting the bank, still holding the door open.

"Thanks very much," I nod to her, tipping my invisible hat as I squeeze under her arm and in through the doorway.

The bank lobby looks like a statue garden in some ice palace courtyard. A couple waits in the teller line behind the velvet rope, morning pumpkin spice lattes and deposit slips in their hands. I skate across the floor. Pink Hipster is leaning over slightly with his rear end sticking out, one finger raised, a derpy expression sculpted onto his face.

"Just a little withdrawal," I call as I glide past him. "I remember the way, thanks."

I gaze at the sealed vault entrance. Curls of my breath waft rhythmically upward.

A frozen vault.

Eighteen inches of solid steel and concrete, now cocooned under a thick wall of ice.

One option – I could thaw some chemicals and blow up the vault door. But there's a guy in a cowboy hat standing about four feet to my left, filling out a deposit slip. He's too close. Too much of a chance that I'd blow up that knucklehead in the process.

I pace slowly in front of the vault entrance, back and forth like a shark, pulling off my sock-mittens and running my fingers along the door's smooth surface.

Merrick floats into my mind. He would have an idea.

I gaze at the ice-encased phones on the teller desks.

I could call Merrick... What was his cell number again? I close my eyes, conjuring up the image of Deadhead Kyle's death note. 555-1012. Pretty sure that was it. But even if I somehow miraculously managed to dial an ice cube, Merrick is surely frozen like everybody else. There's no way he's picking up his phone.

I punch my knuckles against the vault door. Maybe I should just try the "blow it up" method. Screw that cowboy guy; it's his own fault he's standing so close. And the blast might miss him. Maybe.

Anyway, neutralizing the wildcard is debatably more important than saving one life... Right? Sure. And flossing is debatably more important than brushing.

But that's the question that keeps gnawing at me, creeping up from the pits of my brain. The big Question, the one I don't really want to think about, because frankly, it makes me feel like a heartless Klingon.

If people will just reappear fine tomorrow like nothing ever happened...why bother saving them?

I'll have to think about that.

Purely out of curiosity, I hoist up one of the ice-coated office chairs and fling it against the vault. The whole chair shatters, peppering me with ice shrapnel. One of the armrests hits me in the face. I taste metallic warmth and spit; little red dots splatter on the floor.

Ugh, lovely. Another "dental floss" analogy. You do the right thing, and you still end up with a mouthful of blood.

I tap my fingertips to my mouth. Just a split lip. Nothing heinous. Nothing like almost taking a battle axe to the head last night. I shouldn't have to worry about bleeding to death a second time here in this bank from some doofy superficial scratch. I wipe my mouth.

Okay, plan B. Coconuts can be cracked open with a bamboo stick, if you can muster the proper leverage. And this ice makes everything extremely brittle.

Using one of my wire coat hangers, I start scraping where the vault door meets the wall frame, over and over. My wire cuts deeper, until it catches on the metal of the door. I wiggle the coat hanger down into the groove between the doorframe. My focus narrows, ignoring everything – no aching numb fingertips, no noise but the steady *skrit-skrit* of my digging. Puffs of my breath spill rhythmically over the tiny white curls peeling from the deepening slit, falling away as fast as they appear. When the slot is sufficiently deep, I toss the gnarled coat hanger aside. This coconut is ready. Now I just need my bamboo.

I find a metal yardstick under a desk. This might do the trick if I can manage to not break it.

Slow as Christmas, I slide the frozen yardstick deep into the slot between the doorframe, leaving it there. Then I grab another office chair, swinging it like a giant hammer and hitting the yardstick dead-on. The chair shatters in my hands, causing the yardstick to reverberate in the slot, fracturing the brittle steel wall. A spectacular avalanche of frozen metal chunks rains down around me, twisted shards spinning and skidding off in different directions across the bank lobby floor.

I crouch there for a moment, waiting for the whole bank to cave in on my stupid rash skull. But it doesn't.

Shivering, I slowly un-crouch and do a quick inventory of my limbs. No cuts or broken bones. Even Cowboy Hat Guy seems to have survived without getting smashed like the wiener dog, and relief washes over me.

The vault is now split open, a jagged, two-foot fissure. I kick out the remaining loose chunks until I can squeeze through the crack, then make my way down the branching honeycomb hallway. My demolition of the vault door has indeed caused structural damage. Hairline fractures snake along the ice tunnel's ceiling rafters, an ominous hint at greater underlying instability.

The quicker I can nab the shotgun and get my butt out of here, the better.

The safety deposit room is open. Two walls of silver drawers on either side of me gleam dimly beneath a sheet of pebbled ice.

A single overhead light flickers weakly, casting a weird, intermittent greenish light on the glimmering white cave. I dig out my 8-ball keychain and hold it up close to my mouth – like a microphone, like Merrick did. After asking it the first yes-no question I can think of ("Can a woodchuck really chuck wood?"), the 8-ball obediently splits open, spitting out the tiny silver key. Rubbing the key between my numb fingers, I locate my drawer. I'm cycling through every possible method I can think of for thawing the keyhole, but it turns out I won't have to bother.

Because the keyhole is open.

Somebody already thawed it.

"I'll be jiggered," I murmur. Slowly, with shaking hands, I insert my key into the keyhole, ready to be electrocuted or blown up. Neither happens.

I snatch the ice-encased safety deposit box out of the drawer and wrench it open.

There, nestled in the chest of ice, like a sleeping baby dragon, is my shotgun. All tucked up into a little compact block, exactly how it looked when Merrick and I found it here yesterday. And it's not frozen. Not a trace of ice, not a crystal. Just like my room at the Red Rooster... Just like this keyhole. My room. My weapon. All things connected to me.

It doesn't make sense.

It doesn't follow the rules.

Of course, I still don't know *what* kind of twisted rulebook this "game" follows. The wildcard always seems to cook up its *own* rules. Until I understand the parameters, no sense lollygagging around.

As I reach into the box, I catch a glimpse of my bare hands. It ain't pretty. My skin is waxy and hard, the blisters have swollen to the size of cherry tomatoes. Ugh, that's a little disturbing. I flex my bloated fingers impatiently, trying to shrug it off. Medical treatment should probably happen right about now, but I don't really have access to any at the moment. It's fine. Frostbite blisters usually look nastier than they really are. My deep tissues should still be unaffected; soft and pink. I should be able to heal up later tonight. Once I've fixed all this craziness.

A deep rumble spreading from the floor to ceiling has currently grabbed my attention, spurring me to snatch up the sleeping beauty weapon and hightail it out of there like a fat rat with cheese. I skid into the street outside. Spinning around in horror, I brace myself to watch the human popsicles crushed to fleshy pebbles as the bank collapses in on itself. But the damaged bank stands strong.

For a moment I just crouch there in the street, huffing and puffing. Then I remember the wildcard detector that I'm clutching in my frostbitten hands. Enough of this hilarious fun. Time to *smash* this wildcard.

With a burst of eagerness, I wedge myself into a shop's frozen doorway and jam my numb, swollen finger into the weapon's button. The shotgun springs open in my hand.

"Alright, give me good news!" My eyes lunge across the screen, hungry for a clue. A juicy red dot, a nice X-marks-the-wildcard. But my hope deflates like a balloon.

The screen is red.

The whole. Freaking. Screen.

"Oh, throw me a bone here!" I wail hoarsely. My screen only confirms what I pretty much already knew: The wildcard is all around me. I'm standing on it. Eating it. Breathing it.

Lowering the weapon slowly into my lap, I raise my gaze and survey my battlefield. I scan the icy town, letting my eyes graze over the gleaming building roofs. I tap the solid-red screen thoughtfully.

If the ice is the wildcard, then obviously I'm supposed to melt it. But that's a pretty tall order. The sheer daunting size of it all brings an excited flutter to my belly.

How do you *melt an entire town?*

I briefly consider carving an enormous version of my ice lens. True, a massive ice lens would probably thaw some cars, maybe even a shop – but how am I supposed to make a lens that big? Whittle it with my fingernails? Not an option. Besides, the whole "town under a giant magnifying lens" thing is a little too supervillain.

My brain cycles through other methods of melting ice.

Salt? It would take thirty dump trucks worth. Ditto for bleach. How about friction? I might as well melt this ice with the power of hopes and dreams. The eager tingle dwindles away, leaving a sick feeling, like a rock sinking deep into my tissue. My rapidly freezing human tissue.

I slap my thighs, kneading the muscles like frozen cookie dough. "Hang in there!" I plead with my limbs. "I'll figure this out."

But all my ideas are too grandiose. Anything big enough to thaw all this ice would also require a snot-load of time to prepare. And time is ticking away. The hours that felt so lazy and plentiful this morning are evaporating fast.

Why did I have to sleep late? Stupid unreliable car alarm... Stupid ice...

But making excuses won't help me. It won't melt a drop. I draw a long, deep breath and hold it until my lungs burn. *Think, Kyle.* Every wildcard has its solution. A big, shiny red reset button. I just need to find it.

I pull my sock-mittens back on, rubbing my fuzzy fists into my temples as I start to walk. The beauty of this morning eludes me. Every darkening alley looks so sinister, every ice-coated shop a tomb.

And the silence. The blasted silence that I relished so much this morning now hangs over me like a heavy lead curtain. It's maddening. You could say it fits into the "be careful what you wish for" category.

I keep on walking. Don't know where, I just keep trudging forward, as if eventually I'll turn a corner and miraculously stumble upon the answer. But the corners just keep coming; an endless string of frozen dead-ends.

My other motivation is keeping my body temperature up. But that's also a losing battle. I'm wearing the signs all over me. My fingers have ballooned and the cherry tomato blisters have filled with blood, taking on a sickly purplish tint. My toes probably look the same. I can't feel them; they quit tingling a long time ago. To someone who didn't know better, this odd loss of sensation might be reassuring, maybe even weirdly peaceful. Too bad I know better.

I watch the afternoon sun move across the sky, its glazed glare reflected in the ice walls all around me. I stop at the curb, swaying a little on my feet. Tuscany Mill sits across the street. The old nineteenth century restaurant towers against the late-day sun like some forbidden ice fortress. Slim chance I could get inside. Its timber wall siding and twisty, wood-railed stairs look slick and totally un-climbable.

I start stumbling toward the restaurant. When I step into the street I automatically look both ways, even though it's not really necessary. None of those frozen, car-shaped lumps will be rolling toward me. Somewhere in the parking lot, one of those lumps is a silver Chevy Tahoe. Not that it matters. But I feel a teensy bit of comfort, just having that familiar nugget to hook my mental tethers onto.

I shamble aimlessly around the frozen parking lot. Around one side of the restaurant is a back door with a small, fenced enclosure, just wide enough for a dumpster. A frozen figure stands hoisting a large trash bag, paused, preparing to toss it over the lip of the dumpster. I think I recognize that kicked-puppy posture and raked-up hair...

Curious, I edge closer.

It's Merrick. Frozen solid, now part of the landscape, like everyone else. Well, what did I expect? That I would find Merrick and something would automagically happen?

I stare at his cold, carved features for a long while.

"Talk to me, Merrick." I whisper. "Tell me the molecular composition of cornflakes. Just say something. *Anything.*"

His glasses have slipped halfway down his nose. Tossing that trash bag must have jostled them loose. Poor kid really should just invest in contact lenses. I reach to push the glasses back up for him, but I stop when my hand touches the thin frame of ice. Everything is so fragile. I don't want to snap off his glasses by accident. Or his head. That would be less than sweet of me.

Sweet...

The word clicks something awake inside my dusty brain. An old file, a twinge of a memory from Cl. Kyle, a memory of when she encountered strange ice before. But much like this ice, it wasn't normal. It looked like ice, sure – but it was synthetic, used to safely preserve living organisms. The artificial ice's chemical composition made it taste salty, even a little sweet. And when exposed to even a tiny amount of rubbing alcohol, it melted like butter.

Could *this* be the same stuff?

I rub my hands voraciously on my legs, spurring on the irresistible hope. If that's what I'm dealing with here, I might have a shot. Luck would swing wildly in my direction.

How can I know for sure?

My eyes skim up and down Merrick's body. If this ice is the same stuff, it should taste sweet...

Hesitantly, I look at Merrick.

"Listen," I warn him. "If you can hear me...this is just an experiment. Okay?"

He stares serenely off into space.

I clear my throat and duck around behind him. Can't believe I'm seriously looking for a place to lick this kid. Preferably where he won't have any chance in Hades of seeing me. Or ever, *ever* knowing about it. Quickly, I touch my tongue to his frozen shoulder. It tastes like...ice. Cold, icy. Other than my tongue briefly sticking to Merrick's shoulder flagpole-style, there's nothing out of the ordinary. It's just ice.

Plain, old ice.

My gut sinks. I'm back to square one. I plop down cross-legged next to Merrick, feeling intolerably lonely. Somehow it seems even colder now. I pull off my sock-mittens and blow into my purple corpse hands. Not that it helps anymore. That purple flesh is just the color of inevitability, barreling at me like a freight train.

Well, that's it. I'm going to have to do something I don't want to. Something desperate.

Something people do in worst-case scenarios.

Firmly, I reach into my pocket and dump out the pen and sheet of notebook paper. My frozen swollen balloon fingers won't bend to grip the pen. After a bit of wrangling, I'm able to hold the pen by squeezing it between both dead hands. I sit there for a moment, pen hovering over the paper. I'm trying to think. Nothing is happening.

My head nods drowsily. I punch myself in the arm. Absolutely, under *no* circumstances, can I allow myself to fall asleep. Hypothermia is finally setting in. If I doze off, I will absolutely freeze to death right here, by this dumpster, in a pile of my own failure.

My head nods again. My nose bumps the paper.

What was I doing, again...?

Ugh, here comes the brain fog. Setting in, taking over. Soon, my cellular metabolic processes will start shutting down. I've been sitting still too long, and death has begun to circle me like vultures.

Just keep kicking, Kyle.

Just write down this one thing...

My pen touches the paper, but I don't write anything.

Because that's when I hear it.

MELTDOWN

The *sound* is loud. Not loud to my ears – the noise itself is distant, dampened – but wherever it's happening, I can tell it's loud. For a second I just sit there, unable to compute what I'm hearing.

A single, deep clang.

Followed by another... Then another.

As if kicked in the tail by some unseen force, I spring to my feet, my head buzzing chaotically. Suddenly, I remember the pen in my hand – and before my brain falls out again, I force myself to scribble onto the notebook paper a single sentence:

Corner of Lincoln and Lee

I just pray it's legible. Battling my tremoring hands, I roll up the note and tuck it between Merrick's frozen fingers, where he'll be sure to see it when he thaws. I clasp both my hands over his, both of us ice-cold.

I'm counting on you, kiddo.

The sound persists. It hammers at my brain as I plunge frantically through the icy tree-lined streets. A long, hollow, resonating clang, deliberately repeated, again and again, briefly growing dimmer and muffled each time I flail around a corner. But always there, always growing in strength as I draw closer.

It sounds synthetic...metallic...

I trip over an ice-covered bike; it topples over, shattering against the pavement. Only when I stumble around that last corner and skid out into Main Street, I find myself staring up at the source of the sound.

The library's bell.

I've been up there. There's no computerized mechanism, just an old-fashioned rope and pulley. If that bell is ringing, it means *someone is up there ringing it.*

Slip-sliding across a car's ice hood (and a good bit of the pavement on the other side), I scramble across the sparkling diamond lawn toward the library, its bell tower silhouetted against a reddening sunset sky, a dark, hulking ice lump concealing the lone gargoyle through the silvery trees. High overhead, the ornate clock glows beneath a glaze of ice, its Roman spade hands halted on 9:27.

The bell stops ringing.

My eyes dart wildly around the belfry.

"Hey!" I shout hoarsely. I immediately double over in pain. Shouting feels like a swig of liquid nitrogen, gasping is like tissue-ripping glass. Despite this, I draw in another stinging breath and cry out again.

"*Hello?* Is someone up there?"

No answer. Are they too weak? Or are they...?

Up in the belfry, the arch-shaped windows remain dark and empty. No...not empty. I blink. Something is sitting on the windowsill. Something metal. Possibly a large can of tomato sauce, or–

Suddenly, my blood goes cold.

It's the canister.

The canister Holliday used to suck out my heart. But why would he leave it sitting out in the open like this? The word "TRAP" screams to mind, but frankly, I don't care. Blame it on my frozen gummy brain. If Holliday is daring me to come...

Try and stop me. I've got nothing left in my options pool.

But getting inside the library's sturdy oak doors, locked *and* sealed under ice... Might as well be another bank vault. Not happening. Plus, those never-ending stairs leading up the bell tower are just too treacherous for any human to tackle, especially now, with the fun added bonus of being coated in slippery, head-cracking ice. Lucky for me, there's a safer way to get up there.

Around the corner in the graveyard, the construction crew is frozen right where they were at 9:27 this morning, repairing the gargoyle's mess. Their scaffolding platforms are stacked oh-so conveniently against the side of the library, right up to the roof. The scaffolding is coated in slippery, head-cracking ice.

Oh, did I say "safer"?

I pull one of my boot shoelaces off, wrapping it several times around both of my mangled hands. Looping the shoelace through each scaffolding pole, I'm able to clumsily hoist myself up the slippery platforms like a mountain climber. Fueled by adrenaline and the notion of seeing another flesh-and-blood human, I begin to pray my exhausted arms don't give out before my precious adrenaline does. Whatever is at the top of this clock tower...

I *need* it.

At last, my elbows are digging into the icy roof shingles. With an almighty roar, I roll myself over the windowsill's edge and tumble breathlessly onto the bell chamber floor, eagerly jerking my eyes up to see–

An empty room. There's nobody here.

And no canister on the windowsill.

For half a panicked second, I wonder if I imagined that bell ringing, just some cold-induced hallucination... But this is Carnival Creeke. I take my crazy with a grain of salt.

I glance up at the ceiling. I can't really see the bronze bell, it's obscured way up in the shadows of the four-point steeple. But I see the rope. It's coated in ice. There's *no way* anyone rang that bell.

"Hello?" I croak. Silence.

I am literally losing my marbles. With effort, I pull myself off the floor to my feet. I'm shivering so violently that it rattles my teeth, threatens to snap my spine. Springing open my shotgun, I check the screen to find it still covered in red. Fury radiates through me. Panting, I pivot slowly in a circle, unable to process my surroundings. I just cashed in all my energy hauling my sorry wasted tail up here in pursuit of some sonic phantom, some stupid canister-shaped beacon of hope. Well, congratulations. Now I'm stuck. There's no climbing back down that scaffolding. I put all my eggs into one basket. Then I blew up the basket.

My fury mingles with desperation. As I stagger round and round, I realize I've been clamping my grip on my shotgun's trigger. Vaguely, I recall how Merrick demonstrated the firing mechanism to me.

"It works like a gear throttle. You squeeze it, aim, then let go and – bwah! It fires."

With a hopeless wail, I aim the weapon and all my fury at the first unlucky object that I see – the forgotten coffee mug, sitting on the railing encased in ice. Then I loose the throttle. A burst of blue light zings from my shotgun and hits the frozen mug with a dull thunk.

But the mug doesn't explode.

It doesn't shatter. Doesn't even crack.

Instead, the blue light absorbs into the ice-covered mug. It sits there, pulsating faintly for a moment. Then the blue glow starts spreading away from the mug, down the railing, seeping outward. And everywhere the blue light touches, the ice dissolves.

I gawk like someone just slapped me with a flat iron.

Melting.

Son of a monkey, my gun is *melting* it! This weapon seems to possess the ability to turn liquids to solid. I've seen firsthand what it does to coffee and blood. But it never occurred to me that it might have the *opposite* effect on solids – at least on solids that *used* to be liquid. Like ice. It makes sense, in a backward, upside-down, Carnival Creekey kind of way.

I watch the room unearth all around me, the wood floor appearing through the melting spots like hot spring in fast-forward. I could laugh. I could crow. I could–

Oh crap-burgers! The glowing edge of that ice is creeping toward my feet pretty quickly. What happens to my (relatively) warm body if that light touches *me?*

An image of Deadhead Kyle flashes into my mind, flopping and convulsing in the street...

I go to step back, but my frozen clay legs don't comply. I tumble backward down the staircase, feet over head. Seriously, do these stairs have it in for me?

It's amazing that I don't break any bones or crack my head open like a walnut. While I'm lying there trying to coax my lungs to breathe, the blue light rushes down the stairs, thawing them. Then it passes harmlessly beneath me.

Well, thank goodness I just fell down the longest flight of steps in history to escape *that* dreadful threat.

What happened next is blur. Literally – I hit my head hard. But it doesn't matter. All I need to see is that lovely image on my shotgun's screen. A hole in the solid red. It starts as a small gray pinprick, steadily growing and spreading outward across the screen, erasing all the red and replacing it with gray.

It's a glorious sight.

The gleaming ice shell encasing the library building melts away, hissing and cracking, revealing brick and stone and grass. About halfway across the lawn, the blue light stops progressing and fizzles out.

"Oh, don't you dare!" I charge the throttle and fire off another blast. That gets things rolling again. So I keep firing. Big, bad wildcard, so overwhelming and daunting this morning... What's that old saying? *How do you eat an elephant?* One bite at a time, of course.

A sideways grin creeps across my face. Forget frozen peanut butter. I'm about to dine on elephant.

"How d'ya like *that*, Carnival Creeke?" I scream with painful effort. "We're playing by *my* rules, now!"

I shoot off blast after blast – into trees, over roofs – aiming as best as I can manage at precise, calculated points. A blast into a corner shop sends blue light spraying off in both directions, thawing the entire intersection and the surrounding streets within a mile radius. All around me, people drop to the ground, collapsing like piles of spaghetti, their hair and clothes miraculously dry. And nothing shatters. The little flags outside the bakery, the potted topiary shrubs on the antique shop's doorstep, an old codger's cigar – all delicate objects that would have been crushed under a real ice blanket – they all appear good as new. Even that streetlamp with all the birdhouses, none of them bear so much as a scuff.

My shotgun's red screen continues to shrink. It's superbly satisfying. Too bad my freeze-dried body decides to be a party pooper. Hope I can remember my way to the corner of Lincoln and Lee…

I stumble drunkenly through the narrow, frozen service alley between the used bookstore and Lau Chow's, firing the shotgun as I go, stopping only when my heroic gun quits spitting blasts. This was the milestone moment that I discovered that this weapon will fire six shots, then it requires about thirty seconds to recharge. Guess nothing is unlimited. Including me.

Especially me.

A street corner wavers hazily in front of me. Townsfolk are slumped all over the sidewalk. I want to run to them, check their pulses, reassure them that everything is okay now. But I can't seem to remember how to do any of that. My legs go numb, my vision irises to black, and I know I'm three seconds from becoming one of those unconscious bodies. Hey, at least I'll blend in.

I hit the ground, my last thought hoping to high heaven that this is the corner of Lincoln and Lee.

*

I awaken with a spastic jerk. I'm lying on upholstery, the unmistakable lulling feel of a car moving beneath me.

Fantastic. I'm in somebody's trunk.

Seatbelts, granola bar wrappers… No, correction, I'm in somebody's backseat.

I boing upright like a jack-in-the-box. Merrick sees me in the rearview mirror and slams on the brakes. My face collides artlessly with the back of his leather seat, causing my brain to slosh around inside my skull. Pretty sure I've got a concussion from my tumble down the library's staircase of doom.

"Holy shneikies!" Merrick exclaims, twisting around. "Are you okay?!"

Normally I would have fired back a confident fib, like "Never better." But right now, my brain has officially shut down. And being in the Tahoe feels like warm apple pie. Merrick has the heater on.

Merrick, who showed up.

I gaze at him until I'm pretty sure it's making him uncomfortable. Finally he blushes.

"Um, what?"

I shake it off. "Nothing. Just…you found me."

He shrugs, scratching the back of his neck. "Yeah, well, I got your note. Corner of Lincoln and Lee. That…was *you* who left it, right?"

I nod, rubbing my eyes. My hands look ninety percent better already. The angry swelling has gone down, my skin faded from rotten purplish to a nice scorched flesh color. I feel like a freezer-burned burrito.

Merrick pulls over and parks by the curb. "I mean, glad to help," he says. "But, um, why'd you leave the note with *me*?"

"Because you helped me with the gargoyle."

And a few times since then.

"One crazy day after another, huh?" Merrick chuckles. "They're saying everyone in Carnival Creeke just passed out. Same time, *everyone*. They're calling it a town-wide flock event." He waves his hands dramatically. "As if they could actually classify it, right? But it's big news. Sheriff Gammell's been on the phone with the FBI since five o'clock."

"Wow," I croak drowsily, trying to sound interested. "Back to normal, then?"

"Well, not exactly. Someone broke into the bank. Totally demolished the vault. Apparently, all they took was something from a safety deposit box belonging to some guy named C. Kyle."

"Oh?" I yawn. "Who's that?"

"No idea. But Sheriff Gammell's making some calls, doing some digging. And there's other stuff, too. Weird stuff. Like did you hear Mrs. Grubmueller's dog is missing?"

"Madness!" I splutter, laughing maniacally. Guilt shower.

I glance out the window. "Where are we going, Merrick?"

"To the hospital." He looks confused. "Everyone is supposed to get checked out."

"No thanks. I don't like doctors."

"It's kinda mandatory."

"Mandatory, shmandatory." I squint, grappling for the English language. Stupid concussion. As fun as it would be listening to the authorities' adorable theories about what happened, it's time to wrap up this day. I'm grumpy and hungry, and my rump is colder than a polar bear's pajamas. All I want to do is go back to my room and take a scalding hot bath.

"Listen, I'm fine," I assure Merrick. "I'm super. Okay? Thanks for rescuing me. Gotta go now." I reach for the car door.

"Hold on a sec."

Uh-oh. I know that voice. It's Merrick's deducting voice. Gears clicking into place... I put on my best innocent smile and brace myself for whatever he's about to ask.

He's gazing at me, curiously, as though hypnotized.

"It was you," Merrick utters in a low voice. "You helped us. You *saved* us... Didn't you?"

"What? Pfff."

"Well, either that, or you *caused* it. I mean, you've gotta admit, right after you showed up everything went all freaky B-movie. That gargoyle, now this town-wide snooze..."

Keeping my eyes closed, I smile slyly. "So what makes you think I'm not behind it all?"

"Nah. You're not." As if embarrassed by his moment of confidence, he adds quickly, "For one, if you're the Big Bad... Well, you probably wouldn't let yourself get beaten to a pulp every day."

I open my mouth, then close it again.

Good point.

"So what *do* you know about all this?" Merrick presses eagerly. "We're government guinea pigs, right? Black helicopters, alien tests?"

"I'm as clueless as you, kid."

And I definitely didn't lick your shoulder.

Merrick slumps a little in his seat. He actually looks a little disappointed.

"Look, just be thankful you're alive." I grimace, pushing the car door open with effort. "No alien takeover adventures today, sorry."

I slide out of the Tahoe into the chilly night air. The stars are out. Beneath my boots, the pavement lurches dizzily; I immediately have to grab the doorframe. Merrick has a quick battle with his arch nemesis, The Seatbelt, then scrambles from the truck. He catches me by the arms.

"Whoa, there! Um, maybe you shouldn't–"

"No." I shrug out from his arm. "Just...*don't* carry me. Lord, no. I don't ever want to be carried. I'm not a puppy."

He looks genuinely mortified. I chew my lip.

"Hey, Merrick?"

"Yeah?"

"I mean it. Thank you. For coming and finding me."

A smile crosses his face. "Anytime. All you had to do was ask." His face reddens, suddenly feeling the need to adjust his glasses even though they're already right where they're supposed to be. I smile, stuffing my hands into my pockets.

"Hey!" Merrick pipes brightly behind me as I'm walking away. "They're putting together a town hall social at the high school tonight. Big recovery party. Cookies, hot chocolate, altruism at its finest. Want to come? I mean, if you don't have plans. Everyone in town's gonna be there."

I remind him that I'm not from this town. With a confident grin, I turn and set off into the night on my long walk back to the bed-and-breakfast.

*

After watching me take approximately two steps and do a faceplant, Merrick graciously offers me a ride. He wouldn't take the cash that I tried to give him either, because he's such a gosh-darn nice guy and all.

So here I am. Konked out in the old claw-foot bathtub, nothing but my knees and my nose sticking out of the steamy water. In my bedroom, the Mamas and the Papas are singing "California Dreaming" on the record player. But I can't really hear their garbled, airy musings on brown leaves. I've got my ears submerged. As the flute solo drifts in and out in its dreamy, slightly-sharp way, I lay there marinating, just savoring the sublime feeling of not being dead. Under the water, it's almost like I'm in another world. Or a science fiction regeneration tank. I like it. Maybe Cl. Kyle used to veg just like this at the end of a long day. The amazing shotgun sits on top my pile of clothes on the bathroom floor. The pink kitten notebook is lying beside it, all updated with today's butt-freezing adventure. Another entry, another "greatest story never to be told."

On the record player, the song ends and the needle scratches against the vinyl. I can hear Mrs. Moffatt puttering around down on the main floor, plates clinking, cleaning up after dinner. It's a really good sound.

I've been thinking about The Question. And I think I've decided on an answer. If people just reappear fine tomorrow like nothing ever happened…why bother saving them?

Because nobody should have to go through that.

Even if they won't remember it.

Heck, *I* don't remember chunks of my life, and who can say I'm not royally messed up? Maybe I even died. Will I ever know? If I'm going to keep playing hero and saving these people, I should keep it simple and strict. Under no circumstances should I get attached. Who knows how long I'll be doing this? Eventually, I'll lose one of them. It's just inevitable.

I jig my foot, running my hands through my wet hair.

On the other hand, I can't deny how rotten it felt being alone today. Some people, you just know you can count on. Merrick is that kind of person. But can I protect Merrick?

My foot jigs faster.

I should cut off these unsafe relationships. Definitely. It's the smart thing to do. Better to keep my head in the game.

Reaching from the tub, I feel around my pants for a quarter.

Heads, I'm solo from now on.

Tails…

DAY 20: BUGABOO

Through the crowd, I meet Merrick's desperate look. Everyone presses in, one roiling, terrified, compacted mass of bodies. The people on the outer edges closest to the chain-link fence are trying to shrink themselves as thin as possible, flinching away from the slashing claws that rattle outside the enclosure. A sea of unintelligible jabbering mixes with panicked shrieks. I want to scream at all of them. For following me here. For trusting me.

I kick the fence, raising my Icemaker at the wall of monsters surrounding us.

I always knew I had an expiration date stamped on me. I just kind of hoped it was a long way off, like a Twinkie. You can't do this crazy blender dance with danger every day and expect to set dates, be picking out curtains someday. Not with my job. I guess I always imagined that my "game over" would look different. Just me, alone – on a deserted street, maybe in an alley somewhere, facing down whichever wildcard drew my number. I never thought it would look like this. Messy and muddled, crammed shoulder-to-shoulder with the whole town. A chaotic climax with a crunchy, bloody filling.

Hello, game over. I won't say it's nice to meet you.

Let's rewind, shall we?

12 HOURS EARLIER

I'm running down King Street. Not a soul in sight.

It's a beautiful day in post-apocalyptic Carnival Creek. The sun is shining on overturned trashcans and garbage strewn across the road. Abandoned cars clog the streets, cattycornered and facing the wrong direction, doors hanging open. My boots crunch on broken glass. The pavement is littered with it – shop displays, car windshields. Most of the restaurant windows are jagged, cavernous holes, their painted front doors hanging off hinges or missing completely. Music is playing somewhere; Patsy Cline's "Walking after Midnight," a deep warble wafting carelessly through the sharp smoke.

Creeptastic.

The squat brick police station is gaping and dark. No sense in digging through that place again. All the police rifles were already gone by the time I got there. Ditto for every handgun and walkie-talkie.

A sharp pang sears my chest. Dropping to a crouch in the police station doorway, I pause to unzip my jacket. With a soft groan, I peel up my red-soaked t-shirt.

The first of the creatures was spotted sometime this morning. Crawled out of a kid's toy box, gave the family a real ugly surprise. And in a matter of mere hours, these creatures have managed to ravage the happy little town of Carnival Creeke into a smoldering wasteland.

It's only ten o'clock.

My bandage is soaked. Most of the tape has lost its sticky, the gauze now hanging off my chest by one corner and flapping in the chilly breeze. I dig a small brown bottle from my pocket. Rubber cement. Unscrewing the cap, I bite my tongue and slop a generous blob of the pungent, sticky goop over my flesh. Stinks like death, but it seals the wound. Effective in a pinch. Don't try this at home, folks.

I'm a fast-healing super-freak, remember?

Ripping off a ribbon of fresh duct tape off with my teeth, I pull it taut across my crusty bandage. My bandage looks worse than the actual wound. The creature could have nicked an artery, but luckily those grim-reaper claws ended up just two inches shy of where my heart should be. I toss the roll of duct tape back on my wrist like a bracelet and zip my jacket, slapping myself across the chest.

I don't know what that stupid meathead was aiming for, anyway. There's nothing beating under my chest but an empty hole.

My zipper ends abruptly where a jagged chunk of leather has been ripped off my jacket. Irks the crap out of me...but whatever. My jacket will be fine tomorrow. I just can't believe one of those ugly critters got a claw in me. I mean, I wasn't even being particularly stupid or saucy.

Rolling my eyes with a grunt, I slide easily back up to a standing position, my hand reaching into my pants for my Icemaker.

"Icemaker." That's the nickname that I've given the weird futuristic Winchester shotgun. Because it turns liquids into solid. Get it? Icemaker?

I know, it's silly.

These days, I've also taken to carrying around the metal battle axe – the one from the Antique Replicas shop. Yep, the very same axe that Deadhead Kyle almost split me open with that night. From what I saw, she seemed pretty adept at handling the heavy weapon. Hey, if the shoe fits, right?

Using a backpack and duct tape, I've rigged up a sheath to carry the axe across my back. Of course, I can't carry it around *every* day. Strolling through town in broad daylight with a medieval battle axe is a surefire way to get thrown in Gammell's jail cell, possibly in a spiffy straitjacket. So I only go buy the axe on those certain "special" days. Days when the wildcard has gone so far haywire that nobody bats an eyelash at some strange chick carrying around a battle axe.

Days like today.

I scurry across the street toward Tuscany Mill's parking lot. By the front streetlamps, the old covered wagon has been sliced open, tattered flaps of cloth hanging off in distinct claw-mark patterns.

Tuscany Mill was a good place to hide. Aside from the water tower, the restaurant's dining room is the highest location in town. A perfect vantage point. Plus, it's a *restaurant* – so there's food in the freezer. Bottled water, too.

I ignore the wooden steps leading up to the restaurant's main entrance, instead slinking around to the dining patio on the side. Green patio umbrellas shade the overturned iron tables, strings of white lights swinging lazily in the breeze.

We don't use the main entrance. We've got that door blocked off with chairs and a wooden bench. For good measure, we jury-rigged it shut with a heavy pulley chain that we hauled down from the antique collection up in the dining room. So, if you need to go outside for any reason (and it better be a *good* reason), you have to crawl out through the window in the food storage cellar downstairs. I've crawled through a lot of windows here in Carnival Creeke. The police station jail cell, the bathroom at the Pinkie Poochie Dog Spa (long story, that one...) It's my new personal goal to climb out a window of every building in town. Everybody needs fun little goals.

I've got a little group up here in the restaurant with me, six in all. There's Twinkie Dad, slumped on a barstool, his big shoulders sagging. Took me a minute to recognize him without his baseball bat. He's got his cute four-year-old daughter with him, her curly dark hair pinned up with little sparkly purple barrettes. Her name is Jemma. No Twinkies to share today, unfortunately.

Mr. Nederson is here, too. He always wears an anxious expression, like a dog tied to a bike rack waiting for his owner to return. Today Mr. Nederson's face is looking puffier than usual behind his glasses, forehead sprinkled with sweat, his polo sweater all rumpled and un-tucked. I guess watching monsters macerate your town will do that to you.

Mr. Nederson has a heart condition. He doesn't know about it yet. Maybe it's the heart thing, but I always feel like I've got to watch his back. Call me a softie.

Right now everyone is sitting around the dining room, their backs against the wall. Not much conversation. At least the homecoming queen finally shut her yap.

Candace Cole, in her cheerleading skirt. Literally, she's tonight's homecoming queen.

Or at least she *would* have been.

Here's a little fact I've discovered: When horrific, ravenous beasts are swarming the streets, most folk's first reaction doesn't involve grabbing their coolers and heading to the bleachers to show their local high school S-P-I-R-I-T.

Candace had a whole lot to say before we got here, when we were still hiding down in the sewers. Mostly screeching in my face, trying to throw her ninety-pound queen bee weight around. Let's just say I made it crystal clear that she was welcome to go join Shepper's group over at the bike shop. Now her majesty is sulking off in the corner, her white shoes all slimy, pretending to be texting on her dead pink phone.

She's right, though. We can't stay here. Sooner or later the creatures will smell us. They're unstoppable eating machines, and their only aim is to gut and guzzle every shred of edible substance in town, flesh included. It's only a matter of time before they figure out how to worm their way into our cozy little restaurant fortress. And then we're a tasty buffet of sitting ducks up here.

I won't go to the bike shop. That place was a dumb idea because of their big glass display window. Might as well hang out a flashing neon "come and get it" sign. Which, rumor has it, they basically did.

At least the bike shop has walkie-talkies. So did the police station, I'm sure of it. Every police station does. But I have no idea where Sheriff Gammell is right now, or Deputy Scarecrow.

What I could *really* use right now is Emmett Tannon. I've been inside that man's farmhouse. I saw his living room, with all his wire-tapping HAM radio gear. A regular clandestine fortress of paranoid. I'll bet you anything Old Man Tannon is hunkered down right now in some secret bomb shelter under his house, raising a glass of 1940 to World War Three.

I'll find us a new hideout. But I'm not taking these people anywhere until my second-in-command returns.

We have a baby monitor sitting on the host podium; its counterpart receiver is downstairs by the main entrance. Not the most high-tech security system, but it's all we've got. If anything tries to come through that door, we'll hear it. Plus, the baby monitors are wireless and can run off batteries. Essential right now, since the power is completely dead in this building. Maybe the whole town.

We all freeze as the baby monitor lets out a sudden sharp crack through the static.

A slow creaking on the floorboards...

Something is moving around downstairs.

Here's another little update about me. I've logged a lot of hours working on my reflexes. Repetitive drills. One of my favorites is to chuck a tennis ball, bounce it off the wall and catch it at the last minute before it hits my face, mimicking a block – then throw a punch immediately after. I do it in my room at night, until Mrs. Moffatt eventually comes knocking to politely ask me to simmer down in her hushed, passive way. I can usually get off about ninety throws before I'm scolded. But I'm sharper now. Quicker. I dare Gammell to try and toss me into his drunk tank *now*.

But back to the creaking sound, which is moving steadily up the stairs toward us. Everyone gathers in a little clump behind me, my Icemaker already sprung open in my hand and aimed at the door.

There's a knock at the door – shave and a haircut.

Everyone relaxes as I smile, lowering my shotgun.

My second and third-in-command have returned.

Everyone crowds around as Merrick and Captain Epic remove their handguns and set them on the table behind me. Other than my Icemaker and battle axe, these guns are the only two actual weapons. The rest of our weapons – tennis rackets, garden hoes, a gold Elven sword – we scrounged up from what was left in the hardware store and off the walls of the Antique Replicas shop. Guess I wasn't the only one who thought to pilfer that place.

Merrick drops cross-legged into a chair, looking like he needs to breathe into a paper bag.

"Sorry," he pants apologetically. "It's just...I've never shot anything before."

"Aw, buck up, bro!" Captain Epic says brightly. "I'm pretty sure you still haven't." He thumps Merrick on the back reassuringly and throws him a wink.

Tall, muscular, and tan, I chose Captain Epic because I've seen him out jumping rope early each morning in his "No Pain, No Gain" t-shirt. Not that jumping rope translates into wielding a weapon, but luckily, he's Army. Plus, he brought guns. So he's like our prize in the cereal box.

"So?" Twinkie Dad presses them. "Did you find a generator at the diner?"

Merrick sighs. "If by 'generator' you mean 'reeking, meat-munching nightmare monsters'... Then yes. We found a generator."

Captain Epic dabs at a gooey gash on his brawny arm. "Yeah dude," he agrees. "Things got pretty hairy. We barely made it back in one piece." He raises his blond eyebrows, adding, "*Majorly* epic."

Everything is epic according to him. Hordes of bloodthirsty monsters, you'd think that would warrant an adjective like "horrific" or "I peed myself." He's just a really optimistic guy. He told me his name – Dylan, or something like that. I didn't bother to remember. Captain Epic works fine for me.

I gesture to Merrick and he trots over. Taking him by the shoulders, I examine him up and down. His glasses are gone.

"Are you hurt?" I demand.

"Geez, no *Mom*..." Merrick shrugs me off, his face beet-red. I'm embarrassing him, I know. But I'm hard and fast resolved to keep his butt alive. Merrick is my special priority.

"What happened to your glasses?" I frown.

"Oh. Long story involving a critter and, uh...a sewer." Shrugging, he adds quickly, "It's no biggie, really. I can actually see fine without glasses."

I shoot him a funny look. "Then why do you wear them?"

Whatever he's about to say takes second fiddle, as a flash of movement on my Icemaker's screen catches my eye.

A red dot, moving along in a straight line. Straight toward us.

I put my hand up and everyone falls silent, looking over with question marks on their faces.

"Hold up." I mutter. "We've got a critter."

We all huddle together at the window, and for a minute, all we see is smoke.

Then we see *it*.

The little stuffed teddy bear toddles down the center of the empty street, swinging its stubby arms like it owns the place. Which it does.

The teddy stops toddling and stands very still. For one panicked second, I think the critter somehow just spotted us all the way up here with its remarkable button eyes. But then I realize it's not *us* the bear is looking at. There's an overturned trashcan spilling garbage out into the street; among the trash is a greasy, crumpled wrapper from a sausage biscuit breakfast sandwich. Apparently still with a scrap of biscuit in it.

"Don't watch, honey," I whisper sternly to Jemma and Twinkie Dad ushers her off to look at some old 1800s sepia photographs on the dining room wall.

The rest of us press our noses against the window. Down on the street, the teddy bear bends over. Seizing the wrapper in its stumpy stuffed paws, it greedily gobbles the breakfast morsel, wrapper and all.

The effect is almost immediate. Convulsing, the fabric on the teddy's back splits open, revealing a row of four-foot barbs. Within seconds, the little beast has doubled – then tripled – in size, its arms and legs elongating to grotesque lengths, masses of furry muscle spilling and bulging like marshmallows in a microwave, until it's the size of a gorilla. All the creatures have similar faces – hog-awful, ugly jackal snouts and massive muscular jaws, lips permanently peeled back over a gnarly mouthful of tangled, tusk-like bushwhackers that jut out in National Geographic angles.

As if testing its new limbs, the creature stretches, flexing a handful of razor-edged claws as long as garden shears, and flicking its demon ears. Then it shakes itself like a dog and goes loping off into the smoky streets.

"Epic," Captain Epic whistles reverently.

Beside me, Merrick's side of the window is fogged up.

"Wait," he utters. "So...*teddy bears* are turning into werewolves?"

I toss him a wry look over my shoulder. "Well, you wanted to see monsters, right?

"On a movie screen, maybe!" Merrick moans. "I'm seriously gonna have nightmares for a week."

My eyes flicker to the floor.

You won't last a week. Not if I can't fix this wildcard in sixteen hours...

I glance at my Icemaker. Clusters of red dots squirm around the screen, representing the streets around us. So many red dots. And my Icemaker can only fire six shots at a time. Initially this morning, I spent all my time in Rambo mode, just trying to knock off as many critters as possible. But they just kept popping up everywhere. Multiplying, like Tribbles. These cuddly little monsters bent us over their knee and spanked us hard.

"HOLD UP...WE'VE GOT A CRITTER."

"Nothing changes," I mutter, turning back to the window. "Our M.O. is still the same. Conserve our food, stay alive...and find the rest of the survivors out there."

In the corner, Candace snorts. "Do you even know what M.O. stands for?"

That girl is grating on my last nerve.

"Candace," I say in a controlled voice. "I know you're tired. And I know you're in a real delicate swing between quietly dealing with it and totally freaking out. But so is everyone else in this room, okay? So I'm asking you nicely to go back to your calm place. And if I hear you so much as fart, I will feed you to the critters outside. Do we understand each other?"

For a second, I think she's actually going to listen to my pearls of wisdom, because she goes over to the restrooms and stands there with her mouth open and her eyes closed.

Then she sneers under her breath, "I'm so glad we elected you."

Without a word, I toss her skinny rump over my shoulder, marching down the wooden stairs and into the dark cellar. I plop her down and jab my finger at the window.

"Out," I order.

She doth protest, so I pick her up again. Candace thrashes and wails, kicking and pounding her fists on my back like girls do when they get all fired up.

"Keep it up," I warn over my shoulder. "I think some critters on the other edge of town haven't heard you yet."

I trudge all the way out past the Tuscany Mill parking lot and as far into the street as I dare before dropping her onto the asphalt like a sack of potatoes.

"Motus operandi," I state flatly.

"What?"

"M.O. It stands for *motus operandi*. Now have fun being a confrontational priss out here by yourself."

I turn and walk away – but not back toward the restaurant yet. My whole reason for coming out here was to try and scrounge up some batteries for the baby monitors, and I'm not returning without them. Toting the cheerleader along was purely for fun and principle.

"Hey!" Candace tosses her glossy platinum hair and scrambles to her knees, assailing me with her eagle-like screech. "Are you a complete psychotic?!"

Nope, not today.

I say, "You can probably make it to the bike shop before dark, if you hustle."

I don't mean it, of course. It's total B.S. to scare her. The bike shop is only about ten minutes away. And it's only noon. That sun won't go down for another seven hours. That's important to me. I'll need to utilize every second of daylight. Got to figure this wildcard out before the sun goes down. Because I *do not* plan on this day ending with me crawling around frantically in the dark while mutated teddies of death scurry through the town from end-to-end.

Behind me, Candace is still hollering her pretty head off.

"Hey, you're not gonna just leave me out here?!"

I don't answer, because I've spotted my prey. Over by the curb, a remote-controlled robot dinosaur is lying in the gutter. Squatting down, I pop open the toy's side flap and slide two nine-volts out into my hand. I tap each battery to my tongue. They give off a little sharp jolt. Good. Still some juice left in them. These should do the trick for the baby monitors.

Candace watches over my shoulder, sidling up close to me. Obviously, she's decided her hatred of being in my presence isn't worse than getting ripped limb from limb.

"Have you ever thought of wearing some makeup?" she broaches quietly.

"Nope."

"Well, you should. I think you're scaring the monsters."

"Thanks for the tip."

She opens her mouth to retort, but never gets a word out because the sudden noise makes us both jump out of our skins.

It's feedback. Echoing off all the broken buildings and empty streets, it sounds like a microphone, or stadium loudspeakers, except we're at least two miles from the high school football stadium.

Then comes the voice. Crackly, as if through a bullhorn:

"Is anyone alive out there?"

Candace and I look at each other.

"What *is* that?" she whispers robotically. I shake my head. The voice booms again.

*"If you can hear me... If **anyone** can hear me... We're all here. Everyone that's left in town."*

I frown. That voice...

There's a long drone of feedback then it cuts off sharply, and we're left in standing in the middle of the street in silence.

Can't shake it. I recognize that voice from somewhere...

"Is there an emergency alert system in Carnival Creeke?" I ask Candace, slipping the batteries into my pocket. She shrugs indignantly.

"Um, hello? Do I *look* like a nerd? That's not what I do for fun, looking for old town relics."

She's right. Merrick would know.

*

They're serving lunch when we get back to Tuscany Mill, portions of olive-rosemary breadsticks found in the pantry and a huge can of stewed tomatoes. The sight of the big fat can brings back memories, mostly of me smashing off the gargoyle's feet in the walk-in freezer, my first night in Carnival Creeke. Ah, good times.

Everyone stands as we tromp into the room, Candace trudging behind me like a dejected puppy.

"Didja get the batteries?"

"Yep," I reply. "But it might not matter anymore. Something happened while we were outside." I pause. They're all staring at me, waiting for my next words. I realize this is the first time I've had a captive audience. I'm usually more of a behind-the-scenes kind of girl. Now all eyes are on me.

I shift uncomfortably, suddenly at a loss for what to say next.

"We heard a voice," Candace says quietly behind me. "Somebody was talking over the old alert system."

I'm oddly grateful to queen bee, because it gave me a moment to pull myself back together.

"Anyone know where the broadcast might've come from?"

Dependably dependable Merrick pipes up.

"Well, there's an old lookout tower near the park. They used it for radio communications and public safety alerts. But, uh, I don't think it's been used since like the 1950s..."

"Well, somebody broke the streak." I state dryly. "Where's the broadcast room?"

"Ugh." Merrick shrugs apologetically. "It could be anywhere in town..."

Welcome to today's needle in a haystack.

Whatever, I could use some fresh air.

"Alright," I mutter to Merrick. "I'm going to go find the lookout tower. If I can, I'll try to radio back to whoever sent that message."

I holster my Icemaker and start toward the stairs. Confusion and all sorts of fun breaks loose. Mr. Nederson shuffles forward, his forehead all knotted up in distress.

"But what if those monsters get in while you're gone? What are we supposed to do?"

"Yeah!" Twinkie Dad heartily chimes in. "Why do *you* have go?"

"Anyone wanna draw straws?" I look at them. "No? Okay then. I'll be back after–"

"Yeah, I do," Merrick interjects.

I scowl impatiently at him. He smiles and raises his eyebrows, silently challenging me.

"I'm just saying you shouldn't go alone," he says. "I volunteer to go with Kyle."

Dang you, Merrick, and your compulsive chivalry.

He ducks behind the bar, emerging a moment later with a handful of neon drinking straws. Everyone gathers around curiously. I pace with my hands on my hips, watching Merrick shuffle the straws. If he draws the short straw, he goes with me. If I draw it, I go alone. But I've got myself a little trick for always drawing the short straw, so I end up drawing it, and that's the end of that.

*

I pause to catch my breath, pressing my back against the ivy-covered patio lattice outside the little French café that I've never eaten at because it's way too honking overpriced.

Alright. The park should be close...just on the other side of this row of shops. I've learned my way around town pretty well, which is how I knew of this access street, a narrow, one-way path that comes out by Gumby's Toys and Hobby shop. There's just one problem.

It's a *toy* shop.

Behind the toy shop's four-paned window, small furry things move around in the dark. They're still teddy bears, heaven help us all.

I pause, narrowing my eyes at the window.

One of them is waving at me. *Waving*, the little demon. And it's holding something in its stumpy paw. Something long and white... I'm just going to assume it's a French fry and not some poor soul's finger. Either way, one nibble and that wicked little bear is going to transform into a giant monster.

I stand there for a minute, rubbing my forehead against the barrel of my Icemaker.

I *could* just plunge in. Run by the shop, gun blazing, and blast those stuffed gremlins. But something about the way those black button eyes are staring at me... It really chills my grill. Almost like they've learned to set a trap...

With a growl, I reluctantly tear myself away from the straight-shot access street and backtrack briskly down the row of shops – but not before pointing my shotgun at the little imp waving at me from the toy shop window. I mimic a firing motion and mutter "boom."

There are narrow alleyways between every four shops or so, just wide enough for back-door trash, like the alley that I dragged my exhausted tail out from Lau Chow's my first night. But most of those alleys are dead ends. Brick walls and padlocked fences.

Hello... Except *that* one.

I halt and jog backward, peering into the alley.

A delivery truck is backed into the narrow passage, its rear roll-up door sitting open like a gaping mouth. There's no way to squeeze around the truck. Its sides are practically inches from the brick walls on each side. Let's hear it for the gutsiest driver in the history of back-alley deliveries.

I drop to a crouch. Can't crawl underneath the truck, either, thanks to the squished cardboard boxes and broken glass littering the ground. Dragging myself across *that* mess, I'd likely kiss my remaining blood supply adios, weakening myself for the critters to sniff me out and come chow on my intestines at their leisure.

A glint of sunlight catches my eye. Inside the truck is a small slide-panel window, connecting the cargo bed to the driver's cab. If I could climb out through the cab...

Tucking my Icemaker into my armpit, my battle axe gripped in one hand, I vault up into the metal truck bed. I'm about halfway in when I feel the truck rumbling under my hands. I jerk my head up just in time to see the truck's roll-up door sliding closed overhead. I try to jump clear, but my boot slips on the truck bed. Crashing onto my stomach, the axe tumbles from my hand, my legs hanging off the back of the truck, the door rattling down at me like a massive guillotine.

An image of a magician sawing a girl in half flickers to mind.

The rumbling door comes crashing to a halt – but nothing chops me in half. I peel one eye open to see what saved me. My battle axe is sitting at the mouth of the truck bed. Amazingly, the heavy steel weapon is propping the roll-up door open, bearing the entire weight on itself.

Well, that was epic.

The truck utters a low, metallic groan. I dive forward, scrambling on my elbows and making an Indiana Jones-worthy grab for my battle axe – but I'm too late. At that moment the axe slips under the weight and topples out of the truck, leaving the door to slam shut. I hear my battle axe clang onto the pavement outside.

For a moment, I just stare at the door like a stunned gopher.

"What the crapfire?!" I yowl.

My attempts to pry the door back open are useless. And I've already established that I can't squeeze under the truck.

Face it. My axe is gone.

A few scattered bread crates lie around the dark truck bed. I punch a few then wriggle myself through the small window into the truck's cab, pausing only to throw a rueful salute to my heroic fallen battle axe before sprinting off down the alley.

*

The park is nestled serenely at the edge of the woods. Swings and interconnecting tube slides glisten beside a small, scenic picnic area, the grass carpeted in yellow leaves and fallen acorns from the surrounding trees. A group of creatures is gathered around one of the picnic tables.

The stench hits me like a roundhouse kick. The creatures smell like a charming mix of sulfur and gas, with just a hint of curry. It's pretty nauseating, even if you like curry.

Their hairy backs rise and fall over the picnic table, occasionally emitting grunts and squeals. I can't see what they're snacking on over there. Frankly, I don't *want* to know.

I narrow my eyes past them. There's the broadcast tower. Beyond the picnic area, at the forest edge, a small shed atop a thirty-foot tall wooden railroad tower is visible over the fiery orange treetops. Affixed to the shed is a rusty speaker shaped like a giant bullhorn, amidst assorted antennae pointing to the sky. That must be my big boy. Now all I have to do is actually *get* to it.

Presently, I've got a picnic table full of bloodthirsty teddy bears sitting smack between me and my goal. I frown at my shotgun's screen. Cluster of red dots. I count six. A good melee weapon sure would come in handy right about now...

Like, say – oh, I don't know – a *battle axe?*

Stupid truck.

There's a small wooden sign near the park entrance. It boasts some historic jargon about how this spot was significant in the Civil War era, and, in larger letters, "Park closes after dark." I yank the sign from the ground and break off the wooden stake, holding it pointy-side up. Slinking low across the playground mulch, I climb silently into the plastic tube slide nearest to the picnic area, stretching out on my belly.

One of them is pink. Most of the creatures are beige or mudskipper brown, but occasionally you'll spot one with dull pink cotton-candy fur mixed in the bunch. Or even rainbow spots. It all depends on what the teddy bear looked like before its evil transformation.

My nose just started running. I don't want risk making my leather jacket creak by reaching to wipe my nose, and goodness knows I don't want to sniff. So I just let it drip. It's dripping on my arm now.

Wildcard hunting at its most glamorous, folks.

At the picnic table, Pinkie suddenly stops munching. It rears back on two legs, taking a big whiff of the air.

My muscles freeze. Pinkie glares at the world for a moment through glinting, beetle-black eyes, then resumes its crunchings and munchings at the picnic table with the others.

What are they eating over there, anyway?

There's a shift of something being slid off the bench, followed by the unmistakable sound of wicker, cracking open upon impact. Picnic baskets. Lovely.

The teddy monsters are having a pic-a-nick.

If I were on a beach right now, thousands of miles away with some coconut drink with a teeny umbrella, I might laugh at this twisted cliché. But I'm not on a beach.

I'm in a frakking tube slide.

Lord, I'm so close I can hear their steaming jaws smacking on peanut butter and jelly sandwiches. The lookout tower isn't far. I could just make a dash for it. But I've only got six shots.

Six creatures.

Six shots.

That's some risky math. I'd have to shoot bang-on perfect, and even if I do, you can bet more critters would hear the hoopla and come crawling out of the woodwork to join the flesh-eating party.

Maybe I can scare them away with my scary no-makeup face. If only. No, there's only one viable strategy here. Sneak across the picnic area and pray to high heaven that they don't notice me.

Holding my breath, I shift my weight in the tube from one hip to the other, one molecule at a time, just enough so I can draw my knee up and begin creeping backward, slowly, out of the slide.

If you've ever been inside a plastic playground slide, there's one little physics lesson that you are now undoubtedly familiar with.

Zap.

The aforementioned frakking tube slide just shocked me.

Outside, the jelly-smacking stops.

I don't know how many times I get zapped in my mad scramble, but by the time I tumble out of the tube onto the mulch, I probably could have taken down the whole bunch of them by shooting lightning bolts from my fingers.

But I run.

The first one blindsides me like a linebacker. The creature's hairy body is as hard as a planet and I actually see stars. For an awful burst of seconds, I flail on the ground against its quill-sharp arm, its rotten-egg stench scorching my nostrils. I'm able to wrestle my Icemaker free from under the creature's stinky bulk; I jam the gun's barrel into its belly and release the throttle. There's a burst of blue light and the creature jerks upright, flailing spastically, spraying foamy filth from its mouth as my weapon curdles its blood into stone. The ugly brute falls onto the mulch, stiff as a dead armadillo in the sun.

Three more critters come galloping across the grass at me. I pop the first two mid-stride, and they hit the ground somersaulting. The third does a mad little duck and two blue blasts sail over its head, but my third blast smacks it square in the kisser. And now I'm officially out of shots.

Squeezing the weapon's throttle and screaming at it to charge faster, I double-back and make for the playground, the last two creatures hot on my heels. The swing rips from my fingertips as I use the chain to clothesline Pinkie, who whips and thrashes, snarling and slobbering and tangling itself up in the chain even tighter. I dart my eyes to the Icemaker's charge gauge.

Fifteen seconds to go…

I wheel around to face the last critter, a hulking brown drool-bucket. My knuckles crack as my left hook connects with the creature's snotty snout, slicing my hand on its snapping razor bushloppers. Lucky for me, the wooden stake is in my other hand. I ram the sharp stake through the creature's temple and take off running for the lookout tower.

I'm at the edge of the woods when Pinkie hammers into me. My feet fly out from under me, my belly hits the ground with enough force to eject every breath I've gulped since arriving at this awful park. Out of the corner of my eye, I glance at my Icemaker. Four seconds left until full-charge. *Four seconds.* That pretty much seals my grisly fate.

Flipping over, I brace my flesh for the needle jaws to sink in.

Imagine my surprise when Pinkie's head pops like a juicy pink grape. Its body goes limp, crashing heavily into the underbrush. The *crack-boom* of the gunshot still rings off the trees. Dazed and breathless, I squint up to see my angel.

His tall gaunt form is bent over me, sprigs of wiry, white hair silhouetted against the bright blue sky in a halo of madness.

It's Old Man Tannon. Armed to the teeth like he's taking on the devil himself, countless rounds of ammo and tactical wilderness pouches slung over his overalls. His face and long sinewy neck are smeared with mud and goodness knows what else.

Tannon works the bolt of his .458 Winchester Magnum rifle, the empty brass round flipping out over the hairy pink mess. He spits on the ground, laughing smugly.

"Trick-or-treat, Boo-Boo."

Seriously, does this town give classes on awesome catchphrases?

Behind him, a small band of townsfolk stand in a cluster over by the trees. Still lying on my back in the grass, I toss a languid wave at them. They snap to attention, smiling and waving back like shell-shocked field mice. I almost laugh.

There's a rustle and a howl across the park. A fresh pack of creatures are pounding over the mulch toward us.

"You gonna just lay there all day like a dead 'coon?" Tannon cocks his mammoth rifle, bellowing at me, "*GO!*"

With an indebted grin, I catapult myself up the lookout tower's wooden steps three at a time. Inside the small shed, a dusty array of amateur radio equipment is tucked under the shelves. There's a radio transceiver with a threshold dial and two sets of lights; yellow, red and green. A lightweight headset, speakers and a packet modem. Piles of wires stacked forgotten in corners like dead snakes. None of which I know what to do with. I should have brought Merrick with me.

Holy guacamole, I'm in trouble.

I let my hands hover over the dials, contemplating what to do next. But I don't touch a daggone thing – because the speaker suddenly blares to life. We all clap our hands over our ears as the voice booms over the trees:

"*Is anyone out there? We're all here... All of us... Everyone... If you're listening... We're at the high school.*"

HIGH SCHOOL REUNION

Getting back to Tuscany Mill was a breeze with Old Man Tannon. Mainly, because he brought his Rambo Mobile.

The old Panhard 178 is fifteen feet long and eight tons of armored can't-touch-this. The heavy turret doesn't work, but the rusted Reibel 7.5 machine gun does just dandy mowing the stuffing out of any critters dumb enough to jump in front of us. It's slow and messy, but who cares. Nothing is penetrating that 20mm bolted hull. The bronze-and-green camo siding is splattered with several nice greasy shades of red, gore splashed all over the "Panhard" factory nose plate, which Tannon has replaced with a "Farm Use Only" plate.

I'm beginning to like this guy more and more.

We only stop once – for me to hop out and retrieve my battle axe from the alley (and only because I threaten to start my menstrual cycle if Tannon doesn't stop).

Everyone gathers in the sun outside Tuscany Mill. Tannon backs his Rambo Mobile right up to the restaurant's patio, its massive armored rear demolishing one of the decorative wooden barrels of begonias. Then he stands off to the side eating dried apricots and surveying us as we start cramming everyone into his vehicle like sardines.

Well, not everyone. Merrick and I aren't riding. We'll be on foot, running alongside as Tannon's wingmen, while Captain Epic brings up the rear. A .22 Hornet rifle is slung across Merrick's shoulders. It hangs awkwardly off his gray hoodie, like some clumsy slab of roadkill. I almost feel sorry for him having to wear it. It may not seem like the most obvious choice, putting a semi-automatic in Merrick's lily-white college boy hands. But I had my reasons. For one, I trust him. This kid will always do the right thing. He's as good as good gets. But let's be honest – in five minutes, we're not going to need him to hold a door for us.

I'm not trying to be a meanie. I just need to know he'll pull the trigger when he has to. And he will.

Stuffing his messenger bag with juice boxes and animal crackers, Merrick calls over to Old Man Tannon. "So how'd you make it all the way from your farm?"

"In the belly of my Pan-Pan," Tannon sniffs. "Naturally."

We all stare at him.

"What?" he barks. "You think I *hiked* into town? No sir, I'da buttered myself with barbecue sauce and rung a dinner bell 'fore I'd do *that.*"

"No, I just mean–" Merrick runs his hand admiringly over the Panhard's rusty siding. "How'd you get this thing to run? It's an antique."

Tannon stands a little straighter in his overalls, a mix of indignation and pride.

"Got my own fuel, of course." He smacks his lips. "Made it m'self. Mixture of jet fuel, gasoline, and my own–"

"Who wants coffee?" Merrick interjects brightly. "Coffee, anyone?"

Mr. Nederson is fretting a little, trying to climb up into the Rambo Mobile. He keeps hiking up his khakis, trying first to step up with his right leg, then his left leg, then back to the right. Poor guy looks like a funny little duck doing a dance.

I offer my hand and help him climb in.

"Much obliged," he bleats appreciatively. "You're a real nice girl. Always helping us."

Yeah, sure.

I saw Mr. Nederson have a heart attack, once. That's how I found out about his heart condition. Of course, since that day technically never happened, he always forgets about it.
But I can't forget.

Clutching my hand, Mr. Nederson wedges himself snugly between the Panhard's 8-speed gear box. Candace cuts her eyes at him. Then she mutters, "If he pees on me, I'm suing the world."

"Hey Candace," Merrick says as he helps her into the vehicle. "You're a cheerleader, right? So, why don't you try spreading a little cheer instead of always clawing everyone's faces like a raging super-witch?"

She glares icily at him.

"Oh, let's see," she snaps back. "*Maybe* because I was supposed to be homecoming queen tonight... Or weren't you aware?" She fakes a pout. "Don't be jealous they won't let you wear the tiara, Merrick."

Merrick puts up his hands in submission and retreats off behind the Panhard.

Lord, I should just tranq the whole bunch of them.

"Merrick has a point," I lean in the doorway toward Candace. "As a cheerleader, you should be used to putting on a smile and lifting people's spirits."

I wink at Jemma, then wrench the hatch shut. It's a sweaty fit. None of us really bothered with delicate things like deodorant today. But that's fine. All these little lambs need to do is make it to the high school alive.

Sweaty or not, here we come.

Tannon starts up the Panhard and the engine roars to life. We all get pumped up in our own way. Captain Epic shouts and slaps himself. Merrick vomits in the flower barrel. I really do feel bad for the kid. He's not cut out for this Sleepy Hollow terminator stuff. But he'll be fine. They'll *all* be fine. Because I've found something more powerful than tranquilizers –

Enthusiasm.

I crack my neck then pump both fists in the air, my Icemaker in one hand, battle axe in the other. "Okay folks, ready to rumble?!"

"Hooah!" Captain Epic answers over the roar.

"Yippee-ki-yay," Merrick gulps weakly.

*

Tannon pilots the Panhard down the center of the street, bashing into cars. Merrick and I jog at either flank, taking potshots at anything with claws. It's like a moving game of whack-a-mole. Or better yet, an Old West arcade shooter.

Bizarrely exhilarating.

Although I doubt Merrick shares my high. I can't see him but every few feet, when we both have to duck and scramble out of the way of Tannon's flying debris. Two things soundtrack our rolling adventure: Over the muddy roar of the Panhard, there's a long, drawn-out screech from Candace – and then there's the Australian song "Down Under" by Men at Work, playing on some renegade car's radio. The bouncy flute echoes through the street with chipper dissonance, random lyrics punched intermittently between our bursts of gunfire. They're singing something about hippies and zombies –

Blam!

Now someone is giving someone else breakfast –

Blam! Blam-plak, boom!

Then a bunch of words rhyming with "under;" "thunder," "chunder"...

Blam-crunch!

Merrick is shouting something, his face covered in soot. "Hey, did you know the flute part in this song is based on a popular Australian children's rhyme?"

"Good to know!" I shout back, even though he probably can't hear me.

We plow forward in our demolition progress. Old Man Tannon hangs out of the hatch and hollers something about a shortcut. None of us protest, because he's Tannon, and he's in a tank. So when he crashes the Panhard through the nail salon and out the other side, none of us are really too surprised.

We finally arrive at the high school under a blood-red sunset. Tannon rolls up onto the school's lawn, leaving deep tire tread marks in the grass.

"Epic victory, everyone!"

Captain Epic sails by, high-fiving me and Merrick and anyone else who's not too jelly-legged to lift their hand. I return his enthused grin, but I won't say what I'm really thinking.

All that squabble we just caused in the street... We should have attracted the attention of every critter within a five-mile radius. But only a handful of garbage-gobblers bothered to show their faces. Heck, I didn't even use up my six shots.

My weary brain is telling me to just shut up and be grateful... But my instinct is whispering that the night's not over yet.

That was too easy.

TEDDY SLAYERS : THE CARNIVAL CREEKE CRAZY 8"

"What's 'chunder' mean?" Jemma asks from the Panhard's hatch. I blink. "Huh?"

"In the song. They said 'men chunder'."

I have no idea. I consider making something up, "to dig up potatoes" or something like that.

"It means to throw up," Merrick says as he lifts Jemma down from the Panhard.

Vocab word of the day, everyone.

The school is secured like a bunker. Men squat on the roof, shouldering farm rifles. Most probably haven't fired a bullet in years, save for chasing some wily fox off their cornfield.

I tilt my head up and look at their faces as we pass under the roof. They peer down at me. I shift awkwardly, trying to angle my body so that it isn't stunningly obvious that I'm carrying a battle axe. It doesn't really help. The wicked butterfly curve of the blade is on proud display over my shoulders. Clearing my throat, I press the button on my Icemaker and it folds into its compact form, making sure they see me slide it back into my pocket.

We're ushered through a side door. Immediately we're prompted to say our names to Gladys, who is flitting around the school lobby with her wrinkled lips pursed, crossing off names on a clipboard. The big glass trophy cabinet has been pushed up against the school's main entrance. There seems to be power in the building, causing everyone in our group to gasp in relief. But judging from the reddish fluorescents dimly lighting the lobby, it's likely the school is using a backup generator. All around, the sharp sound of hammering echoes through the lobby and down the halls. Windows and unnecessary doors are hurriedly being sealed off with planks of wood bearing white painted lettering "Carnival Creeke Drama Department."

Sheriff Gammell greets us in the lobby, followed by a belt-gripping Deputy Scarecrow. Both look sweat-streaked and haggard. A woman stands off in the corner of the lobby. Middle-aged and attractive, she wears a pinstriped business skirt, her pale gold hair spilling in limp waves over her untucked blouse as she mutters important-sounding things to a group of important-looking men. Merrick leans over and whispers to me that the woman is Julie Dove, the school principal.

Dove? Hey, I know that name. She must be Kindly Mustache Sam's wife.

With a handshake, I introduce myself to Deputy Scarecrow and a dubious Sheriff Gammell. My best cheesy-disarming smile usually wins over everyone in Carnival Creeke. But not Gammell. Never Gammell. I've found there's only one thing that gets the sheriff to grudgingly accept me – Merrick. He always vouches for me.

"Kyle's cool, Sheriff," Merrick says casually. "She's actually staying with us. Grandma Cohen just had her surgery, you know. Kyle's here to help."

Sheriff Gammell nods slowly, raising an eyebrow at me. He returns my handshake, but I still feel his silent gaze drilling into me, assessing whether or not I'm the Big Bad Wolf. And the battle axe on my back isn't winning me any trust points.

"Welcome to the party," he grumbles cynically. "Show them around, will you, Joe?"

Gesturing like he's got other things on his mind, Gammell traipses across the lobby toward Principal Dove's group, leaving me and Merrick with Deputy Scarecrow. I explain to him how we came to the school after hearing the broadcast over the lookout tower. Honestly, it's been bugging the heck out of me all day. I'm itching to put a face on that familiar voice. I swear it's on the tip of my tongue...

"So who made the distress call?" I ask the deputy, trying to sound casual.

He just smiles and hands me a Vegamite sandwich.

Just kidding. But how awesome would it be if he did? I'm starving. I seem to burn calories like a forest fire.

Deputy Scarecrow gives me a cockeyed look. "Distress call?" He frowns, shrugging his bowed shoulders. "Well golly, sorry, don't know what to tell you. No one here made no distress call."

Figures.

Carnival Creeke, you continue to give me a headache.

Now that we're standing here safely in the school lobby and bladder function has begun returning to our brains, everyone in my little group has realized they need to pee. Merrick and I do a quick critter sweep of the restrooms, checking each stall. I make my way to the farthest stall, preparing to kick it open. Merrick snickers.

"Remember high school?" he quips. "Nobody uses the far stall, unless you plan on doing something unspeakable."

"Like transform into a cow," I mumble under my breath. Merrick coughs a laugh and shoots me a look.

"Transform into cows?" he says. "Is that like a normal thing on the planet you're from?"

"Don't you?" I deadpan.

Merrick deadpans back, "Only on Tuesdays." He lets the stall door swing shut.

This kid is so much fun.

Suddenly his tone gets serious. "Just so you know," he says. "Back there, when you met Sheriff Gammell... I don't usually lie like that. Lying's not really my thing."

Even though you're really good at it, I want to tease him.

Merrick smiles. "So, I hope at least part of what I said was true."

I flat-out don't know what to tell him. Because the more days go by, the more I suspect that lying *was* Cl. Kyle's "thing." The lies just roll so easily off my tongue, like happy little ice cubes tumbling into sweet tea. I hate that I've fed Merrick stories day after day. I wish I never had to again. But what else can I do? If he's looking for some truthful breadcrumbs about the "real me," I just don't have any to offer. Doesn't matter how much I wish I could. Wish upon a cold, cold star.

I remain silent as I turn on the faucet and start washing the dirt and blood off my hands.

Merrick suddenly breaks into a shy grin, waving it off.

"Ah, it's okay. I know you probably can't blab. Or you'd have to kill me, right?"

We exit the restrooms and everyone files in behind us. Merrick comes alongside me, grinning covertly.

"Okay, okay, don't assassinate me. But I've seen you in action. You're clearly some top-secret superhero. A real-life Catwoman." This earns him an eye-roll from me.

"I'm not a Halloween costume kind of girl."

"C'mon – agile, deadly...Selina...*Kyle?*" When I swat at him he dodges, hopping around to my other side. "Though I'm guessing your first name isn't Selina, huh?"

I stifle a laugh. As if I know my name any better than he does. Then an idea occurs to me. Maybe hearing someone else say it might jog my old memory.

Worth a try...

"Okay Merrick, you want to know my first name?" I don a playful grin. "Take your best shot."

He tilts his head thoughtfully, assessing me, as if my facial features will magically reveal my name.

I smile. "I'll give you a hint. It starts with 'Cl.'"

"Okay, let's see. Claire?"

I cross my arms, shrugging. He tries again.

"Claudia? Clara? Chloe? Wait, no, Chloe isn't 'Cl'..."

His head turns at Sherriff Gammell's shout, beckoning him over across the lobby. Merrick excuses himself like a gentleman and trots over, joining Gammell and taking a tangle of wires from a clueless-looking Deputy Scarecrow.

The hallway bench feels blissful as I plop down. Thanks to my quick-healing superpowers, the slash across my chest is pretty near healed. But nobody needs to know that. They're all freaked out enough as it is; no sense in announcing that I'm a mutant. I carefully rebandage my chest with fresh medical tape from restroom's first aid kit. Best to keep up appearances that I'm normal.

Reclining on the bench, I fish out my compacted Icemaker and consult the screen. Still no red dots. Calm and quiet.

For now, anyway.

I turn my head, gazing idly at the wall. It's been adorned with a painted mascot – a cartoon wolverine, all teeth and claws. Framed in a maroon and orange circle "CARNIVAL CREEKE," the mascot is chomping a bite out of the letter C.

Funny, looking at that snarling cartoon, the first thing that pops into my brain is what those meat-hook claws could do in real life if I turned my back on them.

Sliding off the bench, I rip down a few homecoming flyers and start sticking them back up on the wall, covering up the wolverine until its nasty gnarly teeth are obscured from view.

There. Much better.

I turn the corner to find Merrick doing the same thing in the next hallway. I smile fondly, watching him for a moment. I'm not sure what kind of guys Cl. Kyle used to know, but I've decided Merrick is the best of them.

He looks up, a flyer for guitar lessons in his hand.

"Oh," Merrick drops the flyer sheepishly. "I was just thinking the mascot might scare the kids. I mean, not that teddy bears turning into horrific monsters are nightmare-inducing or anything."

"You're a good man, Charlie Brown." I pop him on the shoulder affectionately and we start heading toward the gymnasium. "Too bad, though," I grin as we round the corner. "Now you won't know what time guitar lessons are."

"I'll survive. Besides, I already play guitar."

"You do?" I look him up and down, trying to picture it.

Yeah, that's right. Merrick did have a surprisingly good singing voice, that night waltzing around my room after narrowly escaping being transformed into a cow.

"You play guitar?" I muse. "I didn't know that about you."

"Why would you?" He laughs, confused.

My boot toe catches and I nearly trip.

"Mm-hm," I manage eloquently.

We swing open the double doors and enter the gymnasium together. From corner to corner, the gym is crowded thick and murmuring with townsfolk of all ages. Randy and his cronies are tossing around a basketball, taking turns shooting hoops. Some people are clutching snacks, boxes of precious Pop Tarts; others with suitcases, like they're waiting for the train to the end of the world. For all they know, they are.

Merrick and I stop in our tracks. Across the gym, above the scoreboard, an enormous, frothing cartoon wolverine has been painted across the entire expanse of the wall.

Merrick and I both look at each other. I shrug and nudge him playfully with my elbow.

"Don't worry about it," I snicker. "It'll grow hair on the kid's chests."

He snorts. "Is that werewolf humor?" We agree to split up and Merrick heads off into the crowd toward Hank, the Jamaican guy in the porkpie hat from the Auto Parts shop. Watching him go, I immediately regret sending him away. I consider calling him back, but I don't. Goodness knows Merrick deserves a little shore leave.

I wander through the milling people. There's Big Kahuna, the husky Hawaiian waiter from Lau Chow's, reclining against the gym wall, fanning himself with a folded-up homecoming flyer. I reckon the poor guy is unemployed now since the gargoyle and I demolished his restaurant. Of course, thanks to the critters, *every* business in Carnival Creeke is now kaput. So maybe I just gave Big Kahuna a mercy head-start. At least that's what I tell myself.

These are good folk. Don't get me wrong, it's not like I'm jumping in the ring to marry this town or anything. But maybe

I've grown accustomed to them. Maybe I'd even miss them if they were suddenly gone.

Like I have any basis for comparison, right?

My 33-day life has consisted of a diet of Carnival Creeke, and nothing else. And sometimes it makes me wonder. What if I lost yesterday, too? I'm talking about the *real* yesterday – "Gargoyle Day," the day Merrick hit me with his truck.

My last real day.

What if all *that* got erased, too? I guess I'd still have a heart. And a future. And a first name. No dislocated shoulder...

And no Merrick.

Do I take it for granted, this bizarre bond between us, so fresh and green and inexperienced each morning, forged on the bumper of his Tahoe?

It occurs to me that although I recognize a lot of these folk, I know almost nothing about them. I've never really asked. Even Merrick. Each day I rope him in, with a bit of guilt for running me over, and a big promise of grand adventures involving monsters and aliens. And yet I couldn't tell you why he chose to study biochemistry. Or his favorite song. Shoot, I didn't even know he plays guitar. Just never seemed relevant to ask.

The citizens of Carnival Creeke, on the other hand, with all their smiley small talk, could probably write a book on me. *If* they could remember me the next day, that is. But they always ask. They always seem to give a hoot. Always seem to care.

Ugh. I'm a slug.

I resolve to spend the next hour meandering the crowd in the gym getting to know these people. I spot Twinkie Dad, sitting cross-legged over by the base of the bleachers. His big shoulders sag, hands slung over his knees. He looks utterly wiped. His little daughter Jemma is sitting on his jacket, playing with a plastic toy horse. I shove my hands in my pockets and trudge over to them.

"Hey, Jemma." I smile. "You like horses, huh?"

She stops making the horse prance around and momentarily slides her eyes up at me. Then she goes back to playing.

Wow. I'm no good at this crap.

Twinkie Dad gives me a wearily apologetic look. "Jemma, you need to use the bathroom?"

She nods. Then the child inexplicably points her finger at me. "Want *her*."

Awkward.

Twinkie Dad immediately starts to apologize.

"It's okay," I wave it off. "I saw the restrooms just around the corner."

I reach for Jemma's hand, but the tiny girl climbs me like a monkey, wrapping her legs around my waist as we push out the single side door from the gym. The hallway is dark, the slick floors reflecting pale light from a single reserve overhead up a short set of stairs. Jemma is clinging to my jacket with both fists. We enter the adjacent hallway. Identical, only flipped – instead of orange, this row of lockers and the walls have been painted maroon, making the hallway appear even darker.

I flip on the restroom light switch. It flickers once, bathing the tiled walls in a weird, synthetic bright green. Once I've tapped open each of four stall doors and I'm satisfied that nothing furry and horrible is lurking in them (especially that last one), I set Jemma down and she trots off to do her thing.

"Uh, do you need any help?" I call from the doorway.

"Nuh-uh." Her little voice echoes from the stall. I lean over the sink, checking out my grimy visage in the mirror. Yikes, Candace wasn't kidding. I look like a wild beast woman.

Raking my hair back into a ponytail, I splash some water on my face from the faucet. It does little to help me look human again. I give up on my decidedly un-ladylike appearance and pace the hallway outside the restroom. Jemma should be finishing up soon.

A muffled thump stops me in my tracks.

There's a Health Ed classroom down the hall. The door is wide open.

Popping my Icemaker open, I tiptoe down the hall and ease into the dark classroom. Rows of half-desks sit empty. A life-sized skeleton grins plastically behind a potted spider plant at the room's far end.

Again comes the noise. I jerk my head immediately toward the source. Seems to be coming from the corner shelf.

A twitchy, muffled scuffling sound…

Using the barrel of my Icemaker, I whack aside a plastic transparent model of the human heart to reveal a teddy bear sitting on the shelf. Swinging its stumpy legs, its tiny demonic eyes glittering at me. Grimacing, I snatch the bear off the shelf. Dang thing wriggles and squirms in my hand. The bear's plush fur is green and orange striped, probably somebody's Halloween toy. I'm contemplating yoinking its little head off when Jemma's voice comes from the doorway.

"I'm all done." She cocks her head at me. "What're you doing?"

"Uh."

Just holding a teddy at gunpoint.

I slide open the teacher's desk drawer, patting my hand all around inside to make sure it's empty, lest it be harboring a stash of Snickers or other potential monster chow. I'm firmly *not* wanting to see what this teddy looks like as a drooling, green and orange striped Halloween hulk-beast. I toss the bear into the drawer, then lock it. We can hear the little creature shuffling around inside, although neither of us wants to mention it.

"Did you wash your hands?" I ask Jemma.

She shrugs. "There wasn't any soap."

We use a few pumps from the sanitizer gel dispenser on the classroom wall, then head back to the comforting commotion and bright fluorescents of the gymnasium. Twinkie Dad tries again to apologize as I pass Jemma to him. She's all sleepy and melty on my shoulder; I have to gently slide her off like a warm cookie sheet.

"It's no biggie," I tell him. "Really."

Twinkie Dad spreads his jacket on the floor and sits down, holding his daughter in his lap. He lets out a slow sigh, raising his eyes to me.

"Jemma's momma ain't around anymore," he says. "I try to do the tea parties and kiss every stuffed animal she sends my way. But...there's only so much daddy can do, you know? It's like she's already a teenager, looking up at me. Scares the wits outta me." He pauses, wiping a hand across his face. "Aw, you're just a kid yourself. You don't need my rainclouds."

"I don't mind."

"You're good with her, though – Jemma. You like kids?"

"Sure, I've got three under my bed," I joke, then try not to cringe hearing myself.

Geez Louise, what's wrong with me? I should just cash in my chips and walk away right now. My bones ache and I really need to go off by myself and do some heavy thinking.
Wildcard thinking.

"Listen," I say gently. "There's only so much one parent can do. And you're doing it. Period. If Jemma was with her mom instead, I'm sure she'd still go to sleep dreaming of her daddy. Just like she's doing right now."

He looks down at his daughter, snoozing against his chest.

"Thanks."

"You'll be fine."

I slink to the top of the bleachers and lean my battle axe against the wall, then cover it with my leather jacket. Surprising how cold I feel without Jemma monkey'd on me.

Discreetly, I pull down the collar of my shirt. The gash across my chest is completely healed up, so I peel off the old rubber cement. Hugging my Icemaker to my ribs, I wedge myself down between two metal bleachers, stretching out lengthwise. I try to organize my thoughts.

I'm starting to get antsy. And it's not just that doggone mystery voice from the lookout tower...

The creatures. These endlessly multiplying monsters. Even if I had a week and I hustled my butt off, I probably still couldn't make a dent in the critter population. I'm trying. But I'm no superhero. I think of Tannon's camo-smeared face, and seriously consider asking him to call in an air strike with those vintage missiles we're all sure he's squirreling away down in his basement. Just bomb the whole town to smithereens, along with every critter in it. Okay, so there are obvious problems with that solution.

I have to face the facts. Can't wiggle my way out with excuses. The truth has become glaringly apparent, staring me so hard in the face that I can practically feel its breath.

*This wildcard has gotten **way** out of my hands.*

There. I said it.

And I don't need to see the library clock to be reminded that I'm running out of time. My pulse has been replaced by the ticking of that wretched clock; its cold, calculated face ticking down the seconds, heedless of us squirming around in our mortality in the streets below.

One o'clock.

I'm forced to feel the weight of a new question, one I've never really yet had to face...

What if I can't fix it this time?

What if I can't neutralize the wildcard?

Stupid question, Kyle. You *know* what happens. One o'clock rolls around, and it stays like this forever. It sticks.

They eat. We burn.

Game over.

I don't have a freaking clue how to get rid of these filthy critters.

I don't know what to do.

I flip-flop around, trying futilely to get comfortable on the hard metal bleacher. It's not happening. It's like these seats were made for the sole purpose of preventing people from being comfortable.

*

I guess I must have dozed off at some point, because I jolt awake, bumping my nose against the bleacher in front of me.

People are still milling around the gym; some settling into sleeping bags or stretching out on the bleachers like me, using their jackets or someone's lap as pillows. Conversation muttered

in low, scattered voices. No craziness, nothing out of the
ordinary.

So, what the heck woke me?

Merrick is climbing up the bleachers. He's being quiet, but I
must have felt the metal rattle under my ear. He slides his rifle
and bag off his shoulder, then crouches to a sitting position on
the next bleacher below mine. I've kept my eyes shut; I'm not
even sure why. But he must think I'm asleep. After a minute,
Merrick speaks in a low voice.

"Hey...Kyle?" There's a pause, then he continues softly. "Okay,
you're sleeping. I'm glad. You deserve it. Plus, it makes this easier
on me." He hesitates again. "Kyle, I've gotta tell you something."

I'm frozen.

Why am I suddenly so nervous? What is it that I'm expecting
him to say?

Most of all, why am I wanting so badly for him to say it?

Keeping my eyes closed, I hear Merrick draw a slow,
quavering breath.

"I'm kinda glad you jumped out in front of my truck
yesterday." He laughs quietly. "Sounds crazy, right? Feels like
ages ago. Another me ago. But if I'm honest with myself... Well,
here goes." His voice is so soft I can barely hear him. "Kyle, I..."

My throat goes dry, and I feel my cheeks flare hot.

The piercing feedback echoes suddenly through the
gymnasium, prompting people all over to groan and sit up from
sleeping bags, looking around with confused expressions and

rumpled sleeping-bag hair. Tannon's twitchy whisper booms over the gym loudspeaker.

"Testing? Yes...ahem. Would Merrick Cohen and Kyle please report to the principal's office immediately!"

TOOTH AND CLAW

Sheriff Gammell, Deputy Scarecrow and Julie Dove are all waiting for us in her office. They're peering out the window blinds, their faces as grave as death eating a cracker. Old Man Tannon is slinking around the room, unscrewing all the light bulbs and shaking the filaments to his ear.

My gaze drifts to a switchboard in the corner of the room. A swivel chair is tucked under the desk, a pair of old padded headphones hung over a microphone.

I narrow my eyes passionately at the board. Whoever made that distress call sat right here, in secret. That familiar voice...

Then it hits me like a ton of bricks.

That softened "a" sound, and how the long "I" became slightly curled into "oi"... Although at first I thought the speaker sounded American, his gentle vowels couldn't completely mask the distinct marks of an Irish accent.

It was Holliday.

Oh, that son of a monkey.

My fingers tighten involuntarily on the switchboard dials. I can almost feel his hands...

"Uh, Kyle?" Merrick clears his throat softly. "You okay there?"

They're all staring at me. Great.

I blink, shaking off the heebie-jeebies. "Yep, present."

"Good," Sheriff Gammell cocks an eyebrow and grabs a heavy Maglite flashlight from the desk. "Because we've got ourselves a problem."

*

We follow him down the hallway to the cafeteria, bunching together in the doorway as we peek in.

The cafeteria is dark. Squares of moonlight gleam across the empty rows of lunch tables, the ceiling all decked out in tinsel streamers for homecoming. Clusters of maroon and orange balloons are twirled around the support columns. Across the cafeteria, we have a clear view through the open door into the kitchen.

We hear the clanking before we see it.

A creature, rooting noisily through the metal kitchen cabinets. A stack of plastic lunch trays slides off the counter, clattering to the tiled floor, and the monster emerges, gnawing a frozen gray slab of Steak-Umm. With one razored hand, it pops open a plastic container of coleslaw like a coconut. I grimace, nearly turning away. That's just awful.

Coleslaw is ghastly stuff.

Aiming my gun, I shoot the critter and it drops its Steak-Umm where it stands. I turn back to Gammell and the others.

"Okay, so, do we know how the Hamburglar over there got into the building?"

"Well," Deputy Scarecrow clears his throat, his voice tense and shrill. "We could reckon it was just some lil' stuffed teddy, already inside the school... Right?" He looks hopefully at us, awaiting agreement. "Sniffed its way here to the food?"

He doesn't want to acknowledge the alternative.

Behind the creature, the kitchen's back door is wide open, propped with a crate of empty cartons. Probably some bozo taking out the trash, then got distracted and forgot to shut the door. Or maybe they got eaten.

Deputy Scarecrow bounds across the cafeteria and bats the kitchen door shut; he rejoins us, his nostrils flaring importantly. But the damage is done. Whoever left that door open has sealed our fate. It's only a matter of time before every critter in Carnival Creeke comes crawling out of the woodwork for a taste of this all-night buffet.

This school is now a sinking ship.

And we're going to have to jump.

*

I climb onto the school roof, one hand on the AC unit to steady myself. Crisp night wind slides over my bloodstained face as I survey our surroundings. The moon is a bright coin. Ropy, fibrous power lines and the domed head of the water tower are silhouetted against the faint purple horizon. Tiny scattered fires flicker in the distance, peppering the dark town below, winking pockets of activity that echo and howl like a river of nightmares.

Whether it's creatures or the wind howling through the houses...
Who knows. I just hope it's not people.

My eyes flicker down to my shotgun's screen. Still no red. Just
the one gray dot, the grave marker of that doofy Hamburglar that
I shot down in the cafeteria.

Calm as a park on Saturday night.

Something feels wrong. Critters should be crawling on us like
white on rice by now. Where *are* they? It's unraveling my nerves.
Like something bad is fixing to happen...

Below I can make out the outlines of school buses, parked in
neat rows along the shadowy back edge of the parking lot.

Eight buses.

Five-hundred souls to evacuate.

And three hours until one o'clock.

This situation should scare me spitless, but it doesn't. Even
though I'm aware of the terror flopping around inside me like a
suffocating fish, I refuse to feel it right now. I've shut that lid.

These creatures... They're just numbers.

This wildcard exists for no purpose but for me to beat it.

Suddenly, something else in the parking lot catches my eye.
Something big.

An enormous beast's head, looming motionless above the
buses. Its black eyes are the size of dinner plates, a wide,
cavernous mouth hangs open, frozen in a yawning snarl so huge
that you could drive a car through it. Rows of white teeth glow in
the moonlight.

A jolt of alarm stabs through me, because for a second, I think I'm looking at some gigantic mutant emperor creature. But staring at the motionless monster, I recognize the other dark shapes parked at its base. Trucks and flatbed wagons, adorned with balloons and streamers. And the paper mâché wolverine.

With a loopy smile, I relax my hand on my Icemaker.

They're homecoming floats.

Maybe we can't cram *everyone* into eight buses...

But we just might give Queen Candace her homecoming parade after all.

"I think I've got a crazy idea," I mutter out loud.

"Right with you." Sheriff Gammell's gravelly grumble comes from the roof beside me. Good thing I don't startle easily, or I might've shot him in the face. How that man keeps managing to sneak up on me is a quandary for another day.

Deputy Scarecrow pops up at Gammell's other side.

"What? You thinkin' we ride all them folk outta here on those frilly floats?" He shakes his orange head. "This ain't no hayride, Frank."

Merrick shrugs. "It's a good idea."

"*All* those people?" Tannon snorts. "Gonna be like stretching a gnat's butthole over a washtub."

"Then get busy stretching some gnat buttholes." Sheriff Gammell heads back to the ladder. "I've got a gym full of people to break the news to."

I smile grimly at the four men.

Looks like I won't be alone.

*

Merrick, Deputy Scarecrow, Old Man Tannon and I skitter across the parking lot like possums, splitting up and darting down the rows of buses. I don't know why we're bothering to tiptoe around. We're about to make a literal truckload of noise.

The walkie-talkie at my hip crackles.

Gammell's voice is low, barely static forming words. Down the rows of buses I hear his hushed growl duplicated on everyone else's radios, creating an echo effect.

"Everyone listen up, because I'm going to say this quick. I want you each to start your bus. If the radio's on, turn it off. No headlights or flashers." He pauses. *"You'll notice I left my big red clown nose at home...so I'm not up for any funny business."*

I know he's talking to me.

"Hook up those floats, shut off the ignition, and leave the key in. Then you get your flaming fannies back into the school as quick as possible."

We all nod in our respective dark.

I take bus 118. The dark cab smells like stale cigars and egg salad. I insert the key into the ignition and hold my breath. Using two fingers I turn the key, very gently, as if it might make it start quietly. The plasticky leather seat vibrates under my butt as the bus's diesel engine rumbles awake. Twisting around, I roll the massive vehicle in reverse until I see a float behind me, illuminated by the bus's red brake lights. The hay wagon is

282

decorated in a cemetery scene, its foam tombstones spray-
painted with *"R.I.P. Pine Valley rivals."* An arch of maroon and
orange balloons stretches over the wagon.

My radio lets out a sharp squawk.

"Float one attached," reports Deputy Scarecrow, whispering
each word slowly and clearly.

Man, he's fast. Must have wings on his loafers.

I shut off the ignition and slink around to my bus's rear
bumper, holding my Icemaker between my knees so I can keep
one eye on the screen. Heady diesel fumes still linger in the air. I
start fumbling the bus's heavy chain through the wagon's tow
hitch. A lanky shape trots by, flashing briefly between the rows of
buses. Deputy Scarecrow, bearing his task like he's carrying the
world on his shoulders, as usual.

Look at them all. Listening to me, going through all this
trouble, following my half-cocked plan. This might not even
work. Maybe we get everyone outside, pack the buses, cram
them onto these floats. What if we still can't fit everyone...?

Then what, genius?

My fingers hesitate on the chain.

I can see Merrick's crouched shape at the next bus, chain
clinking as he works the hitch. His head turns and notices me.

"We're breaking so many safety regulations," he hisses in a
loud whisper. I can't quite muster a laugh, but my frazzled nerves
actually relax a hair. Gotta hand it to him, Merrick is the only
force on this earth capable of calming my butterflies.

Suddenly from inside the school, a high-pitched, piercing bell sound shatters the silent night, along with my no-longer-relaxed nerves.

The fire alarm.

I jerk my eyes down to my Icemaker's screen – and there they are.

Red dots, flowing steadily inward from all sides.

They're here.

The streams of red dots narrow in certain spots, like an hourglass – places where the creatures must be forced to funnel through doorways single-file – then turning in sharp angles and snaking down the hallways, toward the screen's center.

This is what I've been waiting for all night.

We collide with Sheriff Gammell outside the gym, Principal Dove clutching her ears behind him, her gold hair still miraculously glossy despite being mussed. They lock into a panicked huddle and shout a bunch about Plan B, and Plan C, and Plan Z. Not that we can hear each other, anyway. Now that we're inside the building, the fire alarm is deafening.

Let them shout. I turn aside, analyzing my screen. All those streaming lines of red dots... This school is filling up like an anthill under water. Snarling, hot death is coming at us from all sides. Sealing off all our exits.

Then I see it. There's one clear area on my screen, completely free of red dots, near the lower left-hand corner of the screen. Our last escape route.

Our last hope.

I jab my finger at the clear spot.

"What's down there?" I demand over the screeching alarm.

"The weight room," Julie Dove answers, wearing a questioning frown.

Boys and girls, meet our escape route.

*

A murmuring line of people has already formed in the hallways. I wonder what Gammell said to them. Once again, I'm struck by this town's admirable ability to suck it together and follow his civilized order, even under supernatural peril.

The fire alarm cuts off abruptly. Shifting, anxious faces flicker under the dim, red emergency light as I jog the up the hall the opposite direction of the line, a lone fish swimming upstream. I pass a pregnant woman, gasping, two other gals on either side supporting her by the elbows, practically dragging her along. Poor thing looks like she's literally going into labor. Wow, that sucks. Of all the nights.

I reach the last person in line, a teenage girl wearing a safety-pinned denim jacket and black ballet slippers. I glance up the dark hallway, then back at the girl.

"Everyone out up here?"

"Well, um, no actually..." Her face knots up, chewing her bottom lip. "There's a boy."

I stop. "What boy?"

She shakes her head, frowning up the gloomy hall.

"I dunno. I didn't recognize him. He's like a goth or something. Black curly hair, leather jacket...really pale..."

My bones freeze.

It can't be...

"This is very important, okay?" I grab her shoulders. "Where did he go?"

"Just up there. By the science lab. He's not a high schooler. He was–" She blushes, biting her lip. "Kinda hardcore gorgeous."

Gritting my jaw, I let go of her and catapult down the hall.

Holliday. It *has* to be him.

First that radio distress broadcast... Now he's slithering his game into my own playing field.

But why come here? Testing me?

Teasing me...?

I skid to a halt, the squeal of my boots echoing on the floor. Panting, my gaze darts around the empty science lab. There's no one here. *I* shouldn't be here. There's no time.

On my hip, my radio squawks.

"*Kyle, where the heck are you?*" Merrick's voice sounds freaked through the static. "*We're at the weight room...*"

I throw my eyes longingly down the dark hallway, my soul being torn in two directions.

Not this time... Not yet.

I have to choose these people over you, Holliday.

My heart will have to wait.

Turning on my heel, I run back down the hall.

286

*

The weight room is crowded from wall to concrete wall, dark as a dungeon. Incline benches and rack equipment might as well be torture devices in this nightmare. Twinkie Dad squeezes by me, nothing in his hands but Jemma. Taking a metal baseball bat from the locker, I catch Twinkie Dad. He looks at the bat, puzzled, as I tuck it into his hand.

"What's this for?"

"Insurance," I give him a wink and trot off.

Merrick, Tannon and I run ahead and bust open the weight room door into the cold night air.

We're on the far side of the school building. Rows of buses sit in lines around the parking lot, their boxy orange butts visible in the dark just beyond a fenced-in tennis court.

"Get everyone to those buses!"

We prop the door open with an eighty-pound weight disc as people start pouring out. Merrick is behind me, his back against the brick wall. From the other side of the door, Tannon flashes me a wild-eyed laugh through the passing bodies. "Hot damn!" he hoots. "Haven't felt this alive since 'Nam!"

Okay buddy, you just keep feeling alive over there.

I lean my head back to Merrick. "He's genuinely insane, isn't he?"

"Certifiably," Merrick shouts back.

I give Tannon my most winning grin and shoot him a thumbs-up. Merrick and I unlatch the chain-link fence encircling the tennis court, and people start filing onto the green pavement. Directly opposite the court is another gate, leading out to the parking lot where the buses await; nothing but dark woods beyond.

I jog across the court ahead of the crowd and press the button on my radio. "Gammell," I bark. "I'm taking them to the parking lot now."

I'm reaching for the latch on the gate when I happen to glance down at my shotgun – and for a second, I think the screen must be fritzing out.

Red.

So much red, in fact, that individual dots are now indistinguishable. Seething blobs of red quiver from all four corners of my screen, closing in until only one tiny, dark square remains in the screen's center.

That's us.

Holy cats…

My eyes jump up to meet the first creature as it bursts out of the inky woods. It's followed instantly by a heart-sinking wave of them, their hairy palms pounding across the asphalt toward us. I slam the gate latch back down, staggering backward and sprinting back across the tennis court. In a matter of minutes, this cage-like space has filled with people. I jostle my hand up and scream into the radio.

"Sheriff, listen to me! We're locked in the tennis court! They've shut off our way to the buses–" I pant, closing my eyes. "And everything else."

We're surrounded.

"Don't come out here, you hear me?" I beg him. "Everyone that's left – shut the doors and keep everyone inside that weight room."

"Already done," comes his quiet reply.

Through the crowd, I meet Merrick's desperate look as Tannon practically yanks the last stragglers into the tennis court by their ears. Merrick dives on the gate latch, locking us in. Trapped like mice in a cage.

A wall of hairy bodies surrounds us. Everywhere I look, jaws snap and slash, rattling the fence, the creatures half-mad at the scent of our sweet meat, so close and yet out of reach. Whining and baying, thousands of black scarab eyes burn at us through the chain links. The stench is overpowering, that rotten-sweet reek, like a gas stove scorching a pot of curry. I'd make a joke about the stench, the funk of forty-thousand years... But the truth is, you don't find yourself with much humor when grisly doom actually is closing in on you.

Everyone presses in, one roiling, terrified, compacted mass, the people on the outer edges closest to the fence trying to shrink themselves as thin as possible. A sea of unintelligible jabbering mixes with panicked shrieks. I want to scream at all of them. For following me here. For trusting me...

My mind cycles frantically, but any shred of an idea seems stupid and fruitless and only would have worked five minutes ago. Our options have expired.

"Game over!" Merrick wails.

Maybe he's right.

I kick the fence, raising my Icemaker on them all.

Then it happens. Off in the corner of my eye, from the edge of the tennis court, someone tosses a tiny firecracker over the fence. Just a little pocket-size thing; the shape of a hornet, small enough to fit in someone's pocket. A firecracker small enough to sneak into the homecoming football game that was supposed to happen tonight, a firecracker just feisty enough to cause a mini riot, to ruffle some authority figure's feathers without actually hurting anybody.

The tiny hornet bounces on the pavement, emitting a whistle and farting pretty purple and gold sparks under the shuffling paws of a creature.

Then the creature explodes.

For one stunned moment, I swear you could hear a pin drop. But there aren't any pins. Just the wet slapping sound of smoking wereteddy meat raining down.

And that's when we discovered the critters are explosive.

I remember their smell – that gassy, rotten-egg stench seeping from their pores – and suddenly it all makes sense. All the hopelessness of five seconds ago just did a wild pendulum swing. The crowd shifts, and I see Randy, whooping victoriously with his band of cronies, a smug not-sure-if-I-did-something-naughty grin spreading under his shaggy bangs.

I could laugh.

"What the blue blazes is going on out there?" Gammell's growl bursts out my radio. *"Talk to me-"*

I rip off my walkie-talkie.

"Sheriff, just hang tight!" I shout over the uproar. "I think Randy just found us a way out of here."

Merrick is jostling through the crowd toward me. He reaches out and snatches a box of Jell-O pudding mix from a bewildered man's backpack. I frown. Either Merrick has chosen the most inappropriate time to whip up a tasty chocolate dessert for us all, or he's totally lost his nerd mind.

"Listen, listen, listen," he's jabbering breathlessly. "Sucrose particles have a high ratio of surface area to volume! If burning particles in the air mix with combustible gas, the sudden increase of pressure might knock it within appropriate flammable limits–"

"In English, Cohen?"

"What I'm saying," he gasps, ripping the top off the Jell-O box. "Ever seen a campfire marshmallow burn?"

It doesn't matter whether Cl. Kyle has ever toasted marshmallows. We all hold our collective breath as Merrick flips open a Memphis barbecue zippo, lighting the strip of cardboard on fire.

"Stand back," he orders. He hurls the Jell-O box over the fence like a grenade, a streaming cloud of chocolate powder trailing behind it. Then he flicks the flaming cardboard strip into it. There's a *whoosh* as the fire flashes through the sugary cloud, burning it up in an instant.

But the real fireworks are the creatures themselves.

All the surrounding monsters ignite and burst like ripe melons, the force of their exploding bodies enough to trigger a bunch of nearby critters to pop, one after another. A stench of burnt curry fills the air.

He made a bomb.

The crowd erupts into cheers. Merrick and I exchange a stunned grin before turning our eye contact across the court toward Tannon.

"Everyone to the buses!!"

Taking a deep breath, I throw the gate open.

Chaos. Plunging chaos.

People tumble out of the tennis court enclosure and begin streaking toward the parking lot, where the buses sit ready in the moonlight, waiting like patient chauffeurs, the floats attached behind them. Seething hordes of wereteddies lunge at us from all sides, their savage jaws snapping. All around is the thundering sound of bodies shoving and slamming against each other, the deafening clatter of thousands of claws clacking over pavement, filling our ears like a primeval rain. Hacking left and right with my battle axe, I'm firing off a rapid rip of blue blasts when I realize Tannon is nowhere to be seen. My jaw clenches.

That man is slipperier than snot on a doorknob...

But there's no time to cry about that now.

We're almost to the buses.

Merrick's rifle is ringing in sharp pops beside me; I'm downright proud he's still holding onto the weapon. Out of the corner of my eye I see him shove a frozen screaming teen girl down by the head, saving her from a nasty end. Twisting around, I spin my Icemaker by the cocking lever loop and blast a reddish creature lunging for his left ribs. When I face forward again, I find I'm running right up behind another creature, galloping on all fours the same direction as us. It stumbles; I can't stop mid-stride and end up hopscotching over its mountainous hulking back, dodging its four-foot spine barbs as I somersault forward over the beast's head and onto the pavement. The monster dives on me, madder than a wet hornet. I jerk my Icemaker's sawed-off barrel up into its frothing, tangled mouth and release the throttle.

But my charge pack is dry.

How did I end up in this situation twice today? And there's crazy Rambo Tannon to save me this time. Or Merrick, who's running up ahead and also just ran out of ammo, judging from the look of puzzled horror that he just gave his rifle. My axe is lying on the pavement, a few feet away, where it got flung. So unless I can use the Force and magically suction that axe back into my hand, I'm toast. *And jam,* my brain adds wryly.

Oh, you mean that gooey red stuff?

It's coming in a second...

I'm just as surprised as the creature when it's suddenly smacked nose-up, clobbered upside the snout, spattering my face with heavy threads of drool. I cough a grin and look up at Twinkie Dad, who's standing over me. He's looking pretty dazed himself, baseball bat still poised in the air, a saucer-eyed Jemma clinging to his back like a squirrel.

"Whew," Twinkie Dad breathes, exhilarated. He extends a hand to help me up.

"Batter up, baby!" I almost laugh. "I owe you one."

He yells, "Like hell! Now we're even!"

As soon as I've snatched up my axe, I'm running alongside Twinkie Dad, Jemma bouncing on his shoulder as he sprints in long strides across the parking lot. Through the frenzied obstacle course of people, we make like the wind toward the nearest bus, which is hitched to the wagon float with the giant Grim Reaper on it. Merrick actually exhales a moan of relief. We reach for the bus's accordion doors to pull them open.

But the doors are already open.

A creature bursts out like a demon jack-in-the-bus. Jemma screams. In the bright moonlight, I see the beast's fur. Green and orange stripes. It's that little punk from the Health Ed room.

And if that gnarled leer is any indication, I'd swear Stripey recognizes *me*, too.

"IT'S THAT LITTLE PUNK FROM THE HEALTH ED ROOM."

FOY DAVIS - CARNIVAL CREEKE

Well, guess what? My Icemaker is fully charged now. And I've had it up to my ever-loving neck with these filthy critters.

I flip open Merrick's zippo lighter and hold it in front of my Icemaker, firing a shot into the flame. The blue blast ignites, morphing into a fireball that hits the creature point-blank in the face. Stripey explodes in a cloud of chunky salsa.

Beside me, Jemma's jaw drops.

She squeaks, "I think I'm gonna chunder."

"Me too," Merrick utters.

We hastily pick our way through the green and orange entrails splattered across the door and climb aboard the bus. We're joined by a woman in jogging pants and a man wearing silk pajamas and a cowboy hat. They get belted in as I drop into the driver's seat, tossing my axe into the seat behind me and cranking the key in the ignition. The diesel engine rumbles to life.

"Gammell, we've got the buses," I shout into the radio. "You get everyone ready to jump, you understand?" The bus gears whine as I jam the clutch. I chuck the radio onto the dashboard after screaming into it, "*We're* coming to *you!*"

Sheriff Gammell bursts out of the weight room door just as I scrape the bus against the curb, his firearm pointing at the sky, face purple from shouting. A flood of people pours from the school and clamors noisily into our bus, packing three and four to a seat as Merrick and Twinkie Dad do their best to direct the madness. Across the parking lot, the other buses are starting up, each with their own frantic torrent of passengers. I have no idea who's driving those other buses now, but some of them have accidentally turned on their flashers (and one poor bozo just swung open their bus's stop sign). But it really doesn't matter in Crazytown.

In my convex mirror, I see people scrambling up onto our Grim Reaper float wagon.

"Hope you're holding on tight," I mutter under my breath as I yank the lever. The accordion doors close with a hiss.

My bus lurches forward, about as agile as an ogre swinging a telephone pole. Massive hairy bodies thud off the windows, claws scraping across the bus's hood. I'm doing donuts and they're sliding off, but we can't keep lollygagging around this parking lot forever. A shadowy swarm of critters is gathering between the pine trees that mark the parking lot's exit, forming a barricade. Even at full speed, there's no way I'm ramming the bus through that living wall, especially not with a homecoming float full of people.

I'm wheeling the bus around for its third circle when the Panhard suddenly roars out onto the parking lot, its Reibel machine gun strobing like a big camo angel of hope. Everyone cheers. Several buses stop their frantic zigzagging and immediately charge for the parking lot's exit, Tannon leading the way in a blaze of glory.

"*Evening, boys and girls!*" Tannon's voice rasps over mine and Merrick's radios. "*If you will kindly proceed to the exit so we can blow this popsicle stand...*"

Gammell's gravelly voice crackles in response.

"*Nice to see you, Emmett. We'll follow you to the bridge.*"

So Gammell is still alive. Internally, I smile.

We swerve around the debris-cluttered street. Behind me Merrick hollers, "Punch it, Kyle!"

I've got the pedal to the floor. But of course, the school bus is equipped with a speed regulator. This boat can't go over fifty miles per hour. Merrick looks over, his green eyes wide.

"Uh, more...punchy?"

"Regulator," I growl. "Merrick, take the wheel." Then I hesitate. "You *sure* you can see okay without your glasses?"

"Yeah, well um, I can't read that sign over there, but it's dark and I'm sure night vision is a factor that plays into–"

"Okay, okay, super."

We squeeze past each other in the aisle. Using the butt of my shotgun, I punch out the safety glass and hang my upper body out of the rear window. A bracing cold rush of air peels at my face, making my eyes sting.

FYI, forty miles per hour feels a heck of a lot faster with your head out the window.

I blink away the croc tears until my eyes adjust. In front and behind us, an orange caravan of buses weaves around the road, hordes of creatures loping alongside us. We're just barely outrunning them... Barely.

I extend my arm, taking aim with my Icemaker. The bus lurches beneath me, the windowsill bashing me in the ribcage.

"Sorry, crap, sorry!" Merrick moans through clenched teeth from the driver's seat.

"You're doing fine, kiddo," I assure him, ignoring my bruised ribs.

Fighting to keep my shotgun steady amidst the bus's herky-jerky movement, I pick off the nearest critters, the ones trying to jump up and sink their meat-hooks into the float's wagon siding. Our passengers are fighting back, too, kicking the intruders in the teeth as they scramble away. Dark streetlamps and busted windows flash by.

Merrick takes a corner on two wheels; the float fishtails behind us, folk clinging onto the paper mâché for dear life. The Grim Reaper's head falls off, exposing chicken wire and toppling a bunch of critters climbing up over the back of the float. They go sprawling off like bowling pins into the distant road, the Reaper's enormous white skull head rolling off into a cornfield. It's a pretty epic sight. Add that to my list of "things you don't see every day."

I'm out of shots now, anyway.

We speed toward the bridge. Eight pairs of headlights spill out over the hill, revealing the covered bridge. A heavy mist hangs over the dark creek below. We don't hit the brakes. Plunging into the wooden tube like a cannonball, we're thrust momentarily into darkness, the trundle planks under the tires rattling our teeth and tossing everyone a foot off their seats, until we rocket out of the bridge's mouth on the other side of the creek in a cloud of dust.

Once we're clear, I thrust my head back out the window. Cold air rips through my nostrils. Up in the distance, the dark windows of the Red Rooster cottage are reflecting our headlights; beside it, the gas station's floodlights shining like a highway beacon. Wind whips at me, my brain working a mile a minute.

There's no edge of Carnival Creeke.

I've tried.

Oh, you better believe I've tried to leave this town. But it just keeps going and going, that endlessly stretching road.

I swallow hard.

It ends here, or not at all.

Lunging over Merrick's lap, I grab my radio from the dashboard, jamming the setting to "All-Call."

"Sheriff Gammell, Tannon, pull over. *Everyone* pull over!"

"Is this a joke, young lady?"

Oh land sakes, I hope not. I left my clown nose at home, too.

"Just listen to me," I shout. "Everyone needs to *stop their buses*. Please, Gammell, if you've ever trusted me…"

Which is never. But he obeys. They all do, careening their buses into a helter-skelter line at the shoulder of the road, kicking up a massive pillar of dust. We're right in front of the gas station. When Merrick twists around his seat to look at me, his face is full of panicked "now what." They're all giving me that look. Staring at the crazy girl.

Waiting to see why I've lined them up for the slaughter.

I jump off the bus and stand on the dotted line in the middle of the road. Hordes of bloodthirsty creatures pound the pavement – hundreds, no, thousands of them, as far as the eye can see – the front row only fifty yards away and closing fast. A roaring multitude of death is bearing down on us like a tidal wave. I glance at my watch. Twenty minutes to one.

Turning around, I hear myself order everyone off the bus. They're tentative at first, but I wave my battle axe like the nutcase they all think I am, and they hastily scoot out into the street. Alone now, I pounce back into the driver's seat and rev the bus right up to the gas pump.

I wonder if I'm being judged. My performance, each day...
Are you watching, Holliday?

With trembling fingers, I remove the nozzle from the gas pump and use my axe to hack through the rubbery hose. With the dispenser pump severed, the noxious liquid flows freely. I guess this is a plan. I hope to high heaven it's a plan.

I'm on autopilot now.

I spray gasoline into the driver's seat. Down the bus aisle. Drench the hood and roof. Then I drop the hose and leave it gurgling onto the pavement.

The tidal wave of creatures is almost on top of us, so close we can hear the deafening clatter of their disgusting claws.

The battle cry of a wildcard that got way too big for its britches.

Well, when life hands you lemons…

You blow stuff up.

I flip open the Memphis barbecue zippo and toss it into our gasoline-soaked bus. I watch just long enough to see the lighter hit the driver's seat, see the bus engulfed in white-orange flames. But that's the last glance I steal over my shoulder. I'm in full-on harebrained dash away mode when the Quik-Pump gas station goes ka-boom. The force of the blast wallops the road out from under my feet, blowing hot air up my neck. The front row of critters ignites…

And that's an understatement.

I was hoping to take out a bunch of them. But what happens is this – just like Merrick's Jell-O bomb, the fire is causing a trigger effect to ripple through the monstrous mass. The exploding creatures are setting each other off like gassy grenades; a happy accident that just keeps going and going, a chain reaction unfolding before our very wide and bloodshot eyes.

Like dominoes, clusters of critters continue to explode all the way up the road. I hear the old covered bridge collapse with a cavernous crash. I'm about to apologize, but the domino effect keeps going. It reaches town like a powder keg, blowing cars sky-high, spewing pillars of flame while we all just watch.

Then, just like that night everyone became cows, a familiar moment of panic seizes me.

What if I missed one? A lone-wolf critter still out there, rummaging through some freezer, oblivious to the memo that all his buddies were flooding to the school for a midnight feeding frenzy? If one o'clock rolls around, and even *one* wildcard remains... But my Icemaker's glowing screen quells my fear.

Red clusters, going gray.

Red dots, too; they're popping off, one by one – pop, pop – replaced with harmless little gray specks. Popping out of existence, like glorious popcorn. The critters' pack instinct was strong, and it sunk them all together. Good riddance.

So here we are. Standing in the middle of the road, together, watching thunderstruck as their town goes up in flames. Victorious cheers erupt from the assembly. People congratulate me, although I'm a little dazed and I can't fathom why. Somebody hugs me. Folks are camped out on bus roofs and on the homecoming floats, where a huge celebration just broke out because that poor pregnant gal just gave birth to a baby boy. Candace is crouched in the hay beside her, assisting. Her platinum-gold hair is a rat's nest, but I've never seen a bigger smile on her face.

The Quik-Pump flames lick the sky, belching black smoke up into the night. Sheriff Gammell comes crunching over on the dirt and we stand side by side, neither speaking a word, just gazing out over the bonfire.

After a moment he speaks. "I won't forget what you did for our town."

Yeah. I know. I've heard that a few times. But it's okay. Really. I don't hold it against him.

I don't need any medals.

Frank Gammell gives me a curt nod then walks off. Just like that night on Lau Chow's roof. And standing here, *tonight*, maybe I'm ready to admit how much I treasure that simple nod from Gammell. Maybe even crave it. It feels so good, feeling like one of them. Like warm apple cider in my belly.

This is my prize each night.

It's enough.

"Anyone want to lead a song?"

Merrick finds a guitar and by the time the moon is right over our heads, pretty much everyone has joined in a rousing rendition of "Jeremiah Was a Bullfrog." The only thing missing is the marshmallows.

It's surreal.

I find myself wishing this moment could last forever. Wishing time could start moving again. Right now. Start from here – a fresh start. The night the world begins again. I know it's childish, but sometimes you find yourself so full, buzzing so high, it feels like if you wish hard enough on one of those cold stars, it'll surprise you and come true. Stranger things have happened.

But I know it won't.

This day will reset, and I'll wake up and do it all over again.

Am I nearing the finish line?

Or have I only just begun?

I will find my answers. I will get my heart back. I'll find out who Cl. Kyle was, find out exactly why she came here in the first place. And I *will* set Carnival Creeke free from this hellish broken record. But in the meantime, there are more wildcards to slay. Roast. Ice. Something tells me I'm not done yet. Not by a longshot. Bedtime is still a long way off.

Through the chorusing bonfire crowd, Merrick looks over at me and I meet his smile.

I won't be alone.

*

My name is Cl. Kyle. Don't bother looking me up.

On second thought – please do. And if you find anything, let me know.

My face is squashed into my creamy white pillow as the car alarm blasts its usual morning trumpet. Twelve migraine-inducing honks, then it goes silent. For a moment, I just lay there, staring at the porcelain rooster on my dresser.

Then I hear it.

A wet thud against the window. Followed by a soft squishing sound...

Something is moving against the glass...

I handspring out of bed, creeping across the carpet on all fours toward the dark outline of the window.

My arms move. My legs move...

Reaching out slowly, I yank the gingham curtain open.

The wildcard is just the kind of challenge I like...

A tiny green frog is stuck to the outside of the window. It cocks its head at me through the glass, blinking its marble eyes, white throat undulating wildly.

Then it belches a basketball-sized fireball.

Behind it, as if in response, the foggy cobalt field erupts in flashes, sporadic bursts of flame punctuating the still-dark morning. Fire-breathing frogs, hundreds of them. A hellish game board, waiting for me to make the first move. A smile tugs at the corner of my mouth.

Today is my day.

Here we go again.

"Treasure this day, and treasure yourself, truly, for neither will happen again." ~Ray Bradbury

www.ingramcontent.com/pod-product-compliance
Lightning Source LLC
Chambersburg PA
CBHW030341020726
47493CB00003B/632